the Bare Bones

BIBLE® HANDBOOK FOR TEENS

the Bare Bones BIBLE® HANDBOOK FOR TEENS

Getting to Know Every Book in the Bible

JIM GEORGE

MJF BOOKS
NEW YORK

Published by MJF Books
Fine Communications
322 Eighth Avenue
New York, NY 10001

The Bare Bones Bible® Handbook for Teens
LC Control Number: 2012936906
ISBN-13: 978-1-60671-140-8
ISBN-10: 1-60671-140-7

Due to the intentionally brief treatment of each book of the Bible as presented in this handbook, disputed dates, themes, or authorships are not discussed. For such information, please consult more comprehensive reference works that are designed to take such various views and details into consideration.

This edition is published by MJF Books in arrangement with Harvest House Publishers.

Printed in the United States of America.

BG 10 9 8 7 6 5 4 3 2 1

Contents

Welcome to the Bible! 5

The Old Testament 7

The Historical Books 9
Genesis 11
Exodus 17
Leviticus 21
Numbers 25
Deuteronomy 29
Joshua 33
Judges 37
Ruth 41
1 Samuel 45
2 Samuel 49
1 Kings 53
2 Kings 57
1 Chronicles 63
2 Chronicles 67
Ezra 71
Nehemiah 75
Esther 81

The Poetic Books 87
Job 89
Psalms 93
Proverbs 97
Ecclesiastes 101
Song of Songs 105

The Prophetic Books 109
Isaiah 111
Jeremiah 115
Lamentations 119
Ezekiel 123
Daniel 127
Hosea 131
Joel 135
Amos 139
Obadiah 143
Jonah 147
Micah 151
Nahum 155
Habakkuk 159
Zephaniah 163
Haggai 167
Zechariah 171
Malachi 175

The 400 Silent Years 179

The New Testament 181

The Historical Books . . 183
Matthew 185
Mark 191
Luke 195
John 199
Acts 203

The Doctrinal Books . . 207
Romans 209
1 Corinthians 215
2 Corinthians 219
Galatians 223
Ephesians 227
Philippians 231
Colossians 235
1 Thessalonians 239
2 Thessalonians 243
1 Timothy 247
2 Timothy 251
Titus 255
Philemon 259
Hebrews 263
James 269
1 Peter 273
2 Peter 277
1 John 281
2 John 285
3 John 289
Jude 293
Revelation 297

A Final Word 303

Bare Essentials for Using You 305

Themes of All the Books of the Bible 307
How to Study the Bible 309
A One-Year Daily Bible Reading Plan 313

Welcome to the Bible!

The Bare Bones Bible Handbook for Teens

A Personal Letter to You

Welcome to this fun and easy to use book about the greatest book ever written—the Bible! It's the only book in the world written by God, and it contains a history of His saving grace, which extends to you today.

Even though the Bible is an ancient book, its truths are as real and meaningful today as they were thousands of years ago. If you're looking for help for your life and your future, the Bible has all the answers.

I wrote *The Bare Bones Bible Handbook® for Teens* just for young people like you because of something that happened in my own life experience. I grew up going to church. At age six I invited Jesus Christ to be my Savior, and became a Christian. I went to church regularly, was a part of my youth group, even the leader of it. I memorized the names of the books of the Bible and 600 verses to win an award at church. But guess what? Even though I knew about the Bible, I didn't really understand it, and I wasn't using it in my daily life. How could I ever understand everything in a book that big?

Only later did I come to realize that the Bible is simple, and I want you to know that too. God wrote the Bible for everyone. He wanted people of all ages to understand it so it could make a positive difference in their lives. He wanted to make our lives easier and better. Most of all, God wants us to enjoy a forever relationship with Him, which happens when you know and accept His Son, the Lord Jesus Christ, as Savior.

I hope and pray this book will help you to know and love God's Word. Every book of the Bible has a personal message to you today, a message you can use now. So dive in! Enjoy learning more about the book God wrote to help you. It's God's gift to you!

Your friend,
Jim George

The Old Testament

The Historical Books

The first 17 books of the Bible trace the history of man from creation through the birth and destruction of the nation of Israel. In the first five books of the Bible, Israel is chosen, redeemed, and prepared to enter a promised homeland. The remaining 12 historical books record the conquest of that land, a transition period in which judges ruled over the nation, the formation of the kingdom, and the division of that kingdom into northern (Israel) and southern (Judah) kingdoms, and finally the destruction and captivity of both kingdoms.

Genesis

In the beginning God created the heavens and the earth.
(1:1)

Theme: Beginnings
Date written: 1445–1405 B.C.
Author: Moses
Setting: Middle East

The Hebrew word for *Genesis* means "in the beginning," and that is exactly what Genesis is all about. As the first book of the Bible, Genesis lays the foundation for everything that is to follow, including the key truths God wants you to know in order to make sense of your life. Throughout the pages of Genesis you experience the awesome power of God in His creation, the holy judgment of God in the flood sent to punish the disobedience of humanity, and the tender mercy of God in His protection of Noah and his family from the flood. You also witness the fantastic grace of God as He sets in motion His plan to save mankind, first through the founding of the nation of Israel, and ultimately through the sending of Jesus Christ. Genesis is filled with key moments that form the very basis of history.

The Skeleton

▸ Chapters 1–2 *The Creation*

God creates the earth out of nothing, a perfect home for Adam and Eve, the first man and woman. He places them in the perfect Garden of Eden and blesses their relationship.

▸ **Chapters 3–5** *The Fall and Its Aftermath*

The perfection of God's creation is spoiled when Satan tempts Adam and Eve to disobey God and try to become like gods themselves and take control over their lives. When they give in to this temptation—referred to as "the fall"—they damage their relationship with God, are put out from the Garden, and must live outside the original blessing God intended for them. (However, even in the midst of this calamity, God is already setting in motion His long-term plan to redeem humanity and bring man back into a close relationship with Him.) Following the sin of their original parents, the human race sinks into violence, wickedness, and self-destruction.

▸ **Chapters 6–11** *The Flood and a New Beginning*

In His displeasure with man's wickedness, God determines to destroy man with a worldwide flood. Only Noah (a godly man) and his family are spared from the devastation. From Noah's family the earth is repopulated as they spread out and form the first nations.

▸ **Chapters 12–25** *The Story of Abraham*

God calls Abraham to leave his home country and travel to a promised land, and God tells Abraham he will become the father of His chosen people. To Abraham God gives many promises, one of which is that he—a childless old man—will have many descendants who will form a great nation, a people through whom salvation will come. This promise would be fulfilled in Abraham's greatest descendant, Jesus Christ.

▸ **Chapters 24–28** *The Story of Isaac*

Growing old and still without a child, Abraham begins to become discouraged. But true to God's promise, Isaac is born to Abraham and his wife, Sarah, in their old age.

▸ **Chapters 28–36** *The Story of Jacob*

Isaac has two sons, Esau and Jacob. Although Isaac favors Esau, the older brother, Jacob schemes to secure the privileges of the birthright from his father. In fear of Esau's anger at being swindled out of his birthright, Jacob is forced to flee for his life. After many adventures, including a mysterious late-night wrestling match with God, Jacob finally matures into the man God intends him to be. God renames him *Israel,* which means "He who struggles with God." Jacob's 12 sons become the 12 tribes of Israel.

▸ **Chapters 37–50** *The Story of Joseph*

Genesis closes with the account of Joseph, the favored son of Jacob, who is tragically sold into slavery into Egypt by his jealous brothers. But God has plans for Joseph and establishes him as a leader in Egypt, which makes it possible for Joseph's family to later settle there with him and survive a devastating seven-year famine.

Putting Meat on the Bones

In addition to the great events such as the creation of the universe, the fall, the flood, and the founding of Israel, God also wants readers to get to know the individual people who will be a part of His plan for saving the human race. The people He chooses are not perfect saints. They are, at times, deeply flawed in character and action. Genesis records that they lie, deceive others, question God, or are extremely proud—but God is able to use them anyway. This is one of the great messages of the book of Genesis: The God who created us is not finished with us. He is in the business of "re-creating" us, giving us new beginnings and helping us become the kind of people He wants us to be.

Fleshing It Out in Your Life

Just as with Abraham, Jacob, Joseph, and others in Genesis, God can do great things through weak vessels, including you. By His grace and because of His powerful plan, your mistakes and faults do not disqualify you from being part of His grand plan, a plan He is still working out in you!

When did you have a chance to start over? How did it feel? Did you make the most of it?

Can you think of a time when God used you—and your flaws—to reveal His strength and goodness?

Do you sometimes doubt God's promises, like Abraham did? What are some ways you can get past the doubt?

Life Lessons from Genesis

- God, the unique and awesome Creator, made you and knows you better than you know yourself.
- God created you in His image, as an expression of Himself.
- God uses normal people—the imperfect, the failures, the flawed—to accomplish His will.
- God takes evil seriously, and those who reject His love and wisdom will experience His judgment.
- God is able to turn your problems into triumphs.

Where to Find It

The story of creation . . . . Genesis 1:1–2:3
The first prophecy about Jesus . . . . Genesis 3:15
The story of Noah and the ark . . . . Genesis 6:1–8:22
Abraham told to sacrifice his son Isaac . . . . Genesis 22:1-14
Jacob dreams of the ladder to heaven. . . . . Genesis 28:10-22
Jacob wrestles with God. Genesis 32:22-32
Joseph interprets Pharaoh's dreams . . . . Genesis 41:1-36

~ Bible Bio Profile ~
Abraham

- He was a descendant of Shem, one of Noah's sons.
- He married his half-sister, Sarah.
- He courageously rescued his nephew Lot by defeating a powerful enemy.
- His name was changed by God from *Abram* to *Abraham,* meaning "father of multitudes."
- He was known as a friend of God (2 Chronicles 20:7).
- His many acts of obedience and trust showed his faith in God.
- He was the father of the Jewish and Arabic nations.
- He lived 175 years.

Noah's ark was approximately 450 feet long and 75 feet wide and 45 feet high. It probably started to feel much smaller to Noah and his family after they had been on it for a while. It was their home for over a year!

Exodus

I have come down to rescue them from the hand of the Egyptians and to bring them up out of that land into a good and spacious land. . .
(3:8)

Theme: Deliverance
Date written: 1445–1405 B.C.
Author: Moses
Setting: From Egypt to Mount Sinai

The time that passes between the final verse of Genesis and the first verse of the book of Exodus is about 400 years. During those four centuries, the 70 members of Jacob's family (who settled with Joseph in Egypt in order to survive a severe famine) multiply to over two million. New kings who do not know of Joseph and his important role in making Egypt's survival possible are ruling the land. Out of fear of this growing population of Israelites, these new kings force the children of Israel to become slaves. Exodus is a record of God delivering His people from slavery and leading them to Mount Sinai to receive instructions on how to worship and serve Him as God.

The Skeleton

▸ Chapters 1–6 *Bondage*

When the suffering Israelites cry out to God for help, God responds by giving them a spokesman. This man, named Moses, has been uniquely prepared for this task by God. He was born a Hebrew slave, adopted by the Pharaoh's daughter, and educated in the house of the king. He failed when he tried to take charge of the Israelites, and spent 40 years as a shepherd in the desert. At last Moses is ready for leadership and, at a burning bush, receives his call to lead the nation of Israel. After some hesitation and many excuses, Moses obeys God, approaches Pharaoh, and asks that the Israelites be allowed to leave Egypt.

▸ **Chapters 7–18** *Deliverance*

Pharaoh refuses Moses' request, so God shows Pharaoh ten plagues to convince him to let the Israelites go. The final plague is the death of the firstborn male in every Egyptian family. The Angel of Death spares all the households of Israel because they followed God's instruction to sprinkle lambs' blood on their doorposts. Finally, Pharaoh releases the people, but he has an evil change of heart and pursues God's people. In one final showdown with Pharaoh, God displays His power as the Egyptian army and Pharaoh are drowned in the Red Sea. With great rejoicing, the Israelites travel on to Mount Sinai to receive their instructions for worshipping and serving God.

▸ **Chapters 19–31** *Instructions at Sinai*

At Sinai, Moses goes up the mountain to receive the Ten Commandments, God's rules for His people to live by. While Moses is on the mountain, God also gives him many social and religious rules for everyday living. In addition, Moses is given the details for the construction of a tent for worship.

▸ **Chapters 32–34** *God's Commitment Tested*

While Moses is on the mountain receiving God's instructions for holy living, the people below are committing sins of the worst kind—idolatry and immorality. God, in holy anger, desires to destroy the people and start over again with Moses. But Moses prays, appealing to God's character and mercy. As a result, the fellowship between Israel and God is renewed and the people recommit themselves to obeying God.

▸ **Chapters 35–40** *Building the Tabernacle*

After repenting for worshipping a golden calf, the people of Israel willingly give their possessions to build a tent and create tables and bowls, and to sew garments for the high priest. The book of Exodus ends with the completion of the tabernacle and God coming to dwell in the tent and filling it with all His glory.

Putting Meat on the Bones

After being slaves for 400 years, it is difficult for the Israelites to adjust to freedom. Slavery in Egypt had its benefits, as Egypt was the center of the world at that time. All the wealth and learning of the world found its way to Egypt. Even though the Israelites were harshly treated, they did have food and shelter. After they are delivered from Egyptian bondage, the children of Israel often look back on their days of slavery with longing, forgetting that they were treated badly.

Fleshing It Out in Your Life

As God did with the Israelites, He extends deliverance to you from slavery—slavery to sin—through the shed blood of God's perfect lamb, the Lord Jesus Christ. But, like the Israelites, you are often tempted to look back, longing for the pleasures of sin while forgetting the harsh cruelty of living as a slave to sin. Let Exodus remind you of your deliverance. Keep looking forward! Keep remembering the glory of God and His Son's victory over your sin.

What excuses do you make when God asks you to take a stand or to trust Him?

Do you ever hold onto your past experiences just to avoid trying something new?

What sins have you been most enslaved to in your life? How has God delivered you?

Life Lessons from Exodus

- God hears the cries of His people and delivers them.
- Preparation for spiritual leadership takes time.
- When God selects you for a task, no excuses are acceptable.
- God demands your wholehearted, undivided worship.

- Praying for others is a vital part of your Christian life.
- Asking God to forgive your sins restores your fellowship with Him.

Where to Find It

The burning bush . . . . Exodus 3:1-12
The ten plagues . . . . Exodus 7:14–12:33
The death of Pharaoh and his army . . . . Exodus 14:15-28
The provision of manna . . . . Exodus 16
The principle of delegation . . . . Exodus 18:1-27
The Ten Commandments . . . . Exodus 20:1-17
The worship of the golden calf . . . . Exodus 32:1-35

Quiz: Can you name the ten plagues?

1. ____________________ 6. ____________________
2. ____________________ 7. ____________________
3. ____________________ 8. ____________________
4. ____________________ 9. ____________________
5. ____________________ 10. ____________________

Answers 1. Blood (7:20) 2. Frogs (8:6) 3. Lice (8:17) 4. Flies (8:24) 5. Diseased cattle (9:6) 6. Boils (9:10) 7. Hail (9:23) 8. Locusts (10:13) 9. Darkness (10:22) 10. Death of the firstborn (12:29)

Rebekah was probably in her late teens when she was brought from Ur to marry Isaac. Later she gave birth to Esau and Jacob.

Leviticus

I am the LORD your God; consecrate yourselves and be holy, because I am holy.
(11:44)

Theme: Instruction
Date written: 1445–1405 B.C.
Author: Moses
Setting: Mount Sinai

By the time the book of Exodus ends, one year has gone by since God's people left Egypt. During that year, two new developments have taken place in God's dealings with His people. First, God's glory is now living among the Israelites; and second, a central place of worship—the tabernacle—now exists. As Leviticus opens, the Israelites are still camping at the base of Mount Sinai in the wilderness.

However, several elements of worship are still missing, and Leviticus contains the instructions for these. An organized and orderly set of sacrifices and feasts are to be observed. Also a high priest, a formal priesthood, and a group of tabernacle workers must be appointed. In Exodus 19:6, God calls Israel to be "a kingdom of priests and a holy nation." Leviticus is filled with God's instructions on how His newly saved people are to worship.

The Skeleton

▸ **Chapters 1–7** *The Laws of Acceptable Worship*

Leviticus opens with God calling to Moses from the tabernacle. God tells Moses to teach the people how to have personal access to God through the offering of five different types of sacrifices. Then God gives Moses instructions for the priests on how they are to assist the people with these five sacrifices.

▸ **Chapters 8–10** *The Laws Pertaining to the Priesthood*

Up to this point in man's worship, Abraham, Job, and other godly people have offered personal sacrifices to God. But now Aaron (the high priest and Moses' brother) and his sons and their descendants are asked by God to take on the role of those who will offer the sacrifices for the people.

▸ **Chapters 11–16** *The Laws for Uncleanness*

In this section God uses everyday issues of life (such as food and clothes) to impress upon the people the differences between what is holy—or "clean"—and what is unholy—or "unclean." God gives no reasons for His instructions. He merely states that these are His standards and that the people are to obey them.

▸ **Chapters 17–27** *The Laws of Acceptable Living*

Moses continues to emphasize personal holiness to the people as their proper response to the holiness of God. Moses gives details on how the Israelites could make themselves spiritually acceptable to God. He also warns them about sexual behavior, honoring their parents, and other issues related to holy living.

Putting Meat on the Bones

Throughout the book of Leviticus there is continual instruction regarding a commitment to personal holiness in response to the holiness of God. This emphasis is repeated over 50 times through the phrases "I am the Lord" and "I am holy." Israel had very little knowledge of how to worship and live for God. The people had lived in a land filled with many pagan gods and their sensitivity to sin was warped, as witnessed by their "golden calf experience." God could not permit the Israelites to continue to worship in a godless way or to live with godless values. With the instructions in Leviticus, the priesthood would lead the people in acceptable worship and godly living.

Fleshing It Out in Your Life

Whether you realize it or not, your Christian values are being challenged or twisted by the godless culture around you. Your worship and purity are constantly being influenced by an ungodly world. But God gives you His instruction book, the Bible, to correct any wrong values and teach you how to live and worship in a way that is acceptable to Him. Be careful not to disregard God's instructions. Read His instructions in your Bible to understand what a holy God demands.

How would you define holiness? How can you practice holiness at school, home, church, or with friends?

In what ways does the world distort morality? Discuss or list specific examples.

In the Bible, find examples of people who lived for God in spite of those around them.

Life Lessons from Leviticus

- God is holy and demands holy living from His people.
- God states there are acceptable and unacceptable ways to worship Him.
- God has specific standards for living.
- God says obedience to His standards results in blessing, while disobedience is punished.

Where to Find It

The beginnings of the priesthood . . . . Leviticus 8:1-36
The ordination of Aaron as high priest . . . . Leviticus 8:1-36
The sin of Nadab and Abihu . . . . Leviticus 10:1-7
The religious festivals of Israel . . . . Leviticus 23

~ Bible Bio Profile ~
Moses

Meet Moses, who is called the greatest of all Old Testament prophets. He…

- authored the first five books of the Bible
- was a prince of Egypt
- had a sister and brother, Miriam and Aaron
- was educated in all the knowledge of Egypt
- was trained in desert survival as a shepherd
- knew God face to face
- lived 120 years
- received the Ten Commandments twice

The Location of Mount Sinai

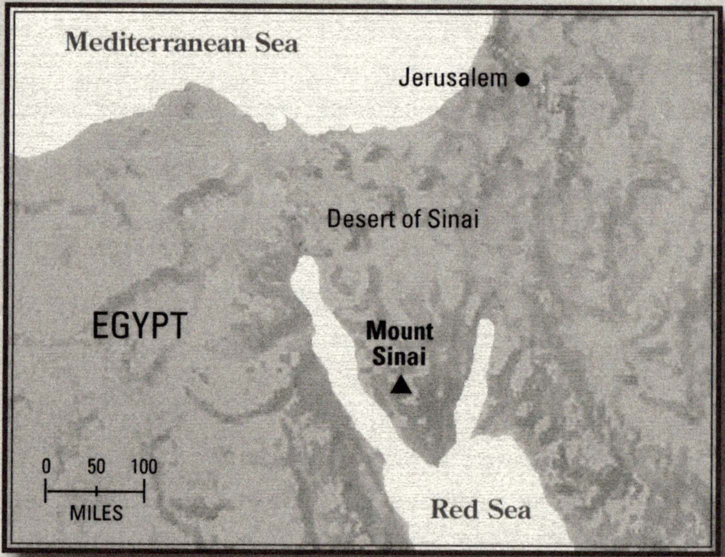

All through the book of Leviticus, the people of Israel live in a camp at the base of Mount Sinai. It is on Mount Sinai that God gives Moses the Ten Commandments and other instructions for right living.

Numbers

Here are the stages in the journey of the Israelites when they came out of Egypt by divisions under the leadership of Moses and Aaron.
(33:1)

Theme: Journeys
Date written: 1445–1405 B.C.
Author: Moses
Setting: The wilderness

The book of Numbers is written in the final year of Moses' life. It concentrates on events that take place after Moses led the nation of Israel out of Egypt to freedom. Moses gives highlights of the Israelites' 39-year journey from Mount Sinai to the plain of Moab and records the experiences of *two generations* of the nation of Israel.

The Skeleton

▸ Chapters 1–14 *The Old Generation*

The first generation of the nation of Israel was involved in the exodus from Egypt. The details of their story begin in Exodus 2:23 when they were slaves in Egypt, and continues through the book of Leviticus and into the book of Numbers. This generation is "numbered" when a census is taken of the available warriors for the conquest in Canaan, the Promised Land. The soldiers are given special instructions and then depart. They march, along with their families, to the borders of the Promised Land. However, when this group of warriors arrives at the edge of their new home, they refuse to enter the land because of a terrifying report from 10 of the 12 men sent to spy out the land. Because of this rebellion against the Lord's orders, all the adults 20 years of age and older are sentenced to die in the wilderness. Only Caleb and Joshua, the two spies who gave positive reports that the land should be taken, will live to enter the new land—the Promised Land.

▸ **Chapters 15–20** *The Tragic Transition*

In these chapters, the *first and second generations* overlap. The first dies out as the second generation grows to adulthood. These chapters provide a sad ending to what began with such promise. In chapter 20, Moses becomes angry with the continual complaining of the people. He then disobeys God's command on how he was to provide water for the people. As judgment, God decrees that Moses will not lead Israel into the land of Canaan. A final act of transition from the first to second generations comes with the death of Aaron, Moses' brother and God's high priest.

▸ **Chapters 21–36** *The New Generation*

Like the first generation, *the second generation* journeys to the borders of the land. They too are given instructions, and again a census is taken before the invasion of the Promised Land. Moses appoints Joshua as his successor and the leader of this new generation. But, unlike the first generation, the second is not fearful of going to war, and within a short time will inherit the land.

Putting Meat on the Bones

In the first few verses of Numbers, God orders Moses to number the men aged 20 years and older who are able to go to war. But before the Israelites go into battle, 12 spies are sent into the Promised Land to determine the strength of the enemy. Ten of the spies give a very negative report, saying God's people were "like grasshoppers" compared to the giants in the land. Even though God promised to give the Israelites the land, most of the spies did not believe the enemy could be conquered.

This negative report spreads and the spies' fear is passed on to the entire army. They focus on the size of their enemy instead of on the size and greatness of their God. As judgment for their unbelief, God determines that all Israelites over the age of 20 must die in the wilderness. Only

Joshua and Caleb are spared because their reports of the land focused on God's power and His promises. They believed God was able to give His people victory. God honored their belief and allowed them to finish their journey and enter the Promised Land.

Fleshing It Out in Your Life

What impossible problem are you facing today? What giant is causing you to be afraid? Learn a lesson from Joshua and Caleb and respond in faith. Focus positively on God's power rather than negatively on the problems at hand as you journey through life. Yes, the enemy is powerful, but God is more powerful! Declare boldly, "With God we will gain the victory, and he will trample down our enemies" (Psalm 60:12).

When have you relied on God's power? What happened?

Think about times when you tried to do everything on your own. How did you feel? How can you lean on God's strength?

How can you relate to Moses and his failure to trust and obey God?

Life Lessons from Numbers

- Following orders and trusting God are essential for successfully completing your journey through life.
- Even when the odds are overwhelming, you can believe in God and His promises.
- Beware of the unbelief of others. It can rub off on you.
- Fearing others and failing to trust God have serious consequences.
- Like Joshua and Caleb, don't follow the negative majority. Instead, have faith in God and reap the blessings.

Where to Find It

The report of the 12 spies . . . . Numbers 13–14

The death of Miriam, Moses' sister . . . . Numbers 20:1

The death of Aaron . . . . Numbers 20:29
The bronze serpent . . . . Numbers 21:4-8
The talking donkey of Balaam . . . . Numbers 22:22-30
The appointment of Joshua as leader . . . . Numbers 27:18-23

The Last Portion of Israel's Journey

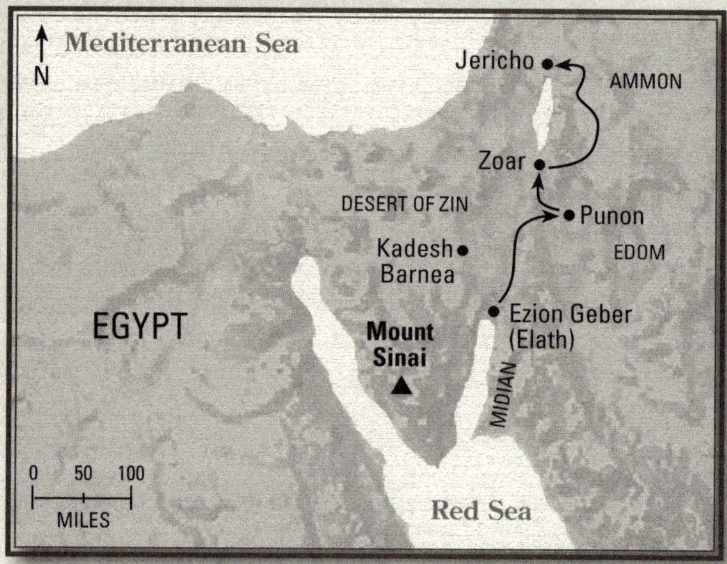

Israel spent 40 years in the wilderness. At the end of the people's journey, they camped on the east side of the Jordan River, ready to enter the Promised Land and conquer the city-fortress of Jericho.

Deuteronomy

And now, O Israel, what does the LORD your God ask of you but to fear the LORD your God, to walk in all his ways...
(10:12)

Theme: Obedience
Date written: 1405 B.C.
Author: Moses
Setting: The plains of Moab

The book of Deuteronomy takes place entirely in one location over about a month of time. Israel is encamped east of the Jordan River across from the walled city of Jericho. It has been 40 years since the Israelites left Egypt.

Deuteronomy focuses on events that take place in the final weeks of Moses' life. The major event is the verbal review of God's instructions to Moses over the past 39-plus years in the wilderness. His audience is the new generation. They are ready to enter the new land. This new generation needs God's instruction in order to succeed in their new land. The 120-year-old Moses gives three farewell speeches.

The Skeleton

▸ Chapters 1–4 *The First Speech*

Looking back over time, Moses gives a review of the years and events from Mount Sinai to the present time as the children of Israel are camped on the plains of Moab.

▸ **Chapters 5–26** *The Second Speech*

Next, Moses reviews God's Ten Commandments and gives instructions about passing these commands on to every new generation. In addition, God's laws for living and worshipping are reviewed for this new group of people before they inhabit the new land.

▸ **Chapters 27–30** *The Third Speech*

In bold fashion, as part of his final "sermon," Moses placed half the people on one mountain and half on an opposite mountain. Addressing first one side and then the other, Moses describes the immediate future with its blessings for obedience and curses for disobedience. He then describes what will happen in the distant future when Israel disobeys God, and in judgment, the people are scattered among the nations. Then Moses tells the people that, true to His promises, God will eventually bring the people back to their homes in the Promised Land.

▸ **Chapters 31–34** *The Concluding Events*

In these closing chapters of the five books written by Moses, Joshua is again confirmed as the new leader of the Israelites. Moses then makes two more short speeches. The first is called "the song of Moses." In this song about the future, Moses describes Israel's coming rebellion, God's judgment, and God's forgiveness and healing of both Israel and the land. In his second mini-speech, Moses gives his final blessing to each of the 12 tribes. Having fulfilled his role as a leader, Moses goes to the top of a nearby mountain, Nebo, and looks out over the Promised Land on the other side of the Jordan River. Then he dies and is buried by God.

Putting Meat on the Bones

The book of Deuteronomy shows much about the character and nature of God. How blessed the world is to have this written testimony of God and His dealings with His people! Any time we forget about some aspect of God's character or His work in history, we can simply pick up the Bible and read Deuteronomy.

But this was not the case in Moses' day. The only way to remind this new generation of the wonderful nature of God was to rehearse it with them, to verbally review for them how God honors obedience to

His commandments and punishes disobedience. Moses also recounts the people's past history of rebellion and the results of their stubbornness. They are to learn a key lesson from the past: Disobedience brings disaster. But they are also to remember God is present with them, and if they dedicate their lives to Him and obey His laws, they will receive His blessings.

Fleshing It Out in Your Life

Moses' instructions concerning the nature of God are still needed today. Learning about God will aid you in your love for Him and your pursuit of personal holiness. God is the standard. He is holy, and He expects holy behavior from His people. As a Christian, you are called to be holy as God is holy. You are to "love" Him "with all your heart and with all your soul and with all your strength" (Deuteronomy 6:5).

Pretend you are writing an online bio for God. How would you describe His character to those who don't know Him?

Is there a promise from God that is hard for you to believe in and trust? Why?

In what areas of your life are you obedient? Disobedient? How can you be more obedient to God?

Life Lessons from Deuteronomy

- Let your past failures prepare you for future victories.
- Realize God can blot out any sin, but He does not always take away its result.
- Never forget what you were saved from.
- Review God's Word regularly—it will guide your steps.

Where to Find It

The Ten Commandments reviewed . . . . Deuteronomy 5:7-22
"The Lord is one" . . . . Deuteronomy 6:4

The command to love God . . . . Deuteronomy 6:4-9

The death of Moses . . . . Deuteronomy 34:5

The Ten Commandments

1. Worship God alone (Exodus 20:3)
2. Do not worship images (Exodus 20:4)
3. Do not swear (Exodus 20:7)
4. Observe the Sabbath (Exodus 20:8)
5. Obey your parents (Exodus 20:12)
6. Do not murder (Exodus 20:13)
7. Do not commit adultery (Exodus 20:14)
8. Do not steal (Exodus 20:15)
9. Do not bear false witness (Exodus 20:16)
10. Do not covet (Exodus 20:17)

Moses is the only person in the Bible who was buried by God—see Deuteronomy 34:5-6.

Joshua

As for me and my household,
we will serve the Lord.
(24:15)

Theme: Conquest
Date written: 1405–1385 B.C.
Author: Joshua
Setting: Canaan, the Promised Land

When Moses passed the baton of leadership on to Joshua (Deuteronomy 34), Israel was at the end of its 40 years in the wilderness. Joshua had been Moses' faithful helper for most of that 40 years and was approaching 90 years of age when Moses calls him to become Israel's new leader. Joshua's task is to lead Israel into the land of Canaan, drive out the inhabitants, and divide the land among the 12 tribes.

The Skeleton

▸ **Chapters 1–5** *Preparing to Conquer the Land*

The book opens with the people of Israel on the plains of the country of Moab, east of the Jordan River, preparing for the conquest of the land. Joshua and the Israelites are facing a powerful and fierce enemy who lives in heavily fortified cities. Yet God will give Israel the land by conquest. This will fulfill the promise He pledged to Abraham and his descendants. It will be a judgment on the sinful inhabitants of the land for their wickedness (see Genesis 15:16).

The conquest begins much like the exodus from Egypt. The people must first cross a body of water. In this case it is the Jordan River, which is overflowing its banks because of the rainy season. As He did at the Red Sea, God holds back the waters of the Jordan River and the army of God passes through on dry ground.

▸ **Chapters 6–12** *Conquering the Land*

Once across the Jordan and on dry land, the army is ready to begin the battle to gain their Promised Land. Israel's first test comes as the people are asked to trust God to provide the victory at the city of Jericho. After the people walk around the city for seven days, God brings down its walls. This campaign against Jericho drives a strategic wedge between the northern and southern cities, which prevents a massive alliance against Israel.

The Israelites are successful because they allow God to fight for them. The only problem comes from a foolish oath made to the lying Gibeonites, who pretended to be from a far-off country and asked for protection from Israel's armies. Because the Israelites fell for their trick and gave an oath to protect them, Israel is forced to defend the Gibeonites, which causes God's people to disobey God's command to eliminate all the Canaanites from the new land, including the Gibeonites.

▸ **Chapters 13–22** *Dividing of the Land*

Seven years later, after much of the conquest is completed, God tells Joshua to divide the land among the 12 tribes, who then must continue the final conquests in their assigned areas.

▸ **Chapters 23–24** *Last Words of Joshua*

These closing chapters record Joshua's final challenge to the leaders to keep the law, and an exhortation to the people to serve the Lord.

Putting Meat on the Bones

The conquest of the land is to follow a simple "divide and conquer" strategy. Jericho is the key city in the central part of the land. God will use what sounds like a foolish military plan (walk around the city for seven days and then blow trumpets and shout on the last day). This command is a test to see if the people will recognize that a successful conquest must always come from God's power and not from their own abilities. And

God's people passed the test with flying colors! They obeyed, blew their trumpets, and a miracle happens—the walls came tumbling down.

Fleshing It Out in Your Life

The book of Joshua teaches that when it comes to fighting the battles of life and gaining spiritual victory, blessing comes through obedience to God's commands. For you this means living your life by faith according to God's directions. Active faith does not require that you understand all or any of what God is doing in your life. You don't need to understand. You need only to obey and then reap the blessings of that obedience. God required the people to attempt the impossible, and it sounded like a crazy idea. Humanly speaking, walking around a walled city and blowing trumpets should have no effect. But in God's realm, the impossible became possible and the people succeeded and gained the victory—God's victory.

Just as God promised the Israelites victory, so He has also promised to give you victory. And like the Israelites, you must follow God's terms. Trust God. Attempt the impossible by submitting to God's directions. Then watch the walls of your impossible problems miraculously come tumbling down.

When have you needed to conquer something in your life? How did you go about preparing?

Has God brought you through a big or small battle at school or at home? How did this strengthen your faith?

What makes you hold back from following God? Fear? Disbelief? Shame? In prayer, give the obstacle over to God.

What would it feel like to be free from your obstacle?

Life Lessons from Joshua

- Faithfulness is a requirement for service.
- Serving others prepares you to lead others.
- Victory occurs when you let God fight your battles.

- Guidance from God for daily living comes from His Word, the Bible.
- At times you must make a stand for your beliefs.
- Living for God requires ongoing obedience.

Where to Find It

Rahab's protection of the spies .... Joshua 2:1-23
The conquest of Jericho .... Joshua 6:1–8:29
The sun is still for a whole day .... Joshua 10:13
Caleb's request for land .... Joshua 14:10-15
Joshua's stand for the Lord .... Joshua 24:14-15

~ Bible Bio Profile ~
Rahab

Meet Rahab, who risked her life by hiding the two spies that Joshua sent to Jericho.

Rahab's courage...
was inspired by her faith in God's ability to deliver.
Rahab's faith...
made her one of only two women listed (Rahab and Sarah) in the Hall of Faith in Hebrews 11.
Rahab's descendants...
included David and later, Jesus.

Judges

When they cried out to the LORD,
he raised up for them a deliverer...
(3:9)

Theme: Deliverance
Date written: about 1043 B.C.
Author: Samuel
Setting: Canaan

Judges opens with the closing days of the life of the leader of God's people, Joshua, and gives a review of Joshua's death (see Joshua 24:28-31). Judges is a tragic addition to the book of Joshua. In Joshua, the people were obedient to God and enjoyed victory in their conquest of the land. In Judges, however, they are disobedient, idolatrous, and often defeated and oppressed.

Like Genesis through Joshua, Judges presents historical facts, but in a very selective and thematic way. Foremost among its themes is God's power, mercy, and grace in delivering the Israelites from the consequences of their failures, which they suffered because of their sinful compromises (see 2:18-19; 21:25).

The book bears the fitting name *Judges,* which refers to 12 special leaders God raises up to deliver His people when they are oppressed because of their disobedience.

The Skeleton

▸ **Chapters 1–2** *The Military Failure of Israel*

The book of Judges opens with a military success after Joshua's death. However, Israel's success quickly turns to repeated failures in their attempts to drive out their enemies. Instead of removing the godless inhabitants of the land, the tribes compromise spiritually. Therefore, God announces judgment and allows the godless nations to remain in the land as a test of Israel.

▸ **Chapters 3–16** *The Rescue of Israel by the Judges*

The people of Israel go through a series of cycles that include four steps:

1. Israel departs from God.
2. God punishes Israel by permitting military defeat and oppression.
3. Israel prays for deliverance.
4. God raises up judges who lead in the defeat of the oppressors.

Afterward, the people fall back into idolatry, which repeats the cycle.

▸ **Chapters 17–21** *The Moral Failure of Israel*

Here the author of Judges ends with two unusual illustrations, one showing religious rejection (17–18) and the other describing social and moral sinfulness (19–21). The last verse of Judges (21:25) gives the key to understanding this period in the history of Israel: "In those days there was no king in Israel; everyone did what was right in his own eyes" (NKJV).

Putting Meat on the Bones

The book of Judges describes seven cycles of Israel's drifting away from the Lord. These cycles of unbelief and deliverance cover the whole land. Each area of the land is specifically identified:

southern (3:7-31)	eastern (10:6–12:15)
northern (4:1–5:31)	western (13:1–16:31)
central (6:1–10:5)	

Even with all the idolatry, immorality, and violence in Israel, God was faithful to deliver the people. In His gracious love for His people, God continued to forgive them every time they cried out to Him.

Fleshing It Out in Your Life

How often can it be said of you that you "do what is right in your own eyes"? It's easy to act in foolishness, stubbornness, and rebellion and then wonder why you suffer. The God of Judges is the same God of today. And as then, when you cry out to God and say you're sorry for your sin, He is nearby and forgives and delivers you. Are you living in spiritual defeat? Cry out to God. He is ready to send deliverance!

Spiritual deliverance is not like pizza delivery—it takes more than 30 minutes! When you get impatient, ask God what you should be doing and learning while you wait. What might His answer be to you right now?

In Israel everyone was following their own sense of right and wrong. How is today's society doing the same thing? And what are some of the results of such behavior?

Life Lessons from Judges

- Don't give in to the world—it leads to defeat.
- Don't sin—it results in suffering.
- Don't wait until you are without hope to cry out to God.
- Don't do what is right in your own eyes—do what's right in God's eyes.

Where to Find It

Deborah, the only female judge . . . . Judges 4–5
Gideon and his 300 men . . . . Judges 7:1-7
Samson and Delilah . . . . Judges 16:4-22
Israel and the war against the tribe of Benjamin . . . . . Judges 20

The Judges	*versus*	**Their Enemies**
Othniel		The Mesopotamians
Ehud		The Moabites and Ammonites
Shamgar		The Philistines
Deborah		The Canaanites
Gideon		The Midianites
Tola and Jair		The evil of Abimelech
Jephthah, Ibzan, Elon, Abdon		The Ammonites
Samson		The Philistines

~ Bible Bio Profile ~ Samson

Meet Samson, the strong man of the Old Testament.

- Dedicated to God as a judge
- Parents talked to God twice
- Used his great strength to free Israel
- Was controlled by worldly desires
- Violated his vows on many occasions
- Used his abilities for selfish purposes
- Put his confidence in the wrong people
- Used by God in spite of his mistakes
- Listed in God's Hall of Faith in Hebrews 11

Ruth

Your people will be my people
and your God my God.
(1:16)

Theme: Redemption
Date written: 1030–1010 B.C.
Author: Unknown/possibly Samuel
Setting: Moab and Bethlehem

The book of Ruth takes place during the spiritually dark days of the Judges. Ruth is the story of a woman (named Ruth) who lives during this evil period in Israel's history. But Ruth does not give in to its evil. Her story is one of honesty, holiness, and faithfulness. It covers about 11 to 12 years. She and Esther are the only women who have books of the Bible named after them.

The Skeleton

▸ **Chapter 1** *Ruth's Faithfulness*

Ruth's story opens with a famine in the land of Israel, including the town of Bethlehem. This famine forces an Israelite named Elimelech to move his wife, Naomi, and their two sons to Moab. While living there, both sons marry Moabite women but later die. So does Elimelech. Now left alone, Naomi decides to return to her homeland and tells her two daughters-in-law, Ruth and Orpah, to remain with their people and kin. Orpah chooses to stay and is never heard of again. Ruth, however, chooses to cling to Naomi and follow the God of Israel. Because of her desire to be faithful to Naomi, Ruth gives up her false gods, her culture, and her people.

▸ **Chapter 2** *Ruth's Service*

Naomi returns to Bethlehem a bitter woman, thinking God is her enemy because of her losses. But God has plans she doesn't know about. These plans begin to unfold when Ruth volunteers to go into the fields to pick up the grain left on the ground by the harvesters. Such gleaning was allowed to provide for the poor. In God's plan, Ruth enters the field of a man named Boaz, a relative of Naomi's. Boaz has heard of Ruth's faithfulness toward his relative Naomi and gives instructions to his workers to leave extra grain behind and therefore provides for her and Naomi.

▸ **Chapter 3** *Ruth's Proposal*

Over a period of several months of harvest, Ruth willingly works in Boaz's fields to provide for her and Naomi. But now it is time for Naomi to repay Ruth's kindness and provide for Ruth's future. Naomi devises a plan that will force Boaz to make a more serious decision about Ruth. Ruth is instructed by Naomi to engage in an ancient custom of asking Boaz to take her for his wife in the place of her dead husband because he is a close relative (see Deuteronomy 25:5-6).

Ruth's proposal is accepted when Boaz throws a garment over her.

▸ **Chapter 4** *Ruth's Reward*

Boaz agrees to marry Ruth, but reveals that he must first ask another man who is a closer relative to see if that man wanted to fulfill the custom. In this final chapter we see Boaz come before the local elders and, with them as witnesses, ask the closer relative about Ruth. The man declines, making Boaz free to marry Ruth. God blesses Ruth's faithful devotion by giving her Boaz as a husband and a son, Obed, who would later be the grandfather of the famous future king of Israel, David.

Putting Meat on the Bones

The book of Ruth gives an example of godly behavior in the midst of widespread ungodliness during the time of the Judges. Ruth's faithfulness to follow the God of Israel leads to great blessing for her, for Naomi, for Boaz, and ultimately for the world as she takes her place in the family line of Jesus Christ.

Fleshing It Out in Your Life

In addition to seeing Ruth's faithfulness to God and to Naomi, we see Boaz's honesty and kindness. Boaz became a "kinsman-redeemer" who "buys back" the Gentile Ruth and gives her a home. Their union produces a son, whose grandson is David and whose ultimate ancestor is Jesus Christ. The book of Ruth gives us an important pattern of the work of Christ. Like Boaz, Jesus is willing to pay the price of redemption. And like Ruth, you must choose to accept redemption and leave the transaction to Jesus. Don't be like Ruth's sister-in-law, who chose to return to her pagan gods and was lost forever. Come to Jesus—who is your Kinsman-Redeemer—and live forever.

What can you learn from Ruth about following God faithfully?

What can you learn from Ruth about following instructions?

Life Lessons from Ruth

- ▶ What you think is a tragedy is God's opportunity to show Himself faithful.
- ▶ Your money is an opportunity to help those in need.
- ▶ God honors faithfulness.
- ▶ Good character is a noble quality that God honors.
- ▶ Every bad situation gives you the opportunity to do the right thing.

Where to Find It

Ruth's loyalty to Naomi . . . . Ruth 1
Boaz's kindness to Ruth . . . . Ruth 2
God's provision of a kinsman-redeemer . . . . Ruth 3
Christ's lineage through Ruth . . . . Ruth 4

~ Bible Bio Profile ~
Boaz: Portrait of a Godly Character

Meet Boaz, the man who took care of Naomi and Ruth.

Diligent	Ruth 2:1	Generous	Ruth 2:15
Friendly	Ruth 2:4,8	Kind	Ruth 2:20
Merciful	Ruth 2:7	Discreet	Ruth 3:14
Godly	Ruth 2:12	Faithful	Ruth 4:1-9
Encouraging	Ruth 2:12; 3:11		

1 Samuel

To obey is better than sacrifice...
(15:22)

Theme: Transition
Date written: 930–722 B.C.
Author: Unknown
Setting: The struggling nation of Israel

The book that precedes 1 Samuel—Ruth—is indeed a bright spot in a dark land and a love story with many happy endings. We now arrive at a transition in the history of God's people with three sets of "doubles"—

1 and 2 Samuel,
1 and 2 Kings, and
1 and 2 Chronicles.

There have been a multitude of books written about the history of great nations. Many of their titles start with the phrase *The Rise and Fall of*...1 and 2 Samuel, along with the other two "doubles" named above could be entitled *The Rise and Fall of the Israelite Kingdom.*

Originally 1 and 2 Samuel were one book in the Hebrew Bible, but later translations separate them into our present two books. First Samuel is named for the first of three important people—Samuel, Saul, and David—seen throughout its chapters.

The Skeleton

▸ Chapters 1–7 *Samuel*

Samuel's life story begins as the period of the judges is coming to an end. Eli is the present judge-priest of Israel and lives at Shiloh, where the tabernacle constructed in the book of Exodus was now located. Samuel's mother, Hannah, is introduced as a woman without children who prays to God for a baby. She promises God that, if He would give her a son, she would dedicate him to the Lord for God's service all the days of his life. God responds to Hannah's prayer and gives her Samuel, who grew to faithfully judge Israel. When Samuel is old the people of Israel, wanting to be like the nations around them, cry out for a king.

▸ Chapters 8–15 *Saul*

God gives the people their request. Their first king, Saul, who is anointed with oil, becomes the nation's new leader. Saul starts out well, but his good qualities begin to erode under the pressures of being king and leading the people in battle. Early in his reign, Samuel tells Saul to wait for his arrival to perform a ritual sacrifice. But because of his pride and lack of patience, Saul takes on the role of a priest and offers up the sacrifice without waiting for Samuel. When Samuel shows up, he tells Saul, "You acted foolishly" (13:13).

Later Saul forces his soldiers to make a rash vow regarding food just before going into battle. Then he disobeys God's command to destroy the Amalekites. Finally and tragically, at the end of his 40-year reign, he foolishly consults a medium, or a witch, for guidance (see chapter 28). The medium foretells Saul's doom, and he and his sons are killed the next day in battle.

▸ Chapters 16–31 *David*

The lives of Samuel, Saul, and David are threaded throughout this book. Although Saul is still king, the main focus of the book is now shifting to David. His story begins as Saul is rejected by God for disobedience and Samuel anoints David as Israel's next king. God's presence with David enables him to kill the Philistine giant Goliath and fight many successful battles. David also becomes a devoted friend to Jonathan, Saul's eldest son.

David becomes a growing threat to the jealous Saul, who actively seeks to kill David. Finally, David flees to a Philistine city, then to a secret hideout, where a band of mighty men protect him. David continues to escape from Saul until Saul and his sons are killed in a great battle with the Philistines.

Putting Meat on the Bones

Samuel is a great illustration of how one man handled changes in his life. He was the last of the judges. Even though Samuel was a man of truth all his life, the people rejected his sons to lead them. Instead, they wanted a king so they could be more like the nations around them. Even with the rejection of his corrupt sons, Samuel commits to praying continually for the people. No matter what is happening to and around Samuel, he never falters in his faithfulness to God or God's people.

Now contrast Samuel's life with that of King Saul. Saul's change from commoner to king is marked by pride, deceit, and an unrepentant heart. He starts out well, but along the way, he decides not to follow God's commands, and chooses to chart his own course. Saul's choice costs him his life and the lives of his sons, and puts the nation of Israel at risk. Samuel was able to make the adjustments necessary for his usefulness to both God and the people. Tragically, King Saul was not able to make the transition. Pride and arrogance were his downfall.

Fleshing It Out in Your Life

Transitions and changes are a critical part of everyone's life. We move from one level or school grade to another. We move from home to school, and from school to work and family. We all pass from one season of life to the next. And ultimately, like it or not, life shifts to death.

Whether you realize it or not, your life is in a constant state of change. Therefore you must recognize how crucial it is to make changes well. And it's not the transition itself that's critical, but how you respond to the changes that come your way. Some people don't handle change or new responsibilities well. They fall apart when faced with a new path or choice.

Like Samuel, you want to stay faithful and close to God through prayer and the study of His Word. Then when a change comes, you will be prepared to draw on God's strength and honor Him with your godly attitudes and actions. And you will never skip a beat in your service to others.

How do you make sure your life and attitudes honor God with each change that comes?

When have you handled change well? Not so well?

When you have success, how can you avoid the pride of King Saul and honor God instead?

Life Lessons from 1 Samuel

- ▶ A close walk with God will help you better handle life's changes.
- ▶ Your faithful service will be rewarded, at least in God's eyes.
- ▶ God wants inward commitment, not outward ceremony.
- ▶ It's not how you start that's important, but how you finish!

Where to Find It

Samuel's mother, Hannah	1 Samuel 1–2
Samuel's service to God as a child	1 Samuel 3
Saul is anointed as king	1 Samuel 10:1
David is anointed as king	1 Samuel 16:13
David's fight with the giant Goliath	1 Samuel 17
David's friendship with Jonathan	1 Samuel 18:1-4
Saul's visit with the witch of Endor	1 Samuel 28:7-19

Why Was Samuel the Most Influential Man of His Day?

- He was wholly devoted to God.
- He was wholly committed to God's people.
- He was wholly honest with the people.
- He was wholly compassionate concerning the people.

David was only a teen when he fought Goliath, who was more than 9 feet tall (maybe 11!), had armor that weighed more than 120 pounds and whose spear weighed 16 pounds. David had a slingshot and 5 smooth stones—but he needed only 1 to bring down the giant!

2 Samuel

Your house and your kingdom will endure forever...
(7:16)

Theme: Unification
Date written: 931–722 B.C.
Author: Unknown
Setting: United kingdom of Israel

Second Samuel picks up where 1 Samuel leaves off. King Saul is now gone, so the people of Judah declare David as their king. The northern tribes, however, acknowledge Saul's youngest son as their king. David rules in Hebron for seven-and-a-half years before all Israel finally acknowledges him as their king. He then reigns in Jerusalem for 33 years. Second Samuel reviews the key events in David's 40-year reign.

The Skeleton

▸ **Chapters 1–10** *David's Success*

Under David's leadership, the northern and southern tribes of Israel are united. David's success is remarkable. Under his leadership the nation adopts a unified government. After David captures the city of Jerusalem, he makes it the nation's capital.

David, a man after God's own heart, rules with justice and fairness and shows mercy to Saul's family. He also brings the ark, which contains the Ten Commandments, to Jerusalem. God honors David's devotion and assures David that one of his descendants would always rule on his throne. This promise is realized in David's distant son, the Lord Jesus Christ.

▸ **Chapter 11** *David's Sin*

David knows that the Lord is responsible for his success. He realizes that God wants to bless His chosen people, Israel. Yet, at the peak of his influence, David commits sexual sin with a woman named Bathsheba. When she informs David that she is going to have a baby, David tries to cover up his sin and, in the process, plots the death of Bathsheba's husband, Uriah, one of David's faithful soldiers. After Bathsheba observes a period of mourning, David marries Bathsheba and she bears him a son. Needless to say, God is displeased. From this point on David will experience continued struggles both within his family and with the nation.

▸ **Chapters 12–20** *David's Struggles*

God confronts David about his sin with Bathsheba and the murder of Uriah by sending the prophet Nathan. Nathan approaches David with a story about a man whose one and only lamb was taken away by a rich man who had many lambs. David righteously condemns the man with many sheep for his actions. At that point the prophet declares, "You are that man."

At last David confesses, but the consequence of his sin would be far-reaching and tragic. His son born by Bathsheba dies. His son Amnon, a child by another of his wives, commits sexual sin with his half-sister Tamar. Absalom, Tamar's brother, kills Amnon and flees for his life. Later Absalom is allowed to return, but he soon schemes to overthrow his father, David. Absalom almost succeeds, but is killed in battle. Civil war continues as a man named Sheba marshals the trust of the northern tribes, but he too is killed and further strife is avoided.

▸ **Chapters 21–24** *David's Reflections*

These chapters catalog David's words and deeds. They show how the moral and spiritual condition of the king affects the physical and spiritual state of the people. The nation of Israel enjoys God's blessings when David is obedient and suffers hardship when David disobeys God.

Putting Flesh on the Bones

In spite of his faults, David remained a man after God's own heart. Why? Obviously it wasn't because he lived a sinless life. Far from that!

He often failed in his personal life, but he never faltered in his desire for an ongoing relationship with God. David was God's man because of his responsive and faithful attitude toward God. After David had sinned, he realized his need to make things right with God through a repentant heart. Unfortunately, his repentance could not repair the damage brought about by his sin. Yes, he was forgiven. And yes, his relationship with God was restored. But the list of those who suffered from and because of David's sins is a long and tragic one.

Fleshing It Out in Your Life

Do you desire to be a young man or young woman after God's own heart? Realize that God isn't looking for perfection, for "all have sinned and fall short of the glory of God" (Romans 3:23). You, as God's teen, have your issues, but you are progressing. Hopefully you love God with all your heart and soul, and even though you stumble and fall at times, you are quick to ask God for forgiveness.

In David's life you see God's grace in action. He forgives David. You can thank God for His grace when you sin. But David's life also gives a sobering look at sin in action. You can learn from David's suffering that sin is never committed in a vacuum. Others are always affected by your sin. Ask God for His strength to help you resist sin so that it doesn't affect your relationship with Him and cause terrible results for others.

How do you feel pressure to be perfect in certain areas of your life? Sports? School? Friendship? Family relationships?

Why is the story of David such an important one for you to know? What does it show you about God's grace?

What is a sin, shortcoming, or failure that you need to give to God?

Life Lessons from 2 Samuel

- Blessing comes to you and those around you when you are obedient to God's commands.
- Conversely, there are always bad results to your sinful actions.

- The role your parents play in your life is a full-time job. Make sure you don't complicate their lives with acts of rebellion.
- Saying you're sorry to God restores your relationship with Him.

Where to Find it

The Davidic covenant . . . . 2 Samuel 7
David's sin with Bathsheba . . . . 2 Samuel 11
David's sin of numbering the people of Israel . .2 Samuel 24:10-17

~ Bible Bio Profile ~
David

Meet David—shepherd, warrior, singer, king, and a man after God's own heart. David was…

- an accomplished musician
- the killer of the giant Goliath with a single stone (while still a teen)
- the possessor of a repentant heart
- the cause of his family's suffering due to his sin
- the greatest king of Israel
- an ancestor of Jesus Christ

Samuel was very young when he first spoke to God. That experience set the tone of his continued relationship with the Lord. Samuel grew up to become an important, influential judge. Revisit 1 Samuel and read chapter 3 for the account of Samuel's conversation with God.

1 Kings

Since this is your attitude and you have not kept my covenant and my decrees, which I commanded you, I will most certainly tear the kingdom away from you. . .
(11:11)

Theme: Disruption
Date written: 561–538 B.C.
Author: Unknown
Setting: Israel

The story of 1 and 2 Kings is basically one of failure. The tiny nation of Israel had gained superiority in its region because God had blessed it. But at the height of their wealth and influence, the people plunge into poverty and insignificance as they turn away from God.

The Skeleton

▸ **Chapters 1–11** *Solomon and a United Kingdom*

The opening chapters describe the glorious reign of King David's son, Solomon. God had refused David's offer to build Him a house and gave that privilege to Solomon instead. David's wars had cleared the way for Solomon, who constructs the temple from materials David had prepared and gathered. The ark of the covenant is placed in the new temple, and the glory of the Lord fills the temple.

Solomon prays and asks God for wisdom and soon becomes the wisest and richest man alive. His many foreign wives, however, turn his heart away from God. God pronounces judgment and declares that Solomon's son would rule only a fraction of the kingdom.

▸ **Chapters 12–22** *The Kings and a Divided Kingdom*

After Solomon dies, his son Rehoboam acts without wisdom and angers the ten northern tribes, which creates a split in the kingdom. As predicted in a warning from God to Solomon, Rehoboam is left with two tribes, Judah and Benjamin. Jereboam, an officer in Solomon's army, leads a revolt and is made king of the northern tribes. This begins a chaotic period of time for the people of Israel, with two nations, two sets of kings, two religions, and two places of worship. The book of 1 Kings reports the reigns of both sets of kings. Of all the kings, only a few from the south did what was right in the sight of the Lord. All the others were idolaters and murderers.

The prophet Elijah ministers during the reign of Ahab, an especially wicked northern king. Ahab's wife, Jezebel, introduces Baal worship to those in the northern kingdom. Elijah confronts Ahab and the prophets of Baal in a showdown on Mount Carmel. There, God sends down fire and consumes a sacrifice drenched with water by Elijah. Elijah goes on to kill the 450 prophets of Baal who were present at Mount Carmel.

Elijah then places his cape on a younger man named Elisha, to let others know that he was to be Elijah's successor. Elijah also continues to condemn Ahab for his wickedness until Ahab's death.

Putting Meat on the Bones

Just before his death, David charged his son Solomon to "walk in [God's] ways, and keep his decrees and commands, his laws and requirements" (1 Kings 2:3). This Solomon did and, when given a choice of riches, long life, or wisdom, Solomon asked for wisdom. As a result, Solomon's reign began with great success. Unfortunately Solomon allowed his many pagan wives to turn his heart away from following after God. Thus the wisest man on earth became a fool.

Rehoboam succeeded his father, Solomon, and had the chance to be a wise and just king. Instead, he accepted foolish advice from his young friends over the advice of his older and wiser counselors, which resulted in the split of the kingdom.

Fleshing It Out in Your Life

How puzzling that the son of the wisest man on earth didn't or wouldn't take the advice of his father's many proverbs which speak of the importance of seeking, hearing, and heeding the advice of good counselors (Proverbs 11:14; 15:22; 24:6). Maybe Rehoboam observed the sin of his father's later life and wanted nothing to do with his father's wisdom from his earlier years. Whatever the reason, Rehoboam listened to his friends rather than to wise counselors—with horrible results.

God has provided you with many ways for obtaining wisdom for the different decisions you must make in your everyday life. Resist your pride and stubbornness to reject help and attempt to do things your own way. You have your Bible, the leading of the Holy Spirit, youth leaders, and the wisdom of your parents available to help in your decision-making. Don't bypass these important resources, for they can help you make decisions that honor God and bless others.

When have you taken wise advice? What happened?

When have you taken foolish advice? What happened?

You have a lot of decisions to make daily. What are practical ways that you can build wisdom?

Life Lessons from 1 Kings

- God has given you the stewardship of your life—use it wisely.
- Obedience to God will bring blessings to you and others.
- Wisdom is not a guarantee you won't act foolishly.
- Beware of having too much worldly fun—it can turn your heart from God.
- Don't let your personal desires overrule the standards in God's Word.
- Unless you serve God, you become a slave to whatever takes His place in your life.
- Pray for those things that will help others.

Where to Find It

Solomon's temple . . . . 1 Kings 5–8
Solomon's meeting with the Queen of Sheba . . . . 1 Kings 10
Jeroboam's golden calves . . . . 1 Kings 12:25-33
Elijah's encounter with the prophets of Baal . . . . 1 Kings 18
Elisha's call to follow Elijah . . . . 1 Kings 19:19-21

Miracles Performed by Elijah

- Multiplies a widow's food
- Raises a widow's son to life
- Calls down God's fire on an altar and its sacrifice
- Calls down fire on evil soldiers
- Parts the Jordan River

Solomon's annual income was 16 tons of gold! To get some idea of how much gold that is, one ton equals 2000 pounds. For comparison's sake, the average weight of a male African elephant is five tons.

2 Kings

I will remove Judah also from my presence as I removed Israel, and I will reject Jerusalem…
(23:27)

Theme: Dispersion
Date written: 561–538 B.C.
Author: Unknown
Setting: Divided kingdoms of Israel and Judah

Without a break, 2 Kings continues the history of the kingdoms of Israel and Judah. Both kingdoms fly headlong toward a collision course with captivity as the glory of the once-united kingdom begins to fade. When the end finally comes (with the northern tribes taken into Assyrian captivity and the southern tribes deported to Babylon), nine different families of kings are described for the northern kingdom, Israel. But, as promised to David, there is only one family of kings in Judah—David's.

The Skeleton

▸ **Chapters 1–17** *The Divided Kingdoms*

These chapters record the continual downward fall of both the northern and southern kingdoms.

The North

All the kings of the north are recorded as evil and wicked. Even the many miracles of Elijah and his successor, Elisha, have little effect. Of Israel's 19 kings, none did what was right in God's sight. Finally, God has enough and brings the Assyrian armies against Israel. They besiege Samaria, the capital of the northern kingdom, and overthrow the nation and take the survivors back to Assyria.

The South

The situation in the southern kingdom of Judah is better but not ideal. Athaliah, the daughter of King Ahab and Jezebel of the north, follows in the wicked footsteps of her mother, and kills all the descendants of David except for Joash. She then takes control of the throne. Then according to God's promise to always have a family member of David sitting on his throne, the priest, Jehoiada, removes Athaliah and places the young lad, Joash, in power. Joash, who is only seven years old, restores the temple and serves God.

▸ **Chapters 18–25** *The Surviving Kingdom*

The account of Judah, the southern and surviving kingdom, reads more easily than the details of the divided kingdoms. Only Judah is left. Six years before the overthrow of Samaria, Hezekiah becomes king of Judah. Because of Hezekiah's faith and reforms, God spares Jerusalem from Assyria and brings some wealth to Judah.

However, Hezekiah's son, Manasseh, is so wicked and his reign is so long that Judah's downfall is certain. Even King Josiah's reforms cannot stop the evil, and the four kings who succeed Josiah are as wicked as Manasseh.

The book of 2 Kings ends with judgment as the people are carried away into exile to Babylonia, and Jerusalem and the temple are destroyed. Yet the book ends on a note of hope as God preserves a small group of people for Himself.

Putting Meat on the Bones

Even though 1 and 2 Kings are two separate books in today's Bibles, they were originally one book with one theme: When kings follow God's ways, they and their people prosper; but kings who refuse to obey God are sure to face judgment. The decline and collapse of the two kingdoms occur because the rulers and the people failed to heed the warnings of God's prophets. God is seen in Kings as the controller of history, and the spiritual climate of the kingdoms determines their political and economic conditions. Because of the disobedience of both the northern and southern kingdoms, God allows His people to be taken captive into exile.

Fleshing It Out in Your Life

Often on a national day of prayer, pastors will quote 2 Chronicles 7:14: "If my people, who are called by my name, will humble themselves and pray and seek my face and turn from their wicked ways, then will I hear from heaven and will forgive their sin and will heal their land." While this scripture is a call for Israel to repent, it can serve as a calling to you as well. Like Israel, you provide a sobering example to others of the necessity of obeying God.

Instead of taking up the ways of the godless, turn from them and call upon God. Nurture a heart of obedience. Willingly humble yourself and pray. Seek God's face. Turn from any practices that are displeasing to the Lord. This is the path to forgiveness and blessing!

In what ways are you obedient to your parents, teachers, and to God in your daily life?

Why is it sometimes hard to follow people in authority?

When have you disobeyed God's Word and paid the consequence? How did you feel? Did it hurt others?

Life Lessons from 2 Kings

- God is patient. He gives you many opportunities to respond to His call to repentance and obedience.
- Even when others around you are disobedient, you are to be obedient, for you are responsible for your own actions.
- An idol is any idea, ability, possession, or person that you regard more highly than God.
- Pride and self-will are sure signs you are going down the wrong path—a path that is not pleasing to God.

Where to Find It

Elijah transported to heaven . . . . 2 Kings 2:11-12
The ministry of Elisha . . . . 2 Kings 2:13–6:23
The stopped sundial. . . . . 2 Kings 20:8-11
The fall of Samaria . . . . .2 Kings 17:5
The fall of Jerusalem . . . . 2 Kings 25

Miracles Performed by Elisha

- Parts the Jordan River . . . . 2 Kings 2:13-14
- Purifies the water at Jericho . . . . 2 Kings 2:19-22
- Multiplies a widow's oil . . . . 2 Kings 4:1-7
- Raises a boy from the dead. . . . . 2 Kings 4:18-37
- Purifies a poisonous stew . . . . 2 Kings 4:38-41
- Multiplies the prophets' food . . . . 2 Kings 4:42-44
- Heals Naaman's leprosy . . . . 2 Kings 5:1-14
- Condemns Gehazi with leprosy . . . . 2 Kings 5:15-27
- Floats an ax head. . . . . 2 Kings 6:1-7
- Blinds Syrian army . . . . 2 Kings 6:8-23

The Three Deportations to Babylon

605 B.C.	Daniel and other Jewish youths of nobility taken to Babylon for training (Daniel 1:1-6)
597 B.C.	Ezekiel and others taken captive after the defeat of Jehoiachin (2 Kings 24)
586 B.C.	Jerusalem falls and the last of the survivors are taken to Babylon (2 Kings 25:8-11)

The Kings of the Northern Kingdom of Israel

Jeroboam I	Jehu
Nadab	Jehoahaz
Baasha	Jehoash
Elah	Jeroboam II
Zimri	Zechariah
Tibni	Shallum
Omri	Menahem
Ahab	Pekahiah
Ahaziah	Pekah
Joram	Hoshea

The Kings of the Southern Kingdom of Judah

Rehoboam	Jotham
Abijah	Ahaz
Asa	Hezekiah
Jehoshaphat	Manasseh
Jehoram	Amon
Ahaziah	Josiah
Athaliah (queen)	Jehoahaz
Joash	Jehoiakim
Amaziah	Jehoiachin
Azariah (Uzziah)	Zedekiah

1 Chronicles

David knew that the LORD had established him as king over Israel and that his kingdom had been highly exalted for the sake of his people Israel.
(14:2)

Theme: Israel's spiritual history
Date written: 450–430 B.C.
Author: Ezra (and possibly other priests)
Setting: Israel after the captivity

The books of 1 and 2 Chronicles were originally one book in the Hebrew Bible. They were divided when they were translated into Greek. That division continues today in English Bibles. First Chronicles covers the same period of Israel's history as the book of 2 Samuel but with one difference. Second Samuel gives a *political history* of the Davidic dynasty, while 1 Chronicles gives the *religious history*.

The Skeleton

▸ **Chapters 1–9** *Royal Line of David*

Chapters 1–4 trace the family tree of David from Adam to Jacob, and through his dynasty during the glory days of the nation. They conclude by giving a list of David's descendants who returned from captivity. These chapters demonstrate God's faithfulness in keeping His promises to maintain the Davidic line through the centuries. Chapters 5–9 provide the genealogies of most of the other tribes of Israel.

▸ **Chapters 10–29** *Reign of David*

David's life is presented here in a more positive way than in 2 Samuel. Because Chronicles is written by priests, the author(s) stresses David's deep spiritual commitment to God and his character. First Chronicles emphasizes David's concern for the things of God—especially his desire to build a temple for God. Even though David isn't allowed to build the temple, he spends the rest of this book (chapters 22–29) making preparations for his son, Solomon, to build the temple.

Putting Meat on the Bones

The previous book, 2 Kings, ends with both Israel and Judah in captivity, a dark period in the history of the Jewish people. But as a small group returns to Jerusalem from exile, the writer(s) of Chronicles summarizes Israel's spiritual history for the Jews, starting from the very beginning with Adam. It's been over 70 years since the people experienced any form of national unity. If the people could be reminded of their heritage and God's promises to them as a nation, they could gain a greater sense of identity and a vision of their future.

Fleshing It Out in Your Life

A review of your spiritual history and God's eternal promises is an important reason for you to read your Bible. Your identity in Christ and God's promises regarding your eternal future are in Scripture for your constant review. Also, just as God was faithful to His people in the past by bringing them out of captivity, you can rely on Him to be faithful in the present to protect and provide for you. You can look ahead with confidence, knowing that God will sustain you and all future generations of believers until His return.

What holds you captive? Is there anything that keeps you from trusting God?

Do you regularly recall God's faithfulness to you in the past? How has He kept His promises?

Do you think about your future with a lot of hope or with worry? How can knowing God's promises help your outlook?

Life Lessons from 1 Chronicles

- ▶ God continues to work out His plans in history through His people.
- ▶ God will be true to His promises in spite of your slip-ups.
- ▶ Your past mistakes provide valuable lessons for your present.
- ▶ Realize God has a future for you, just as He has a future for Israel.

Where to Find It

Davidic covenant . . . . 1 Chronicles 17:7-27
David's numbering of the people . . . . 1 Chronicles 21:1-13
David's preparations to build the temple. . . . . 1 Chronicles 22:1-6
Divisions for the priesthood . . . . 1 Chronicles 24:1

David's Preparations for Building the Temple

- 100,000 talents of gold, approximately 750 tons
- 1,000,000 talents of silver, approximately 37,500 tons
- Bronze and iron beyond measure
- Large amounts of timber and stone
- Workmen, woodsmen, and stonecutters in abundance

2 Chronicles

If my people, who are called by my name, will humble themselves and pray and seek my face and turn from their wicked ways, then will I hear from heaven and will forgive their sin and will heal their land.
(7:14)

Theme: Israel's spiritual heritage
Date written: 450–430 B.C.
Author: Ezra (and possibly other priests)
Setting: Israel after the exile

The book of 2 Chronicles covers much of the same period as 1 and 2 Kings. Second Chronicles highlights the spiritual nature of the Davidic dynasty from the time of the united kingdom of Solomon to the deportation of Judah. It ends with the decree of Cyrus, king of Persia, which allowed the Jews in exile in Persia to return to Jerusalem and rebuild the temple after 70 years. Because this is a spiritual account of David's lineage, the evil kings of the northern kingdom and their history are completely omitted.

The Skeleton

▸ Chapters 1–9 *Solomon's Glory*

A major focus of both 1 and 2 Chronicles is the temple. Much of the last half of 1 Chronicles centers on David's preparation of materials and personnel for the building and the service of the temple. In 2 Chronicles, most of the first nine chapters are devoted to the building and dedication of the temple by Solomon.

▸ **Chapters 10–36** *Judah's Decline and Exile*

The glory of Solomon's temple is short-lived. Soon after Solomon's death, the nation is divided and both kingdoms begin downward spiritual and political spirals. The kingdom of Judah, named for its most prominent tribe, must not only battle idolatry and spiritual rebellion from inside the country, but also the godless hostility of the northern kingdom and the rising powers of Assyria and Babylonia from outside the country.

This section is a priestly account on the 20 kings of Judah. Eight of those kings were good and brought about some level of spiritual revival. However, the effects of the revivals never lasted beyond one generation. Each king is described according to his respect for the temple as the center of worship. When the reigning king serves God, the kingdom is blessed. But if or when that king forsakes the temple and the worship of God, the nation is torn by warfare and unrest.

Putting Meat on the Bones

One of the central themes of both 1 and 2 Chronicles is *remembrance.* The author wants the returning Jews to remember the temple and the role of the law and the priesthood. The two books of Chronicles look back to Israel's former glory and offer encouragement to those rebuilding their heritage. These two books are a history lesson intended to help returning Jews remember a very important lesson: The reasons for the decline and fall of the nation are forgetting about spiritual matters, entering into defection, practicing idolatry, and marrying pagan neighbors. Chronicles must have taught the people at least one lesson, for they never again worshipped idols.

Fleshing It Out in Your Life

Like Israel, you are placed on this earth to represent God. But, again like Israel, it's easy to forget who you are and stumble blindly after the idols of clothes, popularity, and self-centeredness. If you make anything a higher priority than God, you are worshipping it and not God, despite what you say. It took 70 years of exile to break the Jews of the habit of following after the false gods of their neighboring nations. Don't wait for

God's hand of judgment. Examine your heart and put away any distraction to a wholehearted commitment to God.

You might be the only example some of your friends ever have of faith in God. What do you want to show them?

To what do you give most of your time and attention? What are you tempted to worship instead of God?

If others were to examine your heart (and your life), what would they find that represents God? What would they find that represents the world?

Life Lessons from 2 Chronicles

- There is always a result to disobedience.
- You can—and should—learn from the failures of others.
- Yesterday's revival must be renewed today.
- In the same way that the temple was the focal point of worship for Old Testament saints, Christ is to be your focal point today.

Where to Find It

Kings who restored the temple:

Asa . . . . 2 Chronicles 14:1–16:14
Jehoshaphat . . . . 2 Chronicles 17:1–20:37
Joash . . . . 2 Chronicles 24:1-27
Hezekiah . . . . 2 Chronicles 29–32
Josiah . . . . 2 Chronicles 34–35

Revival Under Three Good Kings in Judah

Jehoshaphat—When the nation was facing destruction he challenged the people to get serious with God, and disaster was averted (2 Chronicles 20:1-30).

Hezekiah—Purified the temple, destroyed the idols, and brought tithes to God's house (2 Chronicles 29–31).

Josiah—Made a commitment to obey God's Word and removed sinful influences from the land (2 Chronicles 34–35).

Jehoiachin was 18 when he became king and reigned in Jerusalem. Unfortunately he followed the evil ways of his father Jehoiakim (2 Chronicles 36:9-10).

Ezra

Because the hand of the LORD my God was on me, I took courage...
(7:28)

Theme: Restoration
Date written: 457–444 B.C.
Author: Ezra
Setting: Jerusalem

Ezra, who is also the author of 1 and 2 Chronicles, picks up where he leaves off at the end of 2 Chronicles. He records the two accounts of the returns of a small group of Jews from exile. As a priest, Ezra continues to provide a priestly and spiritual view of Judah's historical events. In addition, Ezra believes a record of the building of the *second* temple could be a helpful reminder of the returning group's link to the *first* temple.

The Skeleton

▸ Chapters 1–6 *The First Return Under Zerubbabel*

The book of Ezra opens with the decree repeated from 2 Chronicles from Cyrus, king of Persia, which allowed the Jews to return to Jerusalem. Ezra lists the families who volunteered to return, tracing their lineage back into Israel's past. This detailed list will help the exiles in years to come know and reestablish their roots and their connection to earlier generations.

Zerubbabel, a direct descendant of King David, heads the list as the leader of the returning Jews. Once this group arrives in Jerusalem, Zerubbabel oversees the laying of the foundation of a new temple. But soon opposition arises, and the work is stopped for 14 years. In the midst of this opposition, the prophets Haggai and Zechariah exhort the people to get back to rebuilding the temple. Zerubbabel and a high priest named Joshua lead the work, and the second temple is finally completed five years later. In a great celebration the temple is dedicated, the sacrificial offerings are started again, the people and priests purify themselves, and the Passover is once again observed.

▸ **Chapters 7–10** *The Second Return Under Ezra*

Approximately 60 years after the temple is rebuilt, another king in Persia, Artaxerxes, gives a decree for yet another return of Jews. The king authorizes Ezra, a priest and teacher, to lead this group back to Jerusalem. The king and his advisors also gave Ezra a large amount of gold and silver to take back with him to help beautify the temple. Before leaving for Jerusalem, Ezra and his small group pause and pray and fast for God's protection during their dangerous four-month journey.

When the group arrives in Jerusalem, God uses Ezra, a skilled teacher, to rebuild the people spiritually and morally. When Ezra discovers that many of the people have intermarried with foreign women, he offers a great public prayer and pleads with God on their behalf. The people quickly respond and make a promise to put away their foreign wives and live according to God's law. The book ends with a great revival and changed lifestyles.

Putting Flesh on the Bones

Ezra had royal documents in hand to support and authorize his work in Jerusalem and on the temple. More than man's documents, Ezra had "the hand of the LORD" helping him. He declared, "The hand of the LORD my God was on me" (Ezra 7:28; see also verse 6). The decrees, proclamations, letters, lists, genealogies, and memos, many of them written by the Persian administration, attest to the powerful hand of God on the two returns of the Jews to Jerusalem and Israel's revival. The main message of the book of Ezra is that God oversaw all of what happened during the past grim situation (the captivity) and would continue to work through pagan kings to give Judah hope for the future. God's administration overrides that of any and all of the kings of this world.

Fleshing It Out in Your Life

The book of Ezra is a message of God's continuing grace to Israel as promised in Jeremiah 29:14: "'I will be found by you,' declares the LORD, 'and will bring you back from captivity. I will gather you from all the nations and places where I have banished you,' declares the LORD, 'and will bring you back to the place from which I carried you into exile.'" God restored His chosen people from their captivity, and God continues to show His mercy and grace to each new generation of His people. No matter how difficult you think life is, you are never removed from God's love and mercy. Help is available each time you turn to Him.

Reflect on a time when God used someone rather surprising to help you learn a faith lesson.

Are there people who give you a hard time about your beliefs? Pray about these people specifically and ask God to work in those circumstances and relationships.

When have you felt the hand of God upon you? In what ways do you feel God's presence in your life today?

Life Lessons from Ezra

- God always keeps His promises to His people…and to you.
- God is at work behind the scenes to lead and direct your life.
- Strong spiritual leadership is necessary to give people spiritual guidance. Take advantage of the guidance of your parents and youth leaders.
- Preparation to teach God's people is a goal that requires dedication.
- Teaching God's Word will always have a positive effect.

Where to Find It

Zerubbabel, the leader of the first return . . . . Ezra 2:2

Urim and Thummim . . . . Ezra 2:63; Exodus 28:30

The temple work begins . . . . .Ezra 3:8-10

Ezra's preparation for ministry . . . . Ezra 7:10

The Two Returns to Jerusalem in the Book of Ezra

Chapters 1–6	Chapters 7–10
Decreed by Cyrus	Decreed by Artaxerxes
538 B.C.	458 B.C.
Led by Zerubbabel	Led by Ezra
Sacred vessels returned	Gold given for temple
Ministry of the prophets Haggai and Zechariah	Ministry of Ezra
Temple rebuilt	People rebuilt

Nehemiah

Then I said to them, "You see the trouble we are in: Jerusalem lies in ruins, and its gates have been burned with fire. Come, let us rebuild the wall of Jerusalem, and we will no longer be in disgrace."
(2:17)

Theme: Rebuilding
Date written: 424–400 B.C.
Author: Nehemiah
Setting: Jerusalem

Nehemiah provides an addition to the story of the book of Ezra. First, Ezra arrives on the scene and brings about spiritual improvements through the teaching of God's Word. Now 13 years later, Nehemiah, a trusted official to the king of Persia, arrives in Jerusalem with a burden to rebuild the wall around the city.

In the book of Ezra we witnessed the rebuilding of the temple under the leadership of Zerubbabel (chapters 1–6), and the restoring of worship under the leadership of Ezra (chapters 7–10). Nehemiah, in turn, has two goals: rebuilding the walls around Jerusalem (which were destroyed by the Babylonians), and re-instructing the Jewish people, whose children were becoming pagan because of intermarriage with Gentile unbelievers.

The Skeleton

▸ Chapters 1–7 *Rebuilding the Walls*

The book opens with Nehemiah living in Susa, the winter capital of the Persian king. There he receives reports of the sad living conditions of the people who had volunteered to return to Jerusalem. Burdened by these reports, Nehemiah prays and, in the process, realizes he is the best one to help. Therefore, he asks for a leave of absence from his duties and receives permission by the king to go to Jerusalem as governor of the city.

Upon arriving, Nehemiah inspects the damaged walls and enlists the support of the people, who eagerly begin helping to rebuild the wall. Nehemiah stands ready against the threat of attack from the Ammonites and Arabians by keeping half of the workers armed with weapons while the other half, armed with work tools, rebuilds the wall. These enemies did not want to see Jerusalem's walls rebuilt, and they tried to discourage Nehemiah and the workers. But the Jews persisted, and a project that had faltered for 70 years was completed in just 52 days! Now that the walls are up, Nehemiah delegates faithful men to have charge over the city and the gates.

▸ **Chapters 8–13** *Re-teaching the People*

With the walls rebuilt, the people gather in a great crowd and ask that the law of Moses be brought out and read to them. Ezra, a priest and the author of the book of Ezra, publically reads the law, and the priests and Levites explain the meaning of what is read. The reading lasts from early morning until noon. In response, the people celebrate the Feast of Tabernacles for seven days, and each day Ezra reads more of the law. As a further response to God's Word, the people fast and put on sackcloth and ashes to demonstrate their humility. They also separate themselves from the Gentiles around them, confess their sins, and enter into a solemn promise to observe the laws of God.

Because Jerusalem is now safe and has lots of open space, the population is shuffled around so that one out of every ten Jews will live in the city. The others are free to live outside the city walls. The rebuilt walls are dedicated with music and thanksgiving. Nehemiah is then recalled to Persia for an undetermined amount of time.

Nehemiah later returns to Jerusalem and is upset to discover that the high priest has allowed an outsider, a Gentile leader, to have a room in the temple—a gross abuse of "the house of God." Nehemiah throws out the man's furniture and cleanses the room. The book ends with Nehemiah continuing to exhort the leaders to fulfill their earlier promises to obey God.

Putting Meat on the Bones

Three major themes can be seen in Nehemiah's account of Israel's struggle to survive in the midst of overwhelmingly hostile odds.

First, the importance of God's Word: There is a constant desire by Israel's leaders to carefully follow God's Word and perform His will. Several times, Ezra and the priests read from "the Book of the Law of Moses" (8:1) and explain its meaning to the people. The leaders desire to "give attention to the words of the Law" (8:13) and are so concerned about how the sacrificial system is to be carried out that they are cautious to perform it exactly "as it is written in the Law" (10:34; see also verse 36). Also, when marriage reforms are needed, the leaders act according to what they read from the Book of Moses (13:1).

Second, Nehemiah's trust in God: Nehemiah is confident that God is leading and directing his every step. Time and time again Nehemiah acknowledges his success and safety to God, referring to "the gracious hand of my God upon me" (2:18; see also 2:8; 6:16), and "my God put it into my heart" (7:5).

Third, opposition from Israel's enemies: The Jews' enemies try hard to make the Persian government withdraw its support of the Jews' efforts to rebuild their social and religious systems. Yet in spite of corruption and disagreement from among the people and bullying from the nations around them, Nehemiah and the people rebuild the walls in only 52 days.

Fleshing It Out in Your Life

When it comes to the building or rebuilding of your spiritual life, follow the example of Nehemiah and the Jews in Jerusalem and remember that God's Word is essential. If you want to build a better spiritual life, look to God's blueprint, the Bible.

From the day he understood his part in God's plan, Nehemiah's trust in God's provision and protection was firm. His confidence was passed on and the people responded by working together to rebuild the city walls. Trust God in the midst of your problems. Maybe your confidence will inspire others toward confidence in God as well.

Also, make sure you don't underestimate your enemy. Jerusalem's enemies had kept the wall from being rebuilt for 70 years. But through prayer and follow-through, the people were watchful, defended themselves, and completed the task. When you face opposition, defend yourself with God's armor (Ephesians 6:14-17) and gain the victory.

How influential is God's Word on the decisions you make? Where does God's truth fit into your building plans?

How strong is your trust in God's provision and protection? Do you trust God in good times and bad?

Your enemies can also be things and desires. What might some of these enemies be in your life?

Life Lessons from Nehemiah

- At times you may become the answer to your own prayers.
- Most things you do for God's purposes will require acts of faith.
- Don't underestimate the importance of reading and understanding God's Word.
- You must keep a constant watch against attacks from the enemy of your soul.

Where to Find It

Nehemiah's prayer for Jerusalem . . . . .Nehemiah 1
Nehemiah's request of the king . . . . .Nehemiah 2
The record of the workers . . . . .Nehemiah 3
The attacks of the Samaritans . . . . .Nehemiah 4
The cancellation of debt . . . . .Nehemiah 5
The completion of the wall in 52 days . . . . .Nehemiah 6
The genealogy of the returning Jews . . . . .Nehemiah 7
The reading of the law . . . . .Nehemiah 8
The people's confession of sin . . . . .Nehemiah 9
The people sign a covenant . . . . .Nehemiah 10
The list of the leaders . . . . .Nehemiah 11
The Levites dedicate the temple . . . . .Nehemiah 12
The Levites serve in the temple . . . . .Nehemiah 13

Nehemiah's Prayer Life

- When discouraged, he prayed (1:4).
- When seeking direction, he prayed (1:5-11).
- When seeking assistance, he prayed (2:1-5).
- When under attack, he prayed (4:4-5,9).
- When weak and powerless, he prayed (6:9).
- When joyful, he prayed (13).

Nehemiah served two terms as governor. One term was 12 years and the other was 14 years. In between the two terms, he served the king of Persia for 9 years.

Esther

Yet who knows whether you have come to the kingdom for such a time as this?
(4:14 NKJV)

Theme: Preservation
Date: 450–431 B.C.
Author: Unknown
Setting: The court of Persia

The three books of Ezra, Nehemiah, and Esther record God's dealings with the Jews after their 70 years of captivity in Babylon. While Ezra and Nehemiah deal with the small group of the people who returned to Judea, the book of Esther deals with the vast majority who decided not to return but to stay in the land of their captivity. Esther is one of two books in the Bible given a woman's name, the other being the book of Ruth. Esther is a Jewish girl who by God's plan becomes queen of the vast Persian Empire that stretches from India to Ethiopia. In the middle of a desperate crisis, Queen Esther exerts her influence and the Jewish people are saved from destruction. Esther's story fits between chapters 6 and 7 of Ezra, and between the first return to Jerusalem led by Zerubbabel and the second return led by Ezra.

The Skeleton

▸ Chapters 1–5 *The Crisis Anticipated*

The drama opens with Queen Vashti refusing to appear before her husband, King Ahasuerus, at a banquet room filled with drunken men. She is banished and an empire-wide search begins for a new queen. Esther, a Jewess, is selected to become the new queen. Meanwhile, Mordecai, Esther's older cousin who raised her, is a government official. Mordecai overhears a plot to kill the king and passes the news on to Esther, who informs the king in Mordecai's name.

Every drama needs a villain, and in the book of Esther, his name is Haman, who is the prime minister, the second in command to the king. Mordecai refuses to bow in reverence to Haman and, in a rage, Haman superstitiously "cast lots" or "Pur" to determine the best day for the Jews to be killed and eliminated. Once he has cast the lots and determined the date, he asks permission from the king to destroy Mordecai and all the Jews.

Haman misleads the king by describing the Jews as a "certain people" who are lawless and deserve to die. The king, not knowing who the people are but eager to eliminate any people who are rebellious, issues an edict condemning the Jews to death. Because Esther has never revealed her Jewish heritage, the king has unwittingly approved the killing of his own queen! When Mordecai tells Queen Esther about the edict, she determines to risk her life to save her people. Esther then plans a banquet and invites the king and Haman, hoping for an opportunity to expose Haman's evil plot.

▸ **Chapters 6–10** *The Crisis Overruled*

The night before Esther's banquet, the king is unable to sleep and asks for records from the royal library to be read to him. While the records are being read, the king learns that some time ago Mordecai had uncovered a plot against him and was never rewarded. The next morning the king asks Haman what should be done to properly honor a hero. Haman thinks the king must be talking about him, so he describes a lavish and public reward. The king then tells Haman to honor Mordecai in this way.

Things go from bad to worse for Haman as Esther reveals that she is a Jew and exposes Haman's plot. In a fury, the king has Haman hanged on the gallows that Haman had prepared for the hanging of Mordecai. The king then gives a new edict that allows the Jews to defend themselves against the attacks which Haman's proclamation had authorized. To celebrate this historic occasion, the Feast of Purim (casting of lots) was established and is still celebrated among Jewish people today. In the final act of this true-life drama, Mordecai is appointed to take Haman's place as prime minister.

Putting Meat on the Bones

The saving of God's people was accomplished through a beauty contest, a pagan king, and a brave woman. Furthermore, regardless of whether the individual Jewish people had chosen to return to Jerusalem or remain in Persia, God protected them according to His plan and promises to His people. God worked through one woman who was willing to risk her life for her people. When Esther realized the need for her to take a stand, she uttered the famous words, "If I perish, I perish" (4:16).

Though God's name does not appear even once in the book of Esther, the clear message that emerges from its pages is that God is totally in control over all things. He faithfully guided and protected His people and overruled harmful human schemes against them, regardless of whether they lived in the capital of Persia or were scattered in one of the 127 Persian provinces that stretched from India to Ethiopia.

Fleshing It Out in Your Life

How much of your security do you think lies in what you have, who you are, what people think of you, or where you live? Wherever you live and whatever you possess, realize God did not place you there or give you those things for your own benefit. No, He has put you there and provided you with the means to serve Him. Esther did not choose to be in King Ahasuerus's palace nor to be his queen. But in her position there, God used her mightily to save His people. Regardless of what you have or don't have, whether your circumstances are good or bad, God can and will protect you. And He can and will use you to help His people. You may not see His mighty hand of provision and protection at home or at school, but you can be sure He is at work on your behalf. He is your ultimate security and provision, and He will take care of you.

Do you ever feel like you are in the plot of a drama? How can you be a hero, with God's help, instead of a villain?

So much happens behind the scenes of your life that you don't know about! Yield to God's control of those unknowns through prayer. Think of a life event or experience when you realized *afterwards* that God was involved the whole time.

Do you ever speak out for the persecuted or ridiculed in your school or neighborhood? How does Esther's story inspire you to stand up for others?

Life Lessons from Esther

- Don't let less-than-perfect circumstances keep you from trusting in God.
- Don't think that a difficult life prevents you from great service to God and His people.
- God's protective hand is always present even though it is not always visible.
- It takes courage to speak up for your beliefs and be willing to suffer any consequences.
- Each of God's people—including you—has been prepared by God for some purpose and important usefulness.

Where to Find It

Mordecai's discovery of a plot against the king .... Esther 2:21-23
Haman's plot against the Jews.................. Esther 3:8-9
Mordecai's statement, "For such a time as this" ..... Esther 4:14
Esther's decision, "If I perish, I perish" .... Esther 4:16
Haman's death on his own gallows .... Esther 7:10
Institution of the Feast of Purim .... Esther 9:20-24

The Feast of Purim

- The first and only non-Mosaic festival
- An annual two-day holiday of rejoicing
- Held in February or March
- Named for the Akkadian word for *lot*

Esther is one of only two books of the Bible named after women. The other book is Ruth.

The Poetic Books

The 17 historical books which make up the first portion of the Old Testament are concluded. They gave the history of civilization from creation to the time of the Persian Empire. They record the history of the Jewish nation from its beginning, through its days of glory and exile, and finally, to its days of survival as a small, unimportant nation surrounded by enemies wanting to destroy it.

Now comes a different set of books, the poetic books of the Bible: Job, Psalms, Proverbs, Ecclesiastes, and the Song of Solomon. They don't talk so much about historical experiences. Rather they describe the experiences of the human heart. They do not continue the story of the nation of Israel. Instead, through the use of Hebrew poetry, they look into the issues of suffering, wisdom, life, love, and most importantly, the character and nature of God. And finally, they have another important function—they serve like a door hinge linking the historical books of the past with the prophetic books of the future.

Job

Therefore I despise myself and repent in dust and ashes.
(42:6)

Theme: Blessings through suffering
Date written: 2000–1800 B.C.
Author: Unknown
Setting: Land of Uz

The book of Job is considered to be the oldest book in the Bible. Job probably lived during the same time period as Abraham in the book of Genesis. Like Abraham, Job is a wealthy and upright man who respects God. This book that bears Job's name describes the death of his pride through the fires of suffering—which include the loss of his family, his wealth, and his health. It also includes a series of debates that take place with his friends over the subject of suffering. Then in a discussion with God, Job stops questioning God's actions in his life and quits trying to prove he is right. He finally acknowledges the greatness, majesty, power, and utter independence of God and sees himself as God sees him. He repents of his pride, and God restores his health, gives him another family, and makes him wealthier than before.

The Skeleton

▸ Chapters 1–3 *The Drama*

The book of Job opens with the facts of Job's honesty, his wealth, and his children. He does not seem like a good candidate for disaster. But in a rare glimpse into the halls of heaven, Satan is seen as the accuser who charges that no one, including Job, loves God out of pure motives. Satan claims that people love God only for what they can get from Him. Satan says, "Take away the blessings, and a person will curse God." To refute Satan's accusations, God allows Satan to strike Job with two series of disasters. The first series takes his wealth and his family, and the second takes his health. Job's wife sees his suffering and tells him to "curse God and die." Four friends hear of Job's adversities and come to give a measure of sympathy. For seven days they sit with Job, watching his suffering. At the end of the seven days, Job breaks the silence by mourning the day of his birth.

▸ **Chapters 4–37** *The Debates*

After Job breaks the silence, three rounds of debates follow with Job's friends. Their charges all have the same theme: Job is suffering because of some deep, dark sin in his life. Having no knowledge of God's discussions with Satan, his friends believe that confession is the only cure. With each round of accusations—and Job's repeated denials—the emotional zeal of the argument increases. Job first accuses his friends of judging him, which they are. Finally out of frustration at their repeated accusations, Job appeals to God as his judge. In the process of defending his innocence, Job becomes guilty of prideful self-righteousness. After Job gives a five-chapter closing argument claiming his innocence, Elihu, the fourth friend, who has been silent up to this point, gives a more accurate view of Job's problem than the other three friends did. Elihu suggests Job needs to humble himself before God and submit to God's work of purifying his life through trials.

▸ **Chapters 38–42** *The Deliverance*

After Elihu's speech, God ends the debate by speaking to Job out of a whirlwind. God gives two speeches. In the first, He describes His power and wisdom as Creator and Sustainer of the physical and animal world. Job could only acknowledge his ignorance and nothingness.

In the second speech, God describes His authority and power. Job responds with a sorrowful heart and again acknowledges his ignorance. There is no way to understand God's ways because they are *God's* ways!

Job finally begins to see his suffering from God's viewpoint. Satan's challenge became God's opportunity to build Job's faith and character. In the end, God restored to Job double what he had initially possessed.

Putting Meat on the Bones

The book of Job is an interesting story of riches-to-rags-to-riches. It helps us to better understand the problem of suffering, the certainty of God's directing hand, the activities of Satan, and a faith that endures. Job was tested, and his faith endured because it was built on the firm foundation of God. His suffering initially caused him to complain, and his self-examination produced pride. But Job's sorrow from his error led to his restoration. In the end, his trial brought about an amazing transformation. Job was a different man after he graduated from God's school of suffering. And in defense of Job's friends, they were the only people who came to his side in his time of need. And Elihu's final speech is never rebuked by God, which means his understanding of Job's problem and God's solution was more accurate than that of the others.

Fleshing It Out in Your Life

God is all-wise and all-powerful, and His will is perfect. However, in our limited minds, we don't always understand His actions. Suffering doesn't make sense to us. After all, we wrongly wonder, aren't God's people supposed to prosper, to always receive blessings, and to enjoy a sorrow-free life? In our misunderstanding of God, we, like Job, lose hope. We question God, and at times even shake our fist at Him in frustration. Job teaches us there are many things we will never understand, including suffering. But one thing we do know: God is never numb to our suffering. His sufficiency makes up for our insufficiency. And, in the end, we are drawn closer to Him.

Is Job hard to read? Why? What suffering have you experienced or witnessed? How have you felt God's comfort?

What insights and gifts of faith does the book of Job offer you personally?

How do Job's friends help you understand what to say and what not to say to a friend who is struggling?

Life Lessons from Job

- Spiritual affairs are going on in heaven that you know nothing about, yet they affect your life.
- Life issues cannot always be understood in human terms.
- God's people do suffer. Bad things do happen to good people.
- You cannot always judge a person's spirituality by his or her pain or prosperity.
- God always has a reason for what you are asked to endure.
- Suffering improves your worship as you draw closer to God and His comfort.

Where to Find It

Satan's debates with God . . . . Job 1:6–2:10
Friends' debates with Job . . . . Job 4–37
God's questions to Job . . . . Job 38–41
Job's confession to God . . . . Job 42
God's blessing of Job . . . . Job 42

Some Sources of Suffering

- The fall of man—Genesis 3:16-19
- The consequences of your sins—Galatians 6:7
- The sins of others—Genesis 37:26-28
- Unavoidable consequences—Luke 10:30
- Unavoidable disaster—Luke 13:1-5
- Consequence of your beliefs—Philippians 1:29; 2 Timothy 3:12
- God's greater plan—Job 1:1–2:13

Psalms

My mouth will speak in praise of the LORD.
Let every creature praise his holy name
for ever and ever.
(145:21)

Theme: Praise
Date written: 1410–450 B.C.
Author: Various authors
Setting: Heaven and earth

The Psalms are poetic expressions of human and religious feeling. They are divided into five books that comprise a total of 150 individual songs or psalms. The Psalms cover the ten centuries from Moses to the days after the Jewish people's exile. They have a wide variety of styles and purposes and emotions (such as lament, thanksgiving, praise, worship, pilgrimage, petition, and penitence). Each of the five books ends with a doxology—a praise to God. The last psalm is the closing psalm for book five of the Psalms and for the book of Psalms as a whole.

The Skeleton

▸ Chapters 1–41 *Book One*

David is named as the author of almost half of the psalms (73 of the 150 psalms). He authored all the psalms in this first book or grouping of psalms. David's wide range of experiences as a shepherd, musician, warrior, and king are seen in his psalms. The psalms in this grouping are basically songs of praise and worship. The most well-known psalm in this section is Psalm 23, which begins with the familiar and well-loved words, "The LORD is my shepherd" (Psalm 23:1). A description of Jesus' future suffering as the "suffering Messiah" can be found in Psalm 22.

▸ **Chapters 42–72** *Book Two*

David and the sons of Korah (a group of singers and composers) wrote most of the psalms in book two. Many of these psalms are hymns of national interest and describe God's nature and His judgment of the wicked and deliverance of the righteous. David's public song of sorrow after his sinful affair with Bathsheba is in this section. In it, David cries out, "Have mercy on me, O God, according to your unfailing love" (Psalm 51:1). These psalms help us gain a sense of wonder and thankfulness toward God in our worship.

▸ **Chapters 73–89** *Book Three*

Asaph was appointed by David as a leader of one of the temple choirs (1 Chronicles 25:1) and is the author of the majority of the psalms in this section. This group of "songs" celebrates the power of God, God's hand in history, His faithfulness, and His promise to David. These psalms remind us that our worship of God should be continual. The psalmist declared, "I will sing of the LORD's great love forever; with my mouth I will make your faithfulness known through all generations" (Psalm 89:1).

▸ **Chapters 90–106** *Book Four*

Although five of these psalms are attributed to David, most of them were written by unknown authors. Primarily these psalms are anthems of praise and reflection. A prayer by Moses is the opening psalm in this section. Moses reminds us that our time on this earth is limited and we are to use it wisely. He tells us to "number our days aright, that we may gain a heart of wisdom" (Psalm 90:12).

▸ **Chapters 107–150** *Book Five*

Many of these psalms are attributed to David and are uplifting songs of praise. They exalt God's works and recount the blessings of righteous living. The longest psalm (Psalm 119) praises God for His wonderful Word, the Bible. The poetry in this grouping reminds us that the most perfect sacrifice we can offer to God is a faithful and obedient life.

Putting Meat on the Bones

Psalms is made up of a variety of songs written by different authors over the course of hundreds of years. Yet they have a common theme of worship—the worship of God for who He is, what He has done, and what He will do in the future. God's goodness extends through all time and eternity. These anthems and songs of praise were written with authentic honesty and openness. In them we hear the psalmists share their deepest feelings for and with God.

Within the Psalms is a group of psalms collectively referred to as the "imprecatory psalms," meaning they "call down a curse." Some people have a problem with these psalms, as they seem to be harsh and unloving. But here are a few things to keep in mind as you read the imprecatory psalms: First, they are in the Bible and are therefore of divine origin. Next, these psalms call for divine justice, not human vengeance. Also, they call upon God to punish the wicked and thus confirm His righteousness. Finally, even Jesus called down a curse on the inhabitants of several cities that rejected the gospel. Summed up, God is the God of love, but He is also the God of justice.

Fleshing It Out in Your Life

The Psalms focus on God and His dealings with His people. The more you read them, the more you understand and are blessed by what you learn of God and His work as Creator, Redeemer, Sustainer, Provider, Protector, and Comforter. Like the psalmists, you should be moved to praise and worship the Lord. The Psalms can guide you into a deeper and more meaningful walk with God.

Our culture follows the example of the psalms and uses songs to express itself all the time! Write your own psalm and communicate why you need God.

How does the book of Psalms give you a better understanding of how God relates to you?

You might not break out into song at school, but how can you "sing" praise to God during the day?

Life Lessons from the Psalms

- The Psalms give you a better understanding of God.
- The Psalms can guide you in your ongoing relationship with God.
- The Psalms are a source of comfort in times of pain and distress.
- The Psalms remind you often of God's control over all things.
- The Psalms provide a model for praise and worship.

Where to Find It

The psalm of the cross .... Psalm 22
The Shepherd's psalm .... Psalm 23
David's psalms of repentance .... Psalm 32; 51
Moses' psalm .... Psalm 90
A psalm about God's Word .... Psalm 119
Songs of travel to Jerusalem .... Psalm 120–134

Members of God's Orchestra

One eclectic list of performers and instruments from Bible times:

Jubal is the first musician listed in the Bible in Genesis 4:21. He'd stop the show with his harp and organ performance.

Miriam was a percussionist. She'd be a multi-talented performer. "Then Miriam the prophetess, Aaron's sister, took a tambourine in her hand, and all the women followed her, with tambourines and dancing. Miriam sang to them" (Exodus 15:20-21).

Aspah would play cymbals (1 Chronicles 16:6).

Benaiah and Jahaziel the priests might blow their trumpets (1 Chronicles 16:6).

David was an amazing musician songwriter. He would make it to the finals in any musical competition. *Psalm* means "song" and David created many powerful songs and arrangements that continue to influence the music and message of churches today.

Throughout the Bible, music is used to honor God. Find ways to celebrate faith and to praise God through song and music. "It is good to praise the LORD and make music to your name, O Most High, to proclaim your love in the morning and your faithfulness at night, to the music of the ten-stringed lyre and the melody of the harp" (Psalm 92:1-3).

Proverbs

The fear of the LORD is the beginning of knowledge,
but fools despise wisdom and discipline.
(1:7)

Theme: Practical wisdom
Date written: 971–686 B.C.
Author: Primarily Solomon
Setting: Everyday life

While David is the author of a majority of the psalms, his son Solomon is the author of most of the book of Proverbs. Early in his rule as king, Solomon was granted great wisdom by God (1 Kings 4:29-34). Much of his wisdom is shared in the 800 proverbs that are in the book of Proverbs.

A *proverb* is a brief statement that offers a short but powerful observation. And it is common for proverbs to use comparisons, contrasts, analogies, or figures of speech to help drive home their point. The book of Proverbs is the most practical book in the Old Testament because it gives simple illustrations and insights about everyday life. The object of Proverbs is to inspire respect for God, a godly fear of His judgments, and a deep love for wisdom and godly living. The book of Proverbs should improve your everyday life just as the book of Psalms should improve your devotional life.

The Skeleton

▸ **Chapters 1–9** *Wisdom for Young People*

A brief introduction spells out the purpose and theme of the book of

Proverbs—to instruct in wisdom and to help in the getting of discernment. In the opening chapters, Solomon enlightens the young men of his day like a father giving advice to his sons or children. He gives a series of ten exhortations, each beginning with the impassioned plea, "My son." Solomon challenges young men and women to treasure wisdom above all else. Wisdom, he explains, will help them avoid crime and evil people. It will provide freedom and safety. It will give discernment on how to avoid sexual sin. It will keep a person from living foolishly. Anyone beginning—and continuing—their journey to discover more wisdom will benefit from these wise sayings. Solomon's goal is "giving prudence to the simple, knowledge and discretion to the young" (Proverbs 1:4).

▸ **Chapters 10–24** *Wisdom for All People*

Solomon wants to impart wisdom not only to the youth of his day, but also to all people, regardless of age, sex, or position in society. This section contains a collection of proverbs from Solomon and a number of lessons from other wise men. These short sayings give practical wisdom for daily living. They contrast good and evil, and right and wrong. They impart advice on child-raising, money matters, and speech. Ultimately, "every prudent man acts out of knowledge, but a fool exposes his folly" (Proverbs 13:16).

▸ **Chapters 25–29** *Wisdom for Leaders*

According to 1 Kings 4:32, Solomon spoke 3000 proverbs and 1005 songs! This section of Proverbs contains more of these proverbs. They were collected after Solomon's death by the men serving under King Hezekiah. While most of these sayings are general in nature, many are directed toward a king and those who deal with him. They are useful for those who are leaders or aspire to be leaders in any area of life—at home, at church, at school, in the government, and on the job. Solomon instructs, "It is the glory of God to conceal a matter; to search out a matter is the glory of kings [or leaders]" (Proverbs 25:2).

▸ **Chapters 30–31** *Wisdom for Disciples*

The last two chapters of Proverbs were written by two unknown sages, or wise men. The first unknown sage is Agur. He gives his advice in clusters of numerical proverbs—"Two things I ask of you...There are three things that are never satisfied...There are three things that are too amazing for me" (Proverbs 30:7,15,18). The last chapter of Proverbs contains wisdom passed on from a wise mother to her disciple—her son, King Lemuel. In the first part of Proverbs 31, the mother advises her son on how to be a good king. In the remaining verses she asks the question, "Who can find a virtuous wife?" (Proverbs 31:10 NKJV), and then gives her son advice on what to look for in a good wife.

Putting Meat on the Bones

Solomon came to the throne with great promise, privilege, and opportunity. God granted him wisdom beyond any other man of his day. In the first part of his reign, Solomon was sought out by kings and queens, by the common people and the upper levels of society, for his wise counsel. It is assumed that Solomon wrote most of his wisdom proverbs during his early years of devotion to God. But amazingly and tragically, in his later years Solomon failed to live out the truths that he knew and wrote about. He became the fool that he so zealously taught about and warned against in Proverbs!

Fleshing It Out in Your Life

As you read Proverbs, keep in mind Solomon's message is that knowing God is the key to wisdom. But don't stop with the book of Proverbs. Read the rest of the Bible to gain more of God's wisdom. Listen to the thoughts and lessons from the Bible's many other teachers. Review these truths repeatedly and apply them always in your life. "The fear of the LORD is the beginning of wisdom, and knowledge of the Holy One is understanding" (Proverbs 9:10).

Wisdom can sound lofty, but wisdom is as practical as street smarts. List three bits of wisdom from Proverbs that directly relate to your life.

You might know what the right thing to do is, but that doesn't mean you'll do it. How can you be sure that you don't end up like Solomon, living foolishly and apart from God's wisdom?

Who do you know that is spiritually wise? How can you learn more from that person? Why is that person a good example to you?

Life Lessons from Proverbs

- Choose God's ways. He will lead you into making right decisions.
- Choose your words carefully. They reveal your inner character.
- Choose to work diligently. God will be honored, and you will profit and gain skills in your labors.
- Choose your friends carefully. They are a reflection of you.
- Choose to develop moral character and devotion to God. This is success in God's eyes.

Where to Find It

Wisdom . . . . Proverbs 2:6; 18:15
Discipline (self-control) . . . . Proverbs 15:18; 16:32; 25:28
Speech . . . . Proverbs 16:23-24; 21:23
Friends . . . . Proverbs 17:17; 18:24; 22:24-25
Money . . . . Proverbs 3:9; 11:28; 13:11
Food . . . . Proverbs 30:7-9
Parenting . . . . Proverbs 20:15; 22:6

A Teen's Tipsheet on the Value of Wisdom from Proverbs 3:1-26

- Wisdom has its source in God.
- Wisdom is seen in God's creation.
- Wisdom looks to God and fears.
- Wisdom looks to God for understanding.
- Wisdom finds favor with God and man.
- Wisdom is established in sound teaching.
- Wisdom produces strength.
- Wisdom welcomes discipline for its benefits.
- Wisdom will add health and peace to your life.
- Wisdom is better than gold.
- Wisdom will keep you on the right path.

Ecclesiastes

Fear God and keep his commandments, for this is the whole duty of man.
(12:13)

Theme: All is worthless apart from God
Date written: 940–931 B.C.
Author: Solomon
Setting: The end of Solomon's life

The title for this next and fourth book in the wisdom series is *Ecclesiastes,* meaning "an official speaker in an assembly." In the case of Ecclesiastes, it is one speaker, "the Teacher" (Ecclesiastes 1:1). There is no doubt this book is a self-description written by King Solomon at the end of his life after he strayed away from God. As if he were reporting the results of a scientific experiment, Solomon, also known as the Teacher, shares his search for satisfaction. In four "sermons," he relates his discovery that life without God is a long and wasted search for enjoyment, meaning, and fulfillment. Solomon hopes to spare his readers the bitterness of learning hard lessons through personal experience. Solomon's "bottom line" is that life's pursuits, apart from God, are empty, hollow, fruitless, and meaningless.

The Skeleton

▸ **Chapters 1–2** *Solomon's Personal Experiences*

The Teacher describes his quest for meaning and happiness as he explores his vast personal resources. He moves from wisdom to laughter and pleasure, and from wine to work, women, and wealth. But all lead to emptiness. He concludes by stating that contentment and joy are found only in God.

▸ **Chapters 3–5** *Solomon's General Observations*

The Teacher next moves from his personal experiences to observe the world and human activity. He discovers the fixed order of events and concludes, "There is a time for every purpose under heaven"—a truth that cannot be understood but needs to be accepted (Ecclesiastes 3:1 NKJV). Solomon then looks at the human conditions of suffering, differences, popularity, wealth, and honor. He again arrives at a similar conclusion: "Much dreaming and many words are meaningless. Therefore stand in awe of God" (Ecclesiastes 5:7).

▸ **Chapters 6–8** *Solomon's Practical Counsel*

Solomon is nearing the conclusion of Ecclesiastes. What is the secret to knowing real satisfaction in life? Any work or pleasures done apart from God are meaningless and will leave us feeling empty. But when we put God first, everything we do becomes meaningful. God designed both work and fun to be good for us, and we will enjoy all our labors and activities when they are done in a way that honors God and obeys His Word. That's the secret to real fulfillment.

▸ **Chapters 8–12** *Solomon's Final Conclusion*

When we look at our lives, we are tempted to find them meaningless and empty. All our labors seem fruitless and passing, and all our pleasures and successes fail to bring true fulfillment. The one thing we can know with certainty is that we will die. The only thing that can help us overcome our hopelessness and achieve true meaning in life is to acknowledge and obey God.

Putting Meat on the Bones

The tone of Ecclesiastes is negative and gloomy—"Meaningless! Meaningless!...Everything is meaningless" (1:2). However, don't conclude that the only chapter worth reading and applying is the last one, which gives Solomon's positive conclusions. The entire book is inspired God, making the entire book a vital source of wisdom. For instance,

Ecclesiastes 3:1-8 is a famous passage that teaches us "there is a time for everything." Remember, too, the Teacher's instruction on spiritual wisdom—"Fear God and keep his commandments, for this is the whole duty of man" (Ecclesiastes 12:13).

Fleshing It Out in Your Life

All of Solomon's remarks that are preserved in the book of Ecclesiastes are for a purpose—to lead you to seek true happiness in God alone. Solomon is not trying to destroy all your hopes. He is instead directing your hopes to the only One who can truly fulfill them. Solomon affirms the value of knowledge, relationships, work, and pleasure. But he also shows us that their value is realized only in their proper place of priority in the light of God's eternity.

What does the world say are the keys to happiness?

What does God's Word say are some of the keys to happiness?

Why is it so important to have a life of meaning? In what ways do you want your life to count?

Life Lessons from Ecclesiastes

- All your activities in life should be seen and measured in the light of eternity.
- Nothing in this life will bring true meaning and happiness—not wealth, fame, pleasure, or success. Only in God can you find real fulfillment.
- There is much less that you can depend on than you might think!
- True happiness comes only from obedience to God.

Where to Find It

"Vanity of vanities" . . . . Ecclesiastes 1:2 NKJV
"There is nothing new under the sun" . . . . Ecclesiastes 1:9
"There is a time for everything" . . . . Ecclesiastes 3:1-8

"Whatever your hand finds to do, do it with all your might" . . . . .Ecclesiastes 9:10

"Remember your Creator in the days of your youth" . . . . .Ecclesiastes 12:1

All Is Vanity—Worthless!

Vanity of godless living
Accumulating wealth
Not heeding God's authority
Ignoring God's timing
Trusting the wisdom of man
Yearning for pleasure

Song of Songs

My lover is mine and I am his.
(2:16)

Theme: Love and marriage
Date written: 971–965 B.C.
Author: Solomon
Setting: Early in Solomon's reign

This is the final of three books written by Solomon, all included in the Bible's wisdom books. Look at these three books with this in mind: *Ecclesiastes* is written in Solomon's old age as he reflects back on his life. The majority of *Proverbs* is written in the maturity of Solomon's life when his focus was on God and on sharing God's wisdom with others. Now, in *Song of Songs,* a youthful Solomon is writing a wedding song to describe his love for a beautiful country girl called the "Shulammite" (Song of Songs 6:13). This song records the conversation between an ordinary Jewish girl and her "beloved," the king of Israel.

The Skeleton

▸ Chapters 1–3 *The Courtship*

This "song" opens at the wedding banquet as the bride thinks about how much she loves her groom. She remembers how they first met, the longing she feels toward him, and all the wonderful romantic memories they shared in their courtship. She recalls her anticipation of her beloved's arrival to take her to Jerusalem for the wedding. As she reflects, we also hear from Solomon and a choir of young women called the "daughters of Jerusalem" (see, for example, 1:5).

▸ **Chapters 3–5:1** *The Wedding Preparation*

In this section, the king does the majority of the speaking. He comes for his bride, in all his splendor, and brings her to Jerusalem. As his bride spoke with admiration and desire for her groom in the earlier chapters, now Solomon speaks with poetic beauty of his bride as he anticipates their union. The wedding takes place, and the couple fulfill their wedding vows.

▸ **Chapters 5:2–8** *The Marriage*

Some time after the wedding, the Shulammite is half-awakened from her sleep by her husband's unexpected return home and his desire to give her a romantic surprise. When she fully realizes that she is not dreaming and gets up to let him in, he is gone. She panics and desperately tries to find him. She asks the "daughters of Jerusalem" to help her find him. They ask her to remember how special he is, which she gladly does. Later the two find each other, and they spend the remainder of the book praising each other and expressing their love for each other.

Putting Meat on the Bones

The world wants to distort what God has created and pronounced as good. Sex has been dirtied and twisted and turned into a casual and selfish activity. Love has turned to lust. Giving has been exchanged for getting. And the commitment of marriage is set aside in favor of "living together." Fortunately, this tender marriage song in the Song of Songs gives God's view on love, sex, and marriage. It celebrates the joy and intimacy of the romantic relationship between a husband and wife. It gives a passionate picture of physical love within the sanctity of marriage. It reveals the importance of verbally and physically communicating love to a marriage partner. Because the affection described between this husband and wife is so beautiful, many Bible scholars have likened it to the great love Jesus Christ shows for His bride, the church.

Fleshing It Out in Your Life

This book of inspired poetry gives you a model of God's intentions for love and marriage. Love is a powerful expression of feeling and commitment between two people. Love doesn't just look for outward physical beauty. It looks for the inner qualities that never fade with time—spiritual commitment, integrity, compassion, and sincerity. Therefore, such love is not to be regarded in a casual manner. Also, the physical expression of this kind of true love should be withheld until marriage. After marriage, it is this genuine, internal love that won't let walls come between a husband and wife. It is a love that communicates, forgives, renews, and refreshes.

How does culture's view of love and sex differ from God's plan?

List ways that God's designs for marriage are better, stronger, and more fulfilling.

Write a poem to God about your future spouse or write a poem *to* your future spouse.

Life Lessons from the Song of Songs

- God takes great joy in the love between a husband and wife.
- A married couple should openly express their love and admiration for each other.
- Christ's love for His church is similar to the kind of commitment that a bride and groom have for one another.
- The physical expression of marriage is special and must be reserved for marriage.

Where to Find It

The couple's courtship .... Song of Songs 1:2–3:5

The couple's first night as husband and wife .... Song of Songs 4:1–5:1

The couple's first disagreement .... Song of Songs 5:2–6:3

The power of love .... Song of Songs 8:6-7

Helpful Hints When It's Time for Marriage

1. Leave others and cleave to one another .... Genesis 2:24
2. Be faithful to your mate .... Proverbs 5:15
3. Remember that two are better than one ...... Ecclesiastes 4:9-10
4. Live together joyfully......................... Ecclesiastes 9:9
5. Honor and prefer one another.................. Romans 12:10
6. The marriage bed is undefiled .... Hebrews 13:4
7. Remember you are heirs together of the grace of life .... 1 Peter 3:7

Quiz: Can you match up the couples?

Abraham	A. Ruth
David	B. Rachel
Isaac	C. Mary
Jacob	D. Sarah
Boaz	E. Bathsheba
Samson	F. Zipporah
Ahasuerus	G. Priscilla
Moses	H. Esther
Aquila	I. Eve
Adam	J. Delilah
Joseph	K. Rebekah

Answers: Abraham D., David E., Isaac K., Jacob B., Boaz A., Samson J., Ahasuerus H., Moses F., Aquilla G., Adam I., Joseph C.

The Prophetic Books

The next 17 books of the Bible contain about one-fourth of Scripture and make up the last division in the Old Testament—the Prophets. The office of *prophet* was begun during the days of Samuel, and those who were prophets stood along with the priests as God's servants. The men who wrote these books were called or appointed to "speak for" God Himself. God communicated His messages to them through a variety of means, including dreams, visions, angels, nature, miracles, and an audible voice. Unfortunately, the messages the prophets shared from God were often rejected and their lives were often at risk. The prophetic books have four major themes and purposes:

1. To expose the sinful practices of the people
2. To call the people back to the law of God
3. To warn the people of coming judgment
4. To look forward to the coming of Messiah

Isaiah

We all, like sheep, have gone astray,
each of us has turned to his own way;
and the LORD has laid on him
the iniquity of us all.
(53:6)

Theme: Salvation
Date written: 700–680 B.C.
Author: Isaiah
Setting: Mainly in Jerusalem

The book of Isaiah is the first of the writings of the prophets. Isaiah is generally considered to be the greatest prophet. His ministry spanned the reigns of four kings of Judah. He was raised in a wealthy home and married to a prophetess. At first he was well liked. But soon, like most of the other prophets, he was hated because his messages were so harsh. In the first 39 chapters Isaiah stresses the righteousness, holiness, and justice of God. The last 27 chapters of Isaiah portray the Lord's glory, compassion, and grace—a similar theme in the 27 books of the New Testament. (Just a note: It's interesting to observe that the Old Testament also has 39 books. And the New Testament has 27 books.)

The Skeleton

▸ Chapters 1–12 *Judgment upon Judah*

The spiritual condition of Israel has declined to the point that the people are offering child sacrifices. The people profess to be religious, but their hearts are corrupt and they engage in idolatry. Isaiah repeatedly warns Israel and Judah of coming judgment if the people do not turn from their evil ways.

▸ **Chapters 13–24** *Judgment upon the Nations*

One of the key reasons for Israel's spiritual downfall is that the people are following the wicked lifestyles of the pagans who live nearby. Warnings are given against Babylon, Philistia, Moab, Egypt, and Ethiopia, among others. In carrying out judgment against the sins of the nations, God affirms His complete rule over all the earth. Ultimately justice will be done, and no one can escape.

▸ **Chapters 25–35** *Judgment and Redemption*

Near the midpoint of the book, Isaiah begins to add words of hope to his words of doom. Through Isaiah, God reveals the first glimpses of His plan to call His people back to Him and restore them.

▸ **Chapters 36–39** *Interlude with Hezekiah*

In the midst of Isaiah's powerful statements of coming judgment is an inspiring story about Hezekiah, a king of Judah (the southern kingdom). At first Hezekiah listens to Isaiah's advice to trust God when Judah is threatened by the Assyrian army. Sure enough, God intervenes and destroys the enemy. Later, when Hezekiah becomes severely ill, Isaiah warns that he would not recover. The king begs God for mercy, and God gives him 15 more years of life.

▸ **Chapters 40–66** *Redemption and Future Glory*

Although judgment upon God's people is coming and will be severe, that is not the end of the story. The people can count on God's promise to one day restore and deliver them. God will freely forgive all those who repent of their sin. Isaiah also predicts Israel's future repentance and its return to glory.

Putting Meat on the Bones

The basic theme of this book is found in Isaiah's name, which means "salvation is of the Lord." The word "salvation" appears 26 times in Isaiah, but only 7 times in all the other prophets combined. In the first 39 chapters of Isaiah, man is pictured as being in great need of salvation—a salvation that is of God, not man. Isaiah describes God as the supreme Ruler, the powerful Lord of history, and man's only Savior. Then in a dramatic shift, the last 27 chapters portray God as being faithful to His promise by preserving a godly group and providing salvation and deliverance through the coming Messiah. The fact that the Messiah is to be both a suffering servant and a sovereign Lord would not be understood until Jesus' time on earth. This Savior is to come out of Judah and redeem, restore, and bless both Jews and Gentiles in His future kingdom.

Fleshing It Out in Your Own

God's judgment is coming, and you too need a Savior. You cannot save yourself. Christ's perfect sacrifice for your sins is foretold and pictured in Isaiah. Just as Isaiah foretold, Christ came in the flesh and paid the price for sin in His death. With His resurrection, He is now willing to save all those who turn from their sin and come to Him. Have you committed yourself to Him? If you have experienced His salvation, continue to be faithful and live looking forward to His soon return.

What do you think Isaiah would point to in your life as sin and sinful behavior?

How can you overcome these sins and sinful behaviors?

What is the hope of the Messiah? Why did the world need a Messiah, and why do you?

Life Lessons from Isaiah

- God is a holy God. He cannot overlook sin.
- God knows the future. His judgment, as predicted in Isaiah, was fulfilled perfectly.
- God is a God of love. He is gracious and forgives you when you repent.
- God always keeps His promises. He will fulfill His plan for you, and for Israel's future salvation.
- The prophecies about Christ's suffering on the cross were accurately

fulfilled, and Christ's work made it possible for you to enter into God's forever family.

Where to Find It

Prediction of Jesus' birth . . . . Isaiah 7:14
A child is born...Prince of Peace . . . . Isaiah 9:6-7
Hezekiah's sickness and recovery . . . . Isaiah 38
Description of the suffering servant . . . . Isaiah 49–57
Prophecy of Christ's death on the cross . . . . Isaiah 53
The wolf and lamb will feed together . . . . Isaiah 65:25

Christ and His Suffering Are Described in Isaiah 53

Verse 2—Unattractive and undesirable
Verse 3—Despised and rejected, a man of sorrows
Verse 4—Bore our grief and sorrows
Verse 5—Wounded, bruised, and beaten for our transgressions
Verse 6—Bore the guilt and sin of all
Verse 7—Like a lamb brought to the slaughter
Verse 8—Tried and led away to His death
Verse 9—Died with the wicked but buried with the rich
Verse 10—Suffered according to God's good plan
Verse 12—Poured out His soul unto death and was counted as a sinner

Isaiah is the prophet who proclaimed "the big one." He said, "Hear now, you house of David! Is it not enough to try the patience of men? Will you try the patience of my God also? Therefore the Lord himself will give you a sign: The virgin will be with child and will give birth to a son, and will call him Immanuel" (Isaiah 7:13-14).

Jeremiah

Now reform your ways and your actions
and obey the LORD your God.
Then the LORD will relent and not bring the
disaster he has pronounced against you.
(26:13)

Theme: Judgment
Date: 627–586 B.C.
Author: Jeremiah
Setting: Jerusalem

Some 80 to 100 years after Isaiah's death, Jeremiah enters the prophetic scene. The book of Jeremiah is Jeremiah's description of his own life and ministry during the reigns of the last five kings of Judah. Jeremiah is the last prophet before the fall of Jerusalem. He is called "the weeping prophet" because of his deep sorrow over the sinful nation, the upcoming destruction of Jerusalem, and the exile of its people. Jeremiah is a picture of faithfulness to God and great personal sacrifice in spite of overwhelming opposition. Jeremiah proclaims not only words of warning, but also words of encouragement as he affirms God's promises to renew His people by renewing their hearts.

The Skeleton

▸ **Chapter 1** *God's Call on Jeremiah*

Jeremiah is called and set apart to be God's prophet even before his birth. This opening chapter identifies the prophet and documents his calling by God. It also outlines his instructions and the protection God promised to give him.

▸ **Chapters 2–45** *God's Judgment on Judah*

Jeremiah's messages are communicated through a variety of stories and object lessons. Some are spoken in the temple, and others are shouted in the streets. The prophet's own life also serves as a daily reminder of the coming judgment of Judah. He is told by God to cut off his hair, to bury a linen sash, to not marry and have a family, to place two baskets of figs—one good and the other bad—before the temple, and to wear a yoke throughout the city. All these visuals are meant to warn the people of certain judgment if the nation does not repent.

Because Jeremiah's message goes unheeded, judgment does come upon Judah in chapter 39, and the city is destroyed. The Jews who flee the destruction of the city take Jeremiah to Egypt against his will. He warns these few survivors not to go to Egypt, for it too would be invaded by Babylon and they would perish there. Sadly, they do not listen.

▸ **Chapters 46–51** *God's Judgment on the Nations*

In Jeremiah 25, Jeremiah proclaimed that all the nations around Judah are to "drink the cup" of God's wrath. (This means these nations would experience the same fate as Judah.) Chapters 46–51 include a series of prophetic statements against nine nations that faced God's judgment. These prophecies were probably given to Jeremiah by God at different times. They are collected and now recorded by nation: Egypt, Philistia, Moab, Ammon, Edom, Damascus (Syria), Arabia, Elam, and Babylonia.

▸ **Chapter 52** *God's Judgment on Jerusalem*

Jeremiah's 40 years of declaring doom conclude with the capture, destruction, and plunder of Jerusalem. The leaders are killed, and the survivors are taken to Babylon. This final chapter is a review of the city's fall and a historical addition to the account given in chapter 39. It confirms the truthfulness of Jeremiah's prophecies concerning Jerusalem and Judah.

Putting Meat on the Bones

Most definitions of success would include the acquiring of wealth, popularity, fame, or power. By these standards, Jeremiah was a complete failure. For 40 years he served as God's spokesman and with strong emotion he urged the people to return to God. But no one listened, especially the kings. Jeremiah was penniless, friendless, and rejected by his family. In the world's eyes, he was not a success. But in God's eyes, Jeremiah was one of the most successful people in all biblical history! Why? Because success, as seen by God, involves obedience and faithfulness. Jeremiah obeyed God and, regardless of being hated and great personal sacrifice, committed himself to fulfilling God's calling on his life.

Fleshing It Out in Your Life

Acceptance or rejection by people is not to be the measure of your success. You must live a life that honors and glorifies God in spite of temptations and pressures that might lead you to do otherwise. God's approval alone should be the standard for your life and your service to Him.

When have you failed in the eyes of your friends but been successful in God's eyes?

Do you strive to please God or your friends when you make choices? Why?

What does faithfulness to God look like in today's world? How can you be an example of such faithfulness?

Life Lessons from Jeremiah

- You must view success from God's perspective, not the world's.
- Commit yourself to being successful in God's eyes.
- Faithfulness to God requires your obedience, even when your friends pressure you to follow them in sin.
- When the time arrives, God will give you the courage to speak up for your beliefs.
- Persecution and rejection are to be expected as you live a godly lifestyle. But don't worry; God will always be there for you.

Where to Find It

David's Branch .... Jeremiah 23:5-6
70 years of exile predicted .... Jeremiah 25:11-12
The time of Jacob's trouble .... Jeremiah 30:7
The New Covenant .... Jeremiah 31:31-33

The Response to Jeremiah's Ministry

Death threats	Isolation
Burning of the prophetic message	Imprisonment
Put in painful stocks	Rejection
Arrested	Starvation
Challenged by false prophets	Chains

Promises God Will Never Take Back

The Noahic Covenant—Genesis 9:8-17
The Abrahamic Covenant—Genesis 15:12-21
The Levitical Covenant—Numbers 25:10-13
The Davidic Covenant—2 Samuel 7:13; 23:5
The New Covenant—Jeremiah 31:31-34

Lamentations

My eyes fail from weeping,
I am in torment within,
my heart is poured out on the ground
because my people are destroyed...
(2:11)

Theme: Lament (a sorrowful chant)
Date written: 586 B.C.
Author: Jeremiah
Setting: Jerusalem

The book of Lamentations contains five poems that describe Jeremiah's eyewitness account of the destruction of Jerusalem by the Babylonian army. Jeremiah predicted this disaster in his earlier prophetic book, Jeremiah. Now he writes these five funeral poems to express his grief. But, as in his previous book, Jeremiah reminds readers that God has not and will not abandon His people. He is faithful, and His mercies continue to remain available to those who respond to His call.

The Skeleton

▸ **Chapter 1** *The First Lament: Jerusalem's Desolation*

In the first poem or lament, Jeremiah describes the city of Jerusalem as having been ruined by its enemies. The destruction, says the Lord, is not the result of bad luck or some accident. No, God sent punishment upon the people because they had abandoned His ways.

▸ **Chapter 2** *The Second Lament: God's Anger at Sin*

Jeremiah moves from the subject of Jerusalem's destruction to an eyewitness account of her ruin. God's anger over the people's sins is described, and this is followed by another round of heartfelt lament by Jeremiah.

▸ **Chapter 3** *The Third Lament: Hope in the Midst of Affliction*

Out of the depths of Jeremiah's grief comes a ray of hope. God's compassion is ever present and His faithfulness is great! Jeremiah realizes that it is only the mercy of God that has prevented total destruction.

▸ **Chapter 4** *The Fourth Lament: God's Wrath Detailed*

The prophet rehearses the siege of Jerusalem and remembers the suffering and starvation of both the rich and the poor. He reviews the causes of the siege, especially the sins of Jerusalem's false prophets and priests. He closes this lament with a warning of punishment on the nation of Edom, a nation next to Judah.

▸ **Chapter 5** *The Fifth Lament: A Prayer for Restoration*

Jeremiah, "the weeping prophet," concludes this sorrowful book with a prayer that God, in His mercy, will remember His people and restore the kingdom in Israel.

Putting Meat on the Bones

Three themes run through the five laments of Jeremiah. The most obvious is the mourning over Jerusalem's destruction. In his sorrow, Jeremiah weeps for himself, for the suffering people, and sometimes for the city as if it were a person. The second theme is Jeremiah's confession of sin and acknowledgment of God's righteous and holy judgment of the nation. The third theme is the hope of God's promised future restoration of His people. God has poured out His wrath, but in His mercy, He will not cease to be faithful to His promises.

Fleshing It Out in Your Life

Most of us don't like to show our emotions, especially our tears. But what makes a person cry says a lot about the person. In Jeremiah's case, the tears are for the suffering of God's people and their rebellion against their God. What causes you to cry? Do you weep because someone has insulted you, or because someone has insulted God? Do you cry because you have lost something that gives you pleasure, or because there are so many people around you who will suffer eternally for their sin? The world is filled with injustice, suffering, and rebellion against God, all of which should move you to tears and action.

Have you ever felt abandoned by God? How did God then reveal His presence to you?

What evidence do you see around you that much of the world is lost? That they aren't following God?

Spend time in prayer for those who are suffering. How can you be a light to these people even if they live far away?

Life Lessons from Lamentations

- The painful cry of lament over the sorrow and suffering of others is a form of prayer, one which God hears and answers.
- There are serious results when a nation—or a person—turns from God's ways.
- You can rest in the knowledge that God is faithful and merciful.
- Prayer is always the right thing to do in times of suffering.

Where to Find It

The announcement of Jerusalem's desolation . . . . . . .Chapter 1
Jeremiah's lamentation over Israel's misery . . . . .Chapter 2
A reminder of God's faithfulness and mercy . . . . .Chapter 3
A description of the siege of Jerusalem . . . . .Chapter 4
Jeremiah's plea for restoration .Chapter 5

Jeremiah's Writings

The book of Jeremiah looks forward...with warning.
The book of Lamentations looks backward...with mourning.

"What do you want to be when you grow up?"

Do you get that question a lot? Teens in Bible times probably weren't asked this question much. They didn't have the choices that you have today. Children were brought up learning the family's trade. If your father was a shepherd, you'd be out tending to sheep and goats. If your family sold and traded goods, you'd likely become a merchant as well.

Here are a few jobs of the time. If you were a teen in Bible days, which occupation would you hope to take on as your own?

baker	blacksmith
carpenter	servant
potter	priest
rabbi	teacher
farmer	midwife
tax collector	merchant
doctor	shepherd

Ezekiel

I got up and went out to the plain.
And the glory of the LORD was standing there,
like the glory I had seen by the Kebar River,
and I fell facedown.
(3:23)

Theme: The glory of the Lord
Date written: 590–570 B.C.
Author: Ezekiel
Setting: Babylon

While Jeremiah is prophesying in Jerusalem that the city would soon fall to the Babylonians, Ezekiel is giving a similar message to the captives who are already in Babylon. Like the people in Jerusalem, the captives could not believe that God would allow Jerusalem to be destroyed. After the news of its fall comes, God changes Ezekiel's messages to one of future hope and restoration for the people. Throughout the book, Ezekiel describes his encounters with God's glory, whether it is His heavenly glory or His earthly glory in the temple of the past or the one predicted for the future.

The Skeleton

▸ Chapters 1–3 *The Call of Ezekiel*

The Babylonian conquest of Jerusalem takes place in stages, and the Jewish people are taken captive in three stages or "deportations" (see page 60). Ezekiel, a priest, is taken to Babylon in the second deportation. While there, Ezekiel has a vision of God's glory. In the vision, God calls Ezekiel to become a prophet to the Jewish people living in Babylon. Ezekiel is clearly warned by God that the people won't listen to his message.

▸ **Chapters 4–24** *The Judgment of Jerusalem*

God's judgment of the people of Judah and Jerusalem is already under way, with many Jewish people already taken captive in Babylon. Through Ezekiel, God continues to warn the people of Jerusalem's coming collapse. He urges them to turn from their wicked ways. Ezekiel announces that God's glory will leave the temple, and that the temple will be destroyed.

▸ **Chapters 25–32** *The Judgment of the Nations*

After pronouncing judgment upon Jerusalem, Ezekiel goes on to pronounce God's anger against several of the enemy nations surrounding Israel. These judgments affirm God's power over all kings and nations.

▸ **Chapters 33–39** *The Restoration of God's People*

Ezekiel announces the fall of Jerusalem and calls the Jewish people to ask God's forgiveness. Though the city and the temple are now in ruins, this is not the end. If the people are willing to turn from their rebellion against God, He will bring them back to their land.

▸ **Chapters 40–48** *The Restoration of Worship*

God gives Ezekiel a vision of Israel's spiritual future and a glorious new temple that will see the return of the glory of the Lord. God promises to bring the people back to Him.

Putting Meat on the Bones

Ezekiel places a strong emphasis on the power, glory, and faithfulness of God, and much of the book focuses on the temple in Jerusalem. Throughout his messages, Ezekiel emphasizes again and again God's statement that all the things to come are happening so that people will know that He is the Lord. Everything that God does—past, present, or future—is to reveal His glory.

Fleshing It Out in Your Life

God's glory is readily visible to anyone who is willing to look up at the heavens (Psalms 19:1). His glory is visible in keeping His people alive and returning them to the land. It is visible in the plans He has made for His future temple and His coming kingdom. And it is visible in His grace toward repentant sinners during the church age. The very thought of God's glory should drive you to praise and worship Him, to make changes that help you better reflect His holy nature.

How is there evidence of God's faithfulness in the world today? In your life?

Why is knowing the Lord so important?

If you do well on a test or in a game, or you act with honesty and are then rewarded for that behavior, how can you give God the glory?

Life Lessons from Ezekiel

- ▶ God normally does not use a person living in sin and rebellion. Through discipline, He can purge such a person, and call him to a new start.
- ▶ God disciplines when necessary, but He always leaves the door open for forgiveness.
- ▶ God has complete control over all people and all nations.
- ▶ God controls every detail of your life, which should be a great comfort to you.

Where to Find It

The vision of God's glory . . . . Ezekiel 1:4-28
God's glory departs from the temple . . . . Ezekiel 11:22-25
The siege of Jerusalem begins . . . . Ezekiel 24:1-14
The watchman and his message . . . . Ezekiel 33:1-9
God's promise of a new heart . . . . Ezekiel 36:26-27
The valley of dry bones . . . . Ezekiel 37:1-14
God's glory returns to Jerusalem . . . . Ezekiel 43:1-9

How Ezekiel Acted Out His Prophecies

- He stayed in his house, tied up and mute.
- He used a clay tablet and iron plate.
- He lay on his left side for 390 days, and on his right side for 40 days.
- He ate in an unclean manner.
- He shaved his head and beard.
- He packed a bag and dug through a wall.
- He could not mourn when his wife died.
- He put two sticks together as one.

Daniel

The Most High God is sovereign over the kingdoms of men and sets over them anyone he wishes.
(5:21)

Theme: God's complete control
Date written: 530 B.C.
Author: Daniel
Setting: Babylon

The book of Daniel is called "the Apocalypse of the Old Testament." It is written to encourage the exiled Jews by showing them God's grand design during and after the period of Gentile (non-Jewish) rule. The "times of the Gentiles" (Luke 21:24) begins with the Babylonian captivity. The Jews will suffer under Gentile powers for a long time, but not forever. A time will come when God will establish the Messianic kingdom, which will last forever. Daniel points out the control and power of God over human affairs. Because Daniel—"O man of high esteem"—is of such great character, God gives him a view of the future.

The Skeleton

▸ Chapters 1–6 *Daniel's Life*

In the first of three deportations (see page 60), Daniel, thought by many to be a teenager at this time, is taken captive to Babylon along with other youths from Jerusalem, including his friends Shadrach, Meshach, and Abednego. King Nebuchadnezzar and the Babylonians want to train these four Jewish teens and others to become part of their pagan culture. However, the four take a bold stand for God in the face of great pressure, and take additional stands as time goes on. God honors these young men for their boldness. For example, at one point Daniel is spared from a den of hungry lions. On another occasion Daniel's friends are preserved from death in a fiery furnace. God also enables Daniel to interpret Nebuchadnezzar's dream of a statue that represents the four major kingdoms that will rule the world until Christ's return. Daniel's character and wisdom earn the respect of Nebuchadnezzar, who places Daniel in a high government office.

▸ **Chapters 7–12** *Daniel's Visions*

Daniel has four visions that look into the future of Israel and the world. He proclaims the famous prophecy of the "seventy weeks" and the seven years of tribulation that will mark the last days. He gives details about the identity of the Antichrist and the eventual return of Israel to its homeland.

Putting Meat on the Bones

Daniel's life is rich in historical experiences and earthly honors. Carried captive to Babylon when he was a teen, Daniel spends his next 70-plus years in public service in a nation filled with idolatry and wickedness. In spite of his surroundings, Daniel lives a godly life and exercises great influence in three kingdoms—Babylon, Media, and Persia. During these years, he could have been sad. He could have thought God had abandoned him. He could have cried, "Where is God?" Instead of giving in or giving up, this courageous man holds fast to his faith in God. Daniel understands that despite his circumstances, God is in control and is working out His plan for all nations, kings, and individuals like you.

Fleshing It Out in Your Life

Daniel and his three teen friends are inspiring examples of how to live a godly life in an ungodly world. Make sure your Christian conduct doesn't get blurred through giving in to the world around you. Be faithful in your study of God's Word. Sustain your prayer life. And maintain God's values. Then, like Daniel, you will have a great influence on those around you, starting with your family, and then your friends at school.

How can you relate to Daniel as a teen?

In what ways does Daniel's faith seem stronger than that of most Christian teens?

How does Daniel's life inspire you to show your friends what faith and faithfulness mean on a daily basis?

Life Lessons from Daniel

- God is in control over all history. Kingdoms rise and fall according to His plan.
- God honors you when you take a stand for what is right.
- God punishes sin.
- God already has a plan for the future, and because He is in control, it will come to pass.

Where to Find It

The fiery furnace .... Daniel 3
The handwriting on the wall .... Daniel 5
Daniel in the lions' den .... Daniel 6
Daniel's vision of the four beasts .... Daniel 7
Daniel's prophecy of the 70 weeks .... Daniel 9

The Four Kingdoms of Nebuchadnezzar's Statue

Body part	Material	Empire
Head	Gold	Babylonians
Chest and arms	Silver	Medo-Persians
Belly and thighs	Bronze	Greeks
Legs and feet	Iron and clay	Romans

The Kings Daniel Served

King Nebuchadnezzar of Babylonia	Chapters 1–4
Belshazzar of Babylonia	Chapter 5
Darius of Medo-Persia	Chapters 6–9
Durius of Medo-Persia	Chapters 10–12

You can be a godly influence like Daniel if you:

- seek God's standards
- live God's standards
- speak God's standards
- defend God's standards
- are willing to suffer for God's standards

Bible School Days

In Bible days, education usually revolved around the home. Families needed the children to help maintain their livelihood, so they didn't send kids off to classes for the day. And in most cases, the families were living a rural or nomad lifestyle. So schooling took place wherever the children were at the time. As you'll see in the references below, educational style varied—from the homeschooling scenario to the very intense training offered by the Jewish leaders.

- Boys were chiefly taught the law and a trade by their fathers. A rabbi said, "He who does not teach his son a useful trade is bringing him up to be a thief."
- Moses was "educated in all the wisdom of the Egyptians" (Acts 7:22) by the teacher of the king's children.
- Samuel set up a school of the prophets at Ramah (1 Samuel 19:19-20).
- Daniel was trained as a young man in Babylon during exile. He attended the schools of the Babylonian court.
- Jesus received His training in His hometown of Nazareth. When He sat with the religious leaders in the temple, they were amazed by His knowledge even as a young man (Luke 2).
- Paul mentions his education and training as a Pharisee. The training received from a rabbi was very disciplined and involved lots of Scripture memorization.
- A stone tablet was discovered in Sumeria (dating from around the time of Abraham) with this description of what a boy did at school: "I read my tablet, ate my lunch, prepared my tablet, wrote it, finished it."

Hosea

I will show my love to the one I called "Not my loved one." I will say to those called "Not my people," "You are my people"; and they will say, "You are my God."
(2:23)

Theme: Unfaithfulness
Date written: 755–715 B.C.
Author: Hosea
Setting: Northern kingdom

Hosea is the first of a series of 12 prophetic books called the Minor Prophets—not because they are less important, but because of their length. Each book in the Minor Prophets is named after its author. Hosea's ministry begins during a time of prosperity in the northern kingdom. But the prosperity is only external. Inwardly, the people are idolatrous and wicked. In less than 30 years, Israel and its capital, Samaria, would fall.

The book of Hosea details the unhappy marriage of a man and his unfaithful wife, Gomer. Their story serves as an example of the loyalty of God and the spiritual faithlessness of Israel. With sorrow, Hosea, whose name means "salvation," exposes the sins of Israel and contrasts them to God's holiness. The nation must be judged for its sin, but it will be restored in the future because of God's love and faithfulness. Hosea has been referred to as the prophet of forgiveness, and the book that bears his name depicts God's willingness to restore the unfaithful.

The Skeleton

▸ Chapters 1–3 *Israel's Adultery and God's Faithfulness*

God commands Hosea to marry Gomer and have children with her. She becomes unfaithful and commits adultery. Her unfaithfulness is a description of Israel's unfaithfulness to God. But just as Hosea shows patient love for Gomer, God still loves His people—even in the middle of their immorality and rebellion! Hosea's wife was so bad that she ends up as a slave. Hosea buys back his wife from the slave market and restores her to her position as his wife. In the same way, a sinful Israel will one day be completely restored in her relationship with God.

▸ Chapters 4–7 *Israel's Guilt*

Because of his painful experience with his wife, Gomer, Hosea can identify with God's sorrow over the unfaithfulness of His people. Though Israel has hardened her heart to God's gracious last appeal to repent, there is still time for God to heal and redeem the people. However, they pridefully continue in their rebellion.

▸ Chapters 8–10 *Israel's Indictment*

These chapters give the verdict of the case that Hosea has just presented for the sinfulness of Israel. The people's disobedience is about to lead them into exile and scattering. Israel has rejected repentance for their sins, and the judgment of God can no longer be withheld. Therefore Hosea rebukes Israel for her sin.

▸ Chapters 11–14 *Israel's Salvation*

Hosea calls Israel to repentance and offers her a spiritual blessing for her return to faith. Though the people are now the objects of stern rebuke, the day is coming when they will receive a powerful blessing.

Putting Meat on the Bones

More than any other Old Testament prophet, Hosea's personal experience illustrates his prophetic message. He has a real compassion for God's people. Also, Hosea's personal suffering because of his wife's unfaithfulness gives him some understanding of God's grief over Israel's sin. Therefore Hosea's words of coming judgment are delivered with firmness yet softened with a heart of affection. Hosea's tenderness illustrates God's faithfulness, justice, love, and forgiveness in contrast with Israel's corruption and defection. With great concern Hosea pleads on behalf of God for the people to return to God, but they will not.

Fleshing It Out in Your Life

Like Hosea, you too may experience times of grief and physical suffering. However, rather than becoming bitter, you can allow God to use your suffering to comfort others in their pain. That's what is at the heart of 2 Corinthians 1:6: "If we are distressed, it is for your comfort and salvation; if we are comforted, it is for your comfort, which produces in you patient endurance of the same sufferings we suffer."

Have you used one of your past hurts to help a friend through a similar problem? How did your experience help?

What can bitterness end up doing to people? Have you witnessed a bitter heart in someone?

In what areas of your life have you strayed from God and His Word? What can you do to get back on God's path?

Life Lessons from Hosea

- God loves you despite your sins and faults.
- You can count on God's faithfulness even when you are unfaithful.
- Saying you are sorry to God is the first step on the path back to fellowship with God.
- God will give you the strength to resist the world's sinful pressure to conform.

Where to Find It

Gomer's marriage and children .... Chapter 1

Israel's leaders rebuked .... Chapter 5

A testimony of God's love . . . . .Chapter 6
Israel's rebellion against God's love . . . . .Chapter 11
Israel's future restoration and blessing . . . . .Chapter 14

Chronological Order and Approximate Dates of the Minor Prophets

Obadiah	840 B.C.	Nahum	660 B.C.
Joel	835	Zephaniah	625
Jonah	760	Habakkuk	607
Amos	755	Haggai	520
Hosea	740	Zechariah	515
Micah	730	Malachi	430

Joel

Return to the LORD your God,
for he is gracious and compassionate,
slow to anger and abounding in love.
(2:13)

Theme: The day of the Lord
Date written: 835–796 B.C.
Author: Joel
Setting: Judah/Jerusalem

Joel appears to be one of the earlier prophets in Judah. He lived and ministered in Judah about the same time as Elisha and Jonah ministered in the northern kingdom of Israel. Joel predicts that the land will be invaded by a fierce army that will make a recent locust invasion seem mild by comparison. On behalf of God, Joel appeals to the people to repent and avoid the coming disaster.

The Skeleton

▸ Chapter 1 *The Plague of Locusts*

Israel experiences a plague of locusts that brings destruction to the land. Joel explains that this is a preview of the coming "day of the LORD" (verse 15). In view of this calamity, Joel calls for humility and repentance.

▸ Chapter 2 *The Day of the Lord*

Joel spells out the events of the coming day of judgment, when an army will invade from the north and a great struggle will occur. He promises that the Spirit of God will be poured out on those who repent.

▸ **Chapter 3** *Judgment and Blessing*

The Lord will judge the nations, especially those which have mistreated His chosen people. Israel will receive a special blessing and be revived and restored.

Putting Meat on the Bones

A single bomb can destroy a large city. A single earthquake or hurricane can destroy whole civilizations. We stand in awe at the power and might of both natural and man-made power. But these forces cannot touch the power of Almighty God. Ever since the first sin was committed in the Garden of Eden in Genesis, man has been in rebellion against God. Judah has now taken its turn in disregarding God's laws. Because the people do not repent, they will surely have their day of judgment, their "day of the LORD." Rebellion continues to be allowed by God, but a future day is coming when all rebellion will be punished.

Fleshing It Out in Your Life

God—not foreign invaders, nature, or the economy—is the one to whom all must give an accounting. One cannot ignore or offend God forever. You must pay attention to His message from His Word. If you don't, you will face "the day of the LORD" later. Where do you stand with God and His coming judgment? Where does Joel's message find you today? It's not too late to ask for and receive God's forgiveness. God's greatest desire is for you to come to Him.

Would a plague of locusts be enough to motivate you to turn to God? Why does it sometimes take a lot before we are willing to listen to God and love His ways?

How do you sometimes try to be the judge of people instead of letting God be the judge?

Repent is not a commonly used word anymore, but in the Bible, we are called to repent, to turn from evil and come to God. Describe how a person can repent of a sin in his or her life. Why is repentance an important part of faith in God?

Life Lessons from Joel

- God always gives a warning before He sends judgment.
- God brings judgment if there is no repentance.
- Humility and repentance are necessary to restore your relationship with God.
- Sin brings God's day of reckoning.

Where to Find It

Judah's invasion and destruction by locusts . . . . .Chapter 1
Judah's destruction by Assyria . . . . .Chapter 2
Judah and Israel's restoration by God . . . . .Chapter 3

The day of God's coming judgment is mentioned 19 times in the Old Testament (5 times in Joel) and only 4 times in all the New Testament.

Amos

Seek good, not evil, that you may live.
Then the LORD God Almighty will be with you. . .
(5:14)

Theme: Punishment
Date written: 790 B.C.
Author: Amos
Setting: Bethel, the northern kingdom

Amos is a shepherd and a cultivator of sycamore trees from a rural area south of Jerusalem. He is gripped by God and called to leave his homeland and preach a harsh message of judgment to the northern kingdom of Israel. He offers eight decrees—three sermons and five visions—warning of coming disaster because of a lack of desire for spiritual things, worshipping other gods, and oppressing the poor. But because of the peace and prosperity of Israel during this period, his message falls on deaf ears.

The Skeleton

▸ Chapters 1–2 *Decrees of Judgment*

The prophet Amos names specific sins of various nations and pronounces eight judgments upon the nations. Then Amos describes the sins of the people of Israel and Judah and warns of future destruction and judgment from the Lord. Among the sins of the nations and the Jewish people is idolatry—the worship of false gods.

▸ **Chapters 3–6** *Reasons for Judgment*

In these chapters, Amos delivers three sermons exposing Israel's sin. Among the problems in Israel are greed, excessive taxation of the poor, and cruel treatment of the poor. God condemns those who "crush the needy" (4:1), take bribes, and "deprive the poor of justice" (5:12). Though the people profess to follow God and offer sacrifices to Him, their two-faced behavior is evident in their excessive lifestyle. There is a total absence of justice and morality.

▸ **Chapters 7–9** *Visions of Judgment and Restoration*

Amos has five visions that show what God will do to punish Israel. Yet in spite of all the people have done wrong, God still loves them and promises there will come a future day of revival and blessing.

Putting Meat on the Bones

Amos is not a professional prophet. He has not been to "prophet school." He says, "I was neither a prophet nor a prophet's son, but I was a shepherd, and I also took care of sycamore-fig trees" (7:14). He is a simple country boy. What is it then that makes him such a powerful spiritual force? In his testimony he gives us the answer: "But the LORD took me...and said to me, 'Go, prophesy to my people Israel'" (verse 15). That's what Amos did. He fearlessly prophesied by the Spirit of God within him (3:8).

Fleshing It Out in Your Life

Amos provides an excellent example for you today. He reminds you that you don't have to be professionally trained to speak up for God when you see human injustice or sinful behavior, especially by those who claim to be Christians. Amos was a fiery spokesman for God not because of education or birth, but because he was obedient when the call of God came. You too can be God's person. Listen for His call and do what He asks. Then watch as the power of God works through you.

It's easy to let a minister or a teacher do all the talking. But what can *you* say and do that is a faith example to others? How can you be a teacher to your peers?

When have you experienced God's strength working through you? How did He turn around the situation?

What prevents people from listening to anything related to faith? What can you do to help them listen?

Life Lessons from Amos

- God cares about the poor and those in need, and so should you.
- Whenever you have the opportunity to show compassion, you should act upon it.
- It is wrong to enrich yourself at the expense of others.
- If your heart is far from God and you are living in disobedience, then your words and actions mean nothing.
- Lack of a love for the things of God happens almost without notice. Check and renew your heart daily.
- Judgment is certain for those who ignore God.

Where to Find It

Prophecy of Israel's coming destruction . . . . .Chapter 3
Israel's reproof and disregard . . . . .Chapter 4
Amos's call to repentance . . . . .Chapter 5
Scattering and restoration of Israel . . . . .Chapter 9

The Five Visions of Amos

1. Vision of the locusts (7:1-3)
2. Vision of the fire (7:4-6)
3. Vision of the plumb line (7:7-9)
4. Vision of the summer fruit (8:1-14)
5. Vision of the Lord (9:1-10)

Project Runway: It's All About Layering

People in the Bible didn't rush to the local mall to get the latest. But they did know how to layer their clothes with style. The layering protected them from the hot sun and during the cold nights. Here's what you would likely be wearing should you have been spotted in Jerusalem in those days:

Guys:

An inner tunic worn during colder weather made of cotton or linen. Think of it as long johns for the robe-wearing set.

The main tunic looked like a big, long-sleeved shirt...down to the ankles. The tunic was cinched with a leather belt.

Don't forget your cloak. This outer layer was like a coat. If men were to add any fashion flair, this is the element that might have some bling.

Your headdress protected you from that blaring sun. Scarves or turbans would be most common.

Girls:

Your layers are similar to those of the men. But you get the finer silks and the detailed embroidery on your cloak and inner tunic.

Your belt and headdress would be made of a more colorful and richer fabric than anything the men would wear.

And you have a touch of leather...your strappy sandals. Every girl should have a pair and a spare. Maybe things weren't so different!

Obadiah

There will be no survivors from the house of Esau.
(Verse 18)

Theme: Righteous judgment
Time: 850–840 B.C.
Author: Obadiah
Setting: Jerusalem/Edom

Obadiah is the shortest Old Testament book—one chapter long—and possibly the earliest prophetic book. It is an example of God's response to anyone who would harm His chosen people. Edom was a mountainous nation to the southeast of Judah. As distant relatives of Esau (Genesis 25–27), the Edomites are blood relatives of the people of Judah. Of all people, they should rush to the aid of Judah when it comes under attack. Instead, they gloat over Judah's problems. They capture and deliver Judah's survivors to the enemy and loot Judah's land. Because of Edom's indifference, rejection of God, and evil actions toward their brothers in Judah, Obadiah gives them God's message of coming disaster.

The Skeleton

▸ Verses 1–16 *Edom's Destruction*

The people of Edom feel secure because their capital city, Petra, is hidden among high peaks that make the city easy to protect. The people of Edom are filled with pride and self-confidence. Their pride is evident in verse 3 as they marvel, "Who can bring me down to the ground?" When Jerusalem is attacked by an unnamed enemy, the Edomites do not come to help the people of Jerusalem. Instead, they encourage the attackers, help take some of the people captive, and plunder the city. This angers God, who promises the Edomites that "though you soar like the eagle and make your nest among the stars, from there I will bring you down" (verse 4).

▸ **Verses 17–21** *Israel's Restoration*

Those who take pride in their power and defy the Lord will face judgment. God promises to completely destroy the Edomites and restore His people to a place of glory.

Putting Meat on the Bones

Bible scholars aren't sure about which invasion of Judah Obadiah refers to in his book. But the message is clear: God judges those who harm His children or aid in their harm. This was true of Edom in the past, and it will be true of any nation in the future.

Fleshing It Out in Your Life

On a more positive and personal note, if you are a child of God through Jesus Christ, you are under His love and protection. Nothing will happen to you that isn't under God's directive hand. Ultimately judgment will fall on all who harm His chosen people, Israel, or His adopted people, believers in Jesus Christ.

Have you ever been joyful about someone else's failure instead of helping them? How would God want you to respond?

We place a lot of emphasis on competition and being the best at something. How can this be both a positive and negative representation of God's love to others?

When have you let pride get in the way of compassion? When have you set your pride aside to obey God?

Life Lessons from Obadiah

▸ Those who persecuted God's people in the Bible were always brought to justice. Likewise, those who are hostile to Christians today can expect to face God's judgment.

- When you see harm being inflicted upon fellow Christians, you should not abandon them, but rather come to their aid.
- Take no pleasure in the misfortune of others.
- Pride and self-centeredness do not please God.

Where to Find It

Edom's destruction . . . . Verses 1-16

Israel's restoration . . . . Verses 17-21

The History of the Conflict Between Israel and Edom

- Israel descended from Jacob, and Edom from Esau.
- Jacob and Esau struggled in their mother's womb.
- Esau sold his birthright to Jacob.
- The Edomites refused to let the Israelites pass through their land after the Exodus.
- Israel's kings faced constant conflict with Edom.
- Edom urged Babylon to destroy Jerusalem.

Jonah

He prayed to the LORD, "O LORD, is this not what I said when I was still at home? That is why I was so quick to flee to Tarshish. I knew that you are a gracious and compassionate God, slow to anger and abounding in love, a God who relents from sending calamity."
(4:2)

Theme: God's grace to all people
Date written: 780–750 B.C.
Author: Jonah
Setting: Nineveh

Jonah is the self-written account of a stubborn prophet who did not want to preach to Israel's enemy, the godless Assyrians, and their capital city, Nineveh. The book is unusual because it is the only Old Testament book whose entire message is to a Gentile nation. God's declaration is that His grace is extended to the Gentiles. Jonah's message to the Ninevites was received with an almost immediate response of repentance exhibited by their fasting and mournful behavior. As a result, the city of 600,000 people is spared from doom and destruction.

The Skeleton

▸ **Chapters 1–2** *Jonah's Call and Disobedience*

God calls Jonah, a resident in the northern kingdom, to go preach repentance in Nineveh, the greatest and most powerful city-state of its time. In his patriotic zeal, Jonah puts his country before God. Rebelling against his instructions from God, Jonah catches a ship to escape his mission. Instead of going 500 miles northeast to Nineveh, Jonah attempts to go 2000 miles west to Tarshish (Spain). The ship is caught in a severe storm, and Jonah is cast into the sea by those on board hoping to escape the wrath of the storm caused by Jonah's presence and disobedience. Jonah is then swallowed by a great fish. God uses the fish to rescue Jonah, get his attention, and finally deposit him on dry land.

▸ **Chapters 3–4** *Jonah's Renewed Call*

Jonah, in obedience to God's second call, preaches to the inhabitants of Nineveh. They repent, mourning their sin, and God spares the city. But Jonah is angry that God has shown mercy to these non-Jewish people. God then lets Jonah know that He intends to offer His grace and mercy to *all* people.

Putting Meat on the Bones

How would you react if you were asked by God to take the gospel message to your country's worst enemy? You now know what Jonah's reaction was. In his heart he knew that no one deserved judgment more than the Assyrians. They were a godless and cruel people, and Jonah wanted their destruction. Eventually, however, with God's helping hand, Jonah does go, and he preaches a one-line message: "Forty more days and Nineveh will be overturned" (3:4). And, much to Jonah's displeasure, the people respond! Then God confronts Jonah's self-righteous pride and lack of compassion.

Fleshing It Out in Your Life

Have you ever been like Jonah? Do you sometimes flee from opportunities to share the truth of your Savior with those around you? Do you move around with heartless indifference, saying nothing about God's saving grace to schoolmates, neighbors, friends, and family? Don't follow Jonah's example! Instead, follow God's example and develop a genuine love and compassion for the lost. Begin praying for those who seem to be the farthest from God. And pray for your enemies. Then look for ways to share "the good news" with them. Who knows, maybe they too will respond to God's message. Pray that they do.

What can you do that will help you feel more comfortable sharing God's truth with others?

Who do you care most about in your life? Do they know God? How can you encourage them toward faith in God?

Do you let jealousy get in the way of celebrating what God is doing in someone else's life? How can you get over jealousy when it rises up?

Life Lessons from Jonah

- You cannot escape God's call on your life. He will pursue you to the ends of the earth...or as in Jonah's case, into the belly of a big fish!
- God's love and mercy are for all people.
- Disobedience leads to big problems in your life.
- It is impossible to run away from God.
- There is no limit to what God will—and can!—use to get your attention.
- Failure does not necessarily disqualify you from God's service.
- Your disobedience affects the lives of others you come in contact with.
- Your personal opinions should never stand in the way of God's plan.

Where to Find It

Fleeing from God's presence .... Chapter 1
In the belly of the great fish .... Chapter 2
Speaking God's truth in Nineveh .... Chapter 3
Hoping for Nineveh's destruction .... Chapter 4

Jonah's Journey to Nineveh

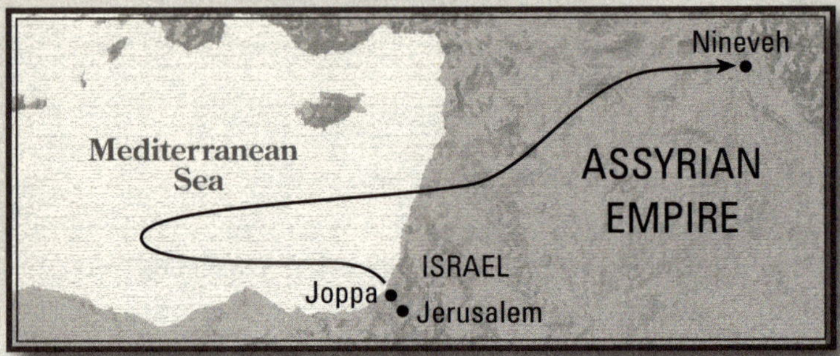

God commanded Jonah to go to Nineveh, but Jonah did not want to go, for the people there were very wicked. Jonah tried to go in the opposite direction by taking a ship to Tarshish. God stepped in and pointed Jonah back toward Nineveh.

Micah

He has showed you, O man, what is good.
And what does the LORD require of you?
To act justly and to love mercy
and to walk humbly with your God.
(6:8)

Theme: Divine judgment
Date written: 735–710 B.C.
Author: Micah
Setting: Samaria and Jerusalem

Micah proclaims a message of judgment to a people continually pursuing evil. He presents his three speeches, or cycles, of doom and hope as if he were in a courtroom. Each message (presented mainly to the southern kingdom of Judah, but also to the northern kingdom) begins with the admonition to "hear." The book begins with judgment for Israel's unfaithfulness, and ends on a strong note that the Lord intends to fulfill the promises He made to Abraham and Jacob in regard to Israel.

The Skeleton

▸ Chapters 1–2 *The Trial of the Capitals*

"Hear, O peoples, all of you" (Micah 1:2). Micah summons all the nations into "court" to hear testimony against Samaria and Jerusalem, the capitals of the northern and southern kingdoms. He points out their oppression of the poor, the two-faced nature of the national and religious leaders, and the bogus words of false prophets. God's people are not living according to God's plan.

▸ **Chapters 3–5** *The Trial of the Leaders*

"Listen, you leaders of Jacob" (3:1). Micah first addresses Israel's corrupt rulers, who should be aware of injustice. Yet their conduct toward the poor is likened to the killing of animals. But Micah also gives a prophetic glimpse of the glorious future, speaking of a "Messianic kingdom" that will be established when the Lord regathers His people. This kingdom will be set up by the coming Messiah, Jesus Christ, who will avenge all wrongs and bring spiritual blessing.

▸ **Chapters 6–7** *The Trial of the People*

"Hear, O mountains, the LORD's accusation" (6:2). Micah rebukes God's people for their ingratitude and for forsaking the practices God had given them. He also reminds them that confession and repentance will lead to a fulfillment of all God's promises.

Putting Meat on the Bones

Micah is a country boy. Unlike the prophet Isaiah, who at this same time is at the king's court in Jerusalem and aware of the *political conditions of the region,* Micah shows a profound concern for the *sufferings of the common people.* Micah stands up for the cause of the poor as he warns the leaders of the results they will suffer for taking advantage of the poor. Because of corruption among the wealthy, Micah's message of coming judgment is not popular. Micah's concern can be summarized in what God wants to see in His people: Justice and fairness balanced with mercy and compassion as the result of a humble and obedient relationship with the Lord (6:8).

Fleshing It Out in Your Life

Micah stresses the relationship between faith and works. True faith in God produces kindness, compassion, justice, and humility. You can please God by living godly and nurturing these qualities in your relationships at school, at church, with your neighbors, and with your family.

What does your faith produce? What evidences of faith do you display to your friends? Family?

When have you witnessed a wrong that needs to be addressed? What did you do?

How can you stand up for others today?

Life Lessons from Micah

- God condemns those who oppress and take advantage of the poor.
- True faith should result in good deeds.
- Your religion cannot be separated from your relationships.

Where to Find It

The trial of Jerusalem and Samaria . . . . .Chapter 1
The reasons for judgment . . . . .Chapter 2
The trial of Israel's leaders . . . . .Chapter 3
The prophecies of a future kingdom . . . . .Chapter 4
The prophecy of a Messiah from Bethlehem . . . . .Chapter 5
The trial of the people . . . . .Chapter 6
God's promise of forgiveness and restoration . . . . .Chapter 7

God's List of Injustices Committed by the Leaders and the People

Devising sin and evil	Micah 2:1
Coveting, oppression, and violence	Micah 2:2
Stealing and dishonesty	Micah 2:8
Casting out of widows	Micah 2:9
Hating good and loving evil	Micah 3:1-2
Abhorring justice and perverting fairness	Micah 3:9
Shedding blood	Micah 3:10
Taking bribes	Micah 3:11

Nahum

The LORD is slow to anger and great in power;
the LORD will not leave the guilty unpunished.
(1:3)

Theme: Assurance of God's justice
Date written: 690–640 B.C.
Author: Nahum
Setting: Jerusalem and Nineveh

About 100 years before Nahum's day, the prophet Jonah visited Nineveh and warned of God's coming judgment. The people listened and repented, and God spared the city. But in time, Nineveh once again becomes a wicked city marked by murder, cruelty, the worship of other gods, and treating people unfairly. Nineveh is the capital of the Assyrian Empire, now the most powerful nation in the world and strongly fortified. But no one can stand against God, who is in control over all the earth. According to Nahum, because of Nineveh's sins, this proud, powerful nation will be utterly destroyed. The end would come within 50 years.

The Skeleton

▸ **Chapter 1** *The Promise of Nineveh's Destruction*

Nahum begins with a very clear description of the character of the Lord. He is holy and fair. He is patient and powerful. He is gracious to all who respond to Him and overthrows all who rebel against Him. God is holy, and Nineveh stands condemned because of its sin.

▸ **Chapter 2** *The Details of Nineveh's Destruction*

Nahum describes how the destruction of Nineveh will take place. Attackers (the Medes and Babylonians) will come and cause great confusion in the city. The people will try to flee and will be taken captive. The city will be stripped of all its wealth. God promises the destruction will be complete. Assyria will be utterly destroyed never to return, but Judah will be restored.

▸ **Chapter 3** *The Reasons for Nineveh's Destruction*

In a series of charges, Nahum explains the reasons for God's punishment of Nineveh. The fact that the people of the city are so wicked proves that God's judgment is deserved.

Putting Meat on the Bones

Nahum portrays the patience, power, holiness, and justice of the living God. He may be slow to express His wrath, but His vengeance is certain. This book gives the kingdom of Judah some rays of hope. Even though Judah has been swallowed up by Assyria, those who trust in the Lord can be comforted to hear of God's coming judgment upon the Assyrians.

Fleshing It Out in Your Life

The book and message of Nahum can also give you great comfort for today. You must constantly remember God's character and nature, and not be afraid of any power or people. God is in control of all events and is able to protect and provide for His children.

God is holy and fair. What is the world's version of power today? How is God like that or not like that?

Think of the most powerful person or nation today. God is far more powerful! In what ways can you trust and rely on God?

How have you tried to be the one in control of your life? How does that work for you?

Life Lessons from Nahum

- Even the most powerful enemies who threaten or oppress God's people will one day fall. No one can hide from God's judgment.
- God not only holds individuals responsible for their actions, but whole cities and nations, too.
- The same God who hated evil in Bible times still hates evil today.

Where to Find It

GOD...		NINEVEH...
is patient, powerful, and holy	**Chapter 1**	is evil, corrupt, and judged
punishes Nineveh	**Chapter 2**	is destroyed
details Nineveh's destruction	**Chapter 3**	is utterly ruined

Good Sports, Valiant Lessons

Life was more physical in Bible times because people depended on athletic ability to get their jobs done and to survive. Think how many laps a shepherd did in a day! And any of the fishermen on the Sea of Galilee would be a fine candidate for a rowing team today. Their physical pursuits paved the way for our present-day recreational and endurance sports. Here are a few examples:

Hunting: Nimrod (Genesis 10:9)
Archery: Ishmael (Genesis 21:20)
Running: Elijah (1 Kings 18:46)
Weight lifting: Samson (Judges 16:29-30)
Fishing: Simon and Andrew (Mark 1:16)
Rowing: The disciples (John 6:19)
Swimming: Paul (Acts 27:43)

Your Call to the Race

Do you not know that in a race all the runners run, but only one gets the prize? Run in such a way as to get the prize. Everyone who competes in the games goes into strict training. They do it to get a crown that will not last; but we do it to get a crown that will last forever.

(1 Corinthians 9:24-26)

Habakkuk

The righteous will live by his faith.
(2:4)

Theme: Trusting a powerful God
Date written: 607 B.C.
Author: Habakkuk
Setting: Judah

Toward the end of the kingdom of Judah, things had gone from bad to worse. Good King Josiah had been killed in battle, and all the reforms he put into place during his reign were quickly overturned by the next four kings—three sons and a grandson—all of whom were bad. This unchecked wickedness causes Habakkuk, a little-known prophet who lived during the same time as Jeremiah, to question God's silence and apparent lack of judgment in purging His special people, Israel. Like Job, Habakkuk asks, "Why?" The second time the prophet asks this, God answers with a flood of proof and predictions. Habakkuk finally catches a glimpse of the character and nature of God, and in response, can only stand back in awe and praise of Him.

The Skeleton

▸ **Chapters 1–2** *Habakkuk's Problem*

Habakkuk has a problem with understanding God's ways: "Why, God, are you allowing the wicked in Judah to go unpunished?" God gives an answer the prophet doesn't expect: God will use the Babylonians to punish Judah.

Now Habakkuk has an even bigger problem: "How can you, the holy

Judge, punish Judah through a nation that is even more wicked?" God answers back that He is aware of Babylon's sins, and assures that the Babylonians will not escape His terrible judgment. But Judah, says God, is guilty of the same kinds of sins and will also be punished.

The Lord concludes His answer to Habakkuk with a statement about His all-controlling majesty: "The LORD is in his holy temple; let all the earth be silent before him" (2:20).

▸ **Chapter 3** *Habakkuk's Prayer and Song of Praise*

The prophet began this short book by questioning God, but now concludes with a psalm or song of praise. He understands and acknowledges God's wisdom at the coming invasion by the Babylonians. The thought of judgment from an evil nation terrifies him, but he will trust God. And why not? God's saving work on the part of the Jewish people should give the prophet confidence in God's purposes and continued hope not to lose heart.

Putting Meat on the Bones

Habakkuk is what many people today would call a "free spirit." He liked to step "outside the box" and wrestle with issues that tested his faith. He looked around and saw the people of Judah in open sin with no restraints. Injustice was widespread. Habakkuk openly and honestly directs his concerns to God and waits to see how God will respond to his questions. God says He will judge the people of Judah, and to Habakkuk's surprise, God says He will use wicked Babylon as His instrument of justice.

Fleshing It Out in Your Own Life

The core of Habakkuk's message resides in the call to trust God—"The righteous will live by his faith" (2:4). God is at work in the lives of His people even when it seems evil has triumphed. Because God is righteous and in control, He will not let injustice continue forever. At times, you may think that God's ways seem unknowable. But just as He was in control in Habakkuk's day, He is still in control today. Your responsibility is to not question God's actions or what seems like a lack of action. Your responsibility is to gain a better understanding of God's character. A true believer—one declared holy by God—will stand firm in faith in spite of what is happening to him or to others. He trusts God to do what is right.

What seems out of control that you should prayerfully give over to God's control? Do it now.

When have you had to trust God completely, even when it seemed scary to do so?

What can you do today that will help build up your faith and godly character?

Life Lessons from Habakkuk

- Faith is not a one-time act. It's a way of life.
- You are called to trust God...even when life seems impossible and doesn't make any sense.
- The wicked may appear to be victorious, but ultimately our righteous God will punish them.
- God's ways are not our ways. They are beyond our understanding.

Where to Find It

Habakkuk questions God . . . . .Chapter 1

"Why do the wicked go unpunished?"

God answers Habakkuk . . . . .Chapter 2

"Judgment, though slow, will surely come."

Habakkuk prays to God . . . . .Chapter 3

"O LORD, I have heard Your speech and was afraid; O LORD revive Your work in the midst of the years! In the midst of the years make it known; in wrath remember mercy" (3:2 NKJV).

The next time you are troubled, remember to...

• Bring your problem directly to God.	Habakkuk prayed.
• Believe and trust in God.	Habakkuk responded in faith.
• Be encouraged.	Habakkuk went from doubt to faith.
• Be sure to realize the problem is never with God.	Habakkuk's problem was a limited understanding of God's ways.

Zephaniah

Seek the Lord, all you humble of the land,
you who do what he commands.
Seek righteousness, seek humility;
perhaps you will be sheltered
on the day of the Lord's anger.
(2:3)

Theme: The "great day of the Lord"
Date written: 635–625 B.C.
Author: Zephaniah
Setting: Jerusalem

Zephaniah is a great-great-grandson of the godly King Hezekiah. Because of his royal background, Zephaniah probably has free access to the court of King Josiah, during whose reign he lives and prophesies. His preaching ministry may have played a key role in preparing Judah for the revival that comes with this last good king of Judah. Zephaniah's message warns of the coming "great day of the Lord" (1:14), a day of judgment, first upon Judah and then upon the Gentile nations. As in the other prophetic books, God also promises to restore the fortunes of His people.

The Skeleton

▸ Chapters 1–3:8 *The Lord's Judgment*

Zephaniah begins his ministry with an awesome statement about God's coming judgment upon the entire earth because of sin. Then Zephaniah zeros in on the immediate judgment of Judah, listing some of the offenses of which she is guilty. Then he pronounces judgment on the nations around Judah. Finally, the prophet comes back to the topic of Jerusalem and describes her as living in spiritual rebellion and moral evil.

▸ **Chapter 3:9-20** *The Lord's Deliverance*

After spending most of his message speaking of God's judgment, Zephaniah changes his tone and proclaims God's future blessing, for this too is an aspect of the day of the Lord. There is coming a day when the nations will be purified and the Gentiles will call on the name of the Lord. A small group of people of the nation of Israel will be regathered, redeemed, and restored. The multitudes will rejoice in their Savior, and He will be in their midst. What starts out in Zephaniah 3:9 as a small chorus gains momentum and swells into a climax that lists the many blessings God will bestow on His redeemed people.

Putting Meat on the Bones

Zephaniah is another of the eleventh-hour prophets in the last days of Judah. The reforms in Zephaniah's day were too little and too late. Wickedness is so ingrained in the people that soon after the death of good King Josiah, they again worship other gods. Zephaniah prophesied that this would happen and that the judgment called "the day of the LORD" would come. This book expands on the similar theme of "the day of the LORD" in the book of Joel. Using varied terms, Zephaniah refers to the day of the Lord 23 times in the three chapters of his book. This day of the Lord would come soon upon Judah, but it would also have a future fulfillment. Jesus alluded to Zephaniah's day of the Lord (Matthew 13:41-43 and 24:29-31) and associated it with His second coming. The first day of the Lord refers to Judah's soon devastation, which is only a prelude to the day when Jesus Christ will come to judge all of creation, all sin, and all the nations of the world. But as promised elsewhere, God will regather and restore His people, and there will come a day of worldwide rejoicing.

Fleshing It Out in Your Life

The message is clear for you today. If you acknowledge Jesus as

Lord, you will escape the coming day of the Lord and one day enter into His blessed kingdom. The rejoicing that will come on that wonderful day can become yours today as you put your faith and trust in Jesus, the coming Messiah.

Do you have relationships you need God to restore? Pray about those today.

What do you need to do to give God full authority over your life? What has kept you from doing that?

You're learning a lot about God and His character. What truths about God make you want to celebrate and rejoice?

Life Lessons from Zephaniah

- No matter how difficult life is now, you can look forward to a day of rejoicing, a day when God will restore all things to what they should be.
- Don't let lots of stuff become a barrier to your commitment to God.
- Losing your spiritual desire will have its consequences.
- You can always find hope in the truths that your God reigns and He will take care of you.

Where to Find It

The fact of Judah's coming day of judgment . . . . .Chapter 1
The call to repentance . . . . .Chapter 2
The coming of wrath and restoration . . . . .Chapter 3

~ The Day of the Lord ~
Two Fulfillments

NEAR	*FAR*
Obadiah 1-14	Obadiah 15-21
Joel 1:15; 2:1,11	Joel 2:31; 3:14
Amos 5:18-20	———
———	Isaiah 2:12
Isaiah 13:6	Isaiah 13:9
Ezekiel 13:5; 30:3	———
———	Zechariah 14:1
———	Malachi 4:5

Haggai

*Now this is what the LORD Almighty says:
"Give careful thought to your ways."*
(1:5)

Theme: Rebuilding the temple
Date written: 520 B.C.
Author: Haggai
Setting: Judah

Haggai opens the last section of the Minor Prophets. He is preaching to the Jewish people who had returned from exile. Prophets of the past had to deal with idolatry, or the worship of other gods. But 70 years of exile had cured the people of this evil. Haggai's message is different. He urges God's people to stop thinking about their own comforts. Instead, they were to put their energies into restoring the temple. They were to build the house of God!

Amazingly, after having rejected the prophetic messages of the past, the people now listen to Haggai. Their hearts are stirred, and they take up the work of rebuilding the temple. God then honors the people's new priorities and blesses their personal lives.

The Skeleton

▸ Chapter 1 *A Call to Completion*

Discouraged by opposition from their neighbors, the Jewish people have lost interest in rebuilding the temple. Instead, they have put their energies into rebuilding their homes and fortunes. Through Haggai, God urges them to consider carefully the results of their wrong priorities.

Haggai points out that the people's selfish concerns have caused many economic hardships, including the fact God has withheld rain for their crops. The people and leaders take Haggai's message to heart. Only 23 days after his first message, the people "obeyed the voice of the LORD" and "feared the LORD." They begin working again on the temple after 16 years of inactivity, and finish it four years later.

▸ **Chapter 2:1-9** *A Call to Courage*

About a month after the rebuilding of the temple starts up, the people, especially the elderly, become sad. Many of them remembered Solomon's temple, a far more glorious structure. This new temple isn't as nice. But the Lord urges the people to hang in there and be courageous. He assures them of His presence and His faithfulness to fulfill His promises, which includes a greater, grander temple in the future.

▸ **Chapter 2:10-19** *A Call to Cleansing*

Two months after encouraging the people to stay strong, God uses the priests and the ceremonial law as an object lesson to further motivate the people to continue working on the temple. The message is that if a holy sacrifice can become impure, so will an offering to God be unacceptable as long as the people neglect the rebuilding of the temple.

▸ **Chapter 2:20-23** *A Call to the Chosen One*

On the same day that Haggai addresses the priests, he gives a second message to Zerubbabel, the leader of the exiles and a distant relative of David. Using a Messianic title that points to Christ, God calls Zerubbabel "my servant" and says He will make Zerubbabel like a "signet ring," which is a symbol of honor, authority, and power.

Putting Meat on the Bones

After 70 years of exile, God's people are being allowed to return to their homeland. Upon arrival, their first order of business is to rebuild the temple. But opposition from their Gentile neighbors and lack of interest from their own people cause the work to come to a halt. Now, 16 years later, God appoints Haggai, along with Zechariah, to stir up the people to rebuild the temple *and* renew their spiritual priorities. During those 16 years the people had focused on themselves and allowed God's temple to lie in ruins. Haggai explains to the people that their lack of commitment to God's priorities is the reason they lack God's blessings.

Fleshing It Out in Your Life

Haggai's message to God's people applies very much to you today. Take a good look at how you spend your money. It will tell a fairly accurate story of where you have placed your priorities. Haggai asks you the same question he asked the people: "Are you spending all your money on yourself and allowing God's church and God's ministries to go neglected?"

What are your top priorities? What priorities do you think God would want you to have?

When you experience blessing, including financial blessing, are you quick to share it?

Imagine God walking beside you throughout your day. (He is, you know!) Would you change the way you treat people? Would you spend more time listening and less time talking? Would you notice the kids at school who seem to have less than others? What else might you notice, change, or do?

Life Lessons from Haggai

- God rewards those who put Him first and seek to do His will.
- You cannot dwell on the glory of the past. Reality is in the present.
- Review your priorities often. Are they in line with God's?
- Your service to God is vitally important.

Where to Find It

The command to build God's house . . . . .Chapter 1
The encouragement to complete God's house . . . . .Chapter 2

Places of Worship in the Bible

TYPE	*EXAMPLE and/or REFERENCE*
Altars	Abraham, Genesis 12:7-8
Tabernacle of God	
Built	Exodus 25–27; 36–39; 40
Set up in Shiloh	Joshua 18:1
Set up in Gibeon	2 Chronicles 1:2-5
Solomon's temple	1 Kings 6
Zerubbabel's temple	Haggai 1:1,14; 2:1; Zechariah 4:9
Zerubbabel's temple further rebuilt by Herod	Matthew 4:5; 21:12
The future millennial temple	Ezekiel 40–44

Zechariah

*I will return to Zion and dwell in Jerusalem.
Then Jerusalem will be called the City
of Truth, and the mountain of the LORD
Almighty will be called the Holy Mountain.*
(8:3)

Theme: God's deliverance
Date written: 520–480 B.C.
Author: Zechariah
Setting: Jerusalem

Zechariah is a priest as well as a prophet. His prophetic ministry overlaps that of his older fellow prophet, Haggai, and includes a series of eight visions, four messages, and two serious proclamations over a two-year period. The first eight chapters of Zechariah are written to encourage the remnant while they were rebuilding the temple. The last six chapters are written sometime after the completion of the temple in anticipation of Israel's coming Messiah. This book is second only to Isaiah in the volume of material about the Messiah, the Lord Jesus Christ.

The Skeleton

▸ **Chapters 1–6** *Eight Night Visions*

In these chapters, Zechariah shares these eight night visions:

- A man among the myrtle trees—God will rebuild Zion
- Four horns and four craftsmen—Israel's oppressors will be judged
- The man with the measuring line—God will protect Jerusalem

- The cleansing of Joshua the high priest—Israel will be cleansed by the Messiah
- The golden lampstand—God's Spirit is empowering God's leaders
- The flying scroll—individual sin will be judged
- The woman in a basket—the nation's sin will be removed
- The four chariots—God's judgment will come upon the nations

There is an interlude during which Zechariah records the crowning of Joshua as the high priest and the anticipation of the coming of the "Branch" who will be both King and Priest (Jesus Christ).

▸ **Chapters 7–8** *Four Messages*

In response to a question from some of the leaders about the continuation of the fasts, God gives Zechariah a series of four messages, which focus on these themes:

- A rebuke for wrong motives associated with fasting
- A call for the people to remember the results of their disobedience—destruction
- A promise of the future restoration of Zion, when God will dwell in Jerusalem
- An announcement that fasting would one day cease and be replaced by joyous feasts celebrating God's blessings

▸ **Chapters 9–14** *Two Serious Messages*

- The first message concerns the Messiah's (or Christ's) first coming and rejection.
- The second message concerns the Messiah's second coming and acceptance. He will come and cleanse the people of their impurities and falsehoods and will judge the nations and reign physically over the whole earth from Jerusalem.

Putting Meat on the Bones

Zechariah is an important book that gives detailed references of a future Messiah that are clearly fulfilled in the life of Jesus Christ. The rebuilding of the temple, Zechariah says, is only the next act in the drama of God's history.

Fleshing It Out in Your Life

God keeps His promises. Jesus, the promised Messiah and great deliverer of Israel, did come. He came first as the suffering Savior predicted by Isaiah. But He is also coming as the Judge and King who will reign forever and ever. The future is certain. Deliverance is coming. Your future can be certain, too, if you trust in Jesus, who is coming again.

Why is it sometimes hard to keep your promises?

What sins has God delivered you from already? What sins do you need deliverance from still?

Why does it mean so much to you personally that God keeps His promises?

Life Lessons from Zechariah

- The future holds no fear when Jesus is your Savior.
- God never fails to keep His promises.
- God's message of the coming Messiah should motivate your present and inspire your future.

Where to Find It

Prediction of Jesus riding a donkey . . . . Zechariah 9:9

Prediction of Jesus' betrayal for 30 shekels of silver . . . . Zechariah 11:4-13

Prediction of Jesus' return to the Mount of Olives . . . . Zechariah 14:4

Prophecies of Christ's Comings

Christ's First Coming:	Zechariah 3:8
	Zechariah 9:9,16
	Zechariah 11:11-13
Christ's Second Coming:	Zechariah 6:12
	Zechariah 12:10
	Zechariah 13:1,6
	Zechariah 14:1-21

Feasts in the Bible

THE FEAST	*THE FULFILLMENT IN CHRIST*
The Feast of Passover	Fulfilled in Christ's death
The Feast of Atonement	Fulfilled in the acceptance of Christ's salvation
The Feast of First Fruits	Fulfilled in Christ's resurrection
The Feast of Pentecost	Fulfilled in the arrival of the Holy Spirit
The Feast of Tabernacles	Is still appropriate to observe during Christ's reign

Malachi

"Bring the whole tithe into the storehouse, that there may be food in my house. Test me in this," says the LORD Almighty, "and see if I will not throw open the floodgates of heaven and pour out so much blessing that you will not have room enough for it."
(3:10)

Theme: Disobedience rebuked
Date: About 430 B.C.
Author: Malachi
Setting: Jerusalem

Malachi attacks the evils that arise in Jerusalem after the temple is rebuilt and its services start up again. He is significant in that his message of judgment on Israel for the people's continuing sin is the last word from God for 400 years until another prophet arrives with a message from God. (Just a note: The 400 years of silence is broken when John the Baptist preaches, "Repent, for the kingdom of heaven is near" [Matthew 3:2]. This was a declaration that the long-promised Christ had come!)

The Skeleton

▸ Chapter 1:1-5 *The Privilege of God's Love*

Because they are wallowing in the problems of their present condition, the people in Jerusalem lose their view on God's work and His love for them in the past.

▸ **Chapters 1:6–2:9** *The Pollution of the Priests*

Consumed by greed, the priests were breaking God's law by offering diseased and imperfect animals on the altar and keeping the best for themselves. Because of their disobedience, God withholds His blessings.

▸ **Chapters 2:10–3:15** *The Problems of the People*

The people are as bad as their priests. They are divorcing their Jewish wives to marry foreign women. They are robbing God of the tithes and offerings due Him, and in pride they challenge God's character.

▸ **Chapters 3:16–4:6** *The Promise of the Lord*

God now spends the rest of the book of Malachi answering the people's challenge concerning His promises. God says a day is coming when it will not be "futile to serve God" (3:14), and those who fear God will be blessed. But there is a time coming when the wicked will be judged. The book ends on a bitter note with the word "curse." Although the people had been cured of idolatry, there was little spiritual progress. Sin was everywhere, and the need for the coming Messiah was greater than ever.

Putting Meat on the Bones

Inspired by the prophets Haggai and Zechariah, the Jews have rebuilt the temple. But years have passed and prosperity has not come. They are beginning to question the rewards of being righteous. On the contrary, in a series of questions and answers, God seeks to pierce their stony hearts. In their disobedience, the people question God and blame Him for their problems. They thought God's lack of concern was the problem, and said He wasn't following through on His promises.

God answers with stinging rebukes that it is the people's compromise and disobedience that have blocked His blessings. He tells them that when they repent and return to Him with sincere hearts, the obstacles to divine blessing will be removed.

Fleshing It Out in Your Life

God is faithful to His children. Even though the children of Israel had witnessed God's faithfulness, they were not worshipping God in a way that pleased or honored Him. Many had lost hope and were losing sight of the promises to come. By speaking through Malachi, God expresses His frustration and anger at His children's lack of faith. He reminds the people that they are not to give up serving the Lord and that the Messiah is coming.

How do you hold back from giving God your best offering?

What should you be giving to God as a sacrifice in your life?

Do you ever feel discouraged because you are still waiting for blessing? Take a look at your life and see how you can be more obedient to God. See how you can serve Him more fully even while you wait.

Life Lessons from Malachi

- God will not bless a disobedient life.
- You cannot out-give God.
- God is true to His promises.
- A lack of interest in God results in faithless motions of worship.

Where to Find It

Reminder of God's love .... Chapter 1
Rebuke of the sinful priests .... Chapter 2
Robbery of God is cursed .... Chapter 3
Return of Christ is prophesied .... Chapter 4

Important Prophecies in Malachi

The coming of God's messenger before the Messiah	Malachi 3:1
The second coming of Christ	Malachi 4:2
The prediction that Elijah would announce the Messiah's arrival	Malachi 4:5

The 400 Silent Years

Over 400 years separate the end of the Old Testament from the beginning of the New Testament. Because there is no spoken or written word from God during these years, they are called the "silent years." However, the history that is predicted in the prophetic book of Daniel continues to move forward with divine precision.

During the span of the 400 silent years the control of the land passes from the Medo-Persian Empire to the Greeks and then to the Romans. The Greeks bring a new trade language to the world, and the Romans bring a system of roads and law and order. Now, at last, the time is right for the coming of Messiah. His message of salvation will be written with precise exactness in the Greek trade language that is in use by most of the known world. His good news will also be communicated and spread throughout the world on the roads built by the Romans.

Even though the voice of God is silent for 400 years, the hand of God is clearly directing the course of history toward the coming of His Son, the Lord Jesus Christ.

The New Testament

The Historical Books

Like the Old Testament, the New Testament is not one book, but a collection of 27 individual books that reflect a wide range of themes, purposes, and writing styles. The first five books in the New Testament—Matthew, Mark, Luke, John (called the Gospels), and Acts—are a narration telling a story. They are the only historical books in the New Testament. The first four books, or the Gospels, are a historical account of the life and times of Jesus Christ, the Messiah, whose birth, life, death, and resurrection were foretold throughout the Old Testament. The book of Acts is a report of the period from Christ's final words to His followers and His ascension into heaven, to the travels and trials of the apostle Paul. Acts describes some of the key events in the spread of the "good news" from "Judea...to the ends of the earth" (Acts 1:8).

Matthew

Jesus began to preach,
"Repent, for the kingdom of heaven is near."
(4:17)

Theme: The kingdom of God
Date: A.D. 60
Author: Matthew (Levi)
Setting: Palestine

It has been 400 years since Malachi gave his last words of prophecy. The world scene has changed. Control of the land of Israel has passed from Medo-Persia to Greece and now to Rome. Greek is still the official trade language of the people, and it is the language in which the New Testament is written. Matthew, whose Jewish name is Levi, is a tax collector until Jesus calls him to become one of the 12 disciples. As Matthew writes, it has been more than 20 years since Jesus returned to heaven (in Acts 1:9). The good news of Jesus has traveled the length and breadth of the Roman world. Jewish Christians are starting to be persecuted. Matthew wants to strengthen their faith in Jesus and give them a tool for evangelizing other Jews scattered throughout the Roman world. He presents Jesus of Nazareth as Israel's promised Messiah and rightful King. With the King comes His kingdom—the kingdom of heaven—which will be occupied by those who acknowledge and obey this King.

The Skeleton

▸ **Chapters 1–4** *Birth and Preparation of the King*

In these chapters we learn that Jesus, a direct and distant family member of David, is born of a virgin in fulfillment of prophecy. He is baptized and proclaimed by God as His Son. Jesus' divine character is tested by the devil after 40 days of fasting in the wilderness. Jesus uses Old Testament scripture to counter the devil's temptations. Having passed these tests, He begins His public ministry by preaching repentance and the coming kingdom of God.

▸ **Chapters 5–6** *Sermon on the Mount*

Jesus gathers His disciples on a hillside by the Sea of Galilee and lays out for them in sermon-like fashion the standard for the kingdom of God. He emphasizes the importance of responding with a heart attitude that goes beyond merely observing a set of rules.

▸ **Chapters 7–20** *Kingdom of God Proclaimed...and Rejected*

Through teaching, telling parables (stories to help the people understand spiritual principles), and performing miracles, Jesus proclaims a new kingdom. He selects 12 disciples (later to become apostles) out of all His followers to share His message. The Jewish religious leaders, known as Pharisees and Sadducees, reject Jesus and His message. Jesus foretells His impending death, resurrection, and second coming.

▸ **Chapters 21–25** *Final Clashes with the Religious Leaders*

Jesus enters into the city of Jerusalem with a royal welcome. He confronts the religious leaders, cleanses the temple, and pronounces doom over the city because it has rejected God's way. He prophesies the future destruction of the temple, the coming days of tribulation and judgment, and His second coming.

▸ **Chapters 26–28** *Death and Resurrection of Jesus, the King*

After celebrating the Passover feast with His disciples, Jesus is arrested. He is then tried in both religious and secular courts, and crucified. All of this takes place in just several hours. Following His death Jesus is buried, but on the third day He rises from the dead. He appears to His disciples and tells them to spread the good news of how He has conquered death.

Putting Meat on the Bones

When Jesus called Matthew, the son of Alphaeus (Mark 2:14), to be one of His disciples, Matthew had a choice to make—Would he give up his rich tax-collecting job with the Roman government and follow Jesus...or not? Matthew chose to leave all and become a subject of the King of kings. As a demonstration of this change, Matthew held a big reception for Jesus at his house so his co-workers could meet Christ and hear about His offer of kingdom citizenship, which Matthew had accepted (Matthew 9:9-13). Later Matthew would write to the whole world about his King—about His miraculous birth, His life and teachings, His miracles, and His triumph over death.

Fleshing It Out in Your Life

Jesus came to earth to die and pay the price for our sins, and, with His resurrection, to begin His kingdom reign. His teachings show you how to prepare for life in His kingdom. His kingdom will be fully realized at His return. Until then, all His subjects will be those who faithfully follow Him. The way to enter God's kingdom is by faith—believing in Christ alone to save you from sin. Then God will change you from the inside out to be a citizen of His kingdom. Are you one of His subjects? If so, are you faithfully sharing your King with your schoolmates, family, and friends as Matthew did?

Just like Jesus called Matthew to follow Him, He calls you to do the same. Have you said yes yet?

Think of three innovative ways that you could share God with friends and family. Try these this week.

When you read through Matthew, what parts of Jesus' life inspire you? What makes you want to follow Him?

Life Lessons from Matthew

- Jesus shows you that the Word of God is your best defense against the devil, the enemy of your soul.

- Jesus has conquered the power of death and provides the only path to overcoming it.
- Jesus has entrusted His message to His disciples, or His followers. You become a follower when you trust in Him as your Savior and Lord.
- Jesus did not merely preach impersonal religious ideas, but a new way of living, through a personal relationship with Him.
- Jesus is coming again!

Where to Find It

The story of the wise men . . . . Matthew 2:1-12
The temptation of Jesus . . . . Matthew 4:1-11
The Sermon on the Mount . . . . Matthew 5–7
The Beatitudes . . . . Matthew 5:1-12
The parable of the sower and soils . . . . Matthew 13:3-23
The prophecies of the end times . . . . Matthew 24–25
The parable of the talents . . . . Matthew 25:14-30
The great commission . . . . Matthew 28:19-20

The Religious and Political Leaders of Jesus' Day

Scribes—	Jewish experts at the understanding of Scripture
Rabbis—	Jewish teachers who passed on the scribes' understanding of Scripture to the people
Pharisees—	A strict Jewish religious party who understood Scripture as literal, but sought to understand it using oral traditions
Sadducees—	Wealthy, upper-class descendants of the Jewish high priestly line who rejected the Old Testament except for the five books of Moses

Herodians— A political party of King Herod's supporters

Zealots— A fiercely patriotic group of Jews determined to overthrow Roman rule

Quiz: Can you answer "Where's the party?"

The religious parties in biblical times had pretty specific interests, preferences, and rules. Select which hangout answers the question "Where's the party?" for each of these three groups. Where would you mostly find the:

Pharisees	A. In the middle of a riot against Roman rule
Zealots	B. At a pro-Roman gathering of the wealthy and powerful
Sadducees	C. Discussing details of the law with scribes and sages

Answers: Pharisees C; Sadducees B; Zealots A.

Mark

*The Son of Man
did not come to be served, but to serve,
and to give his life as a ransom for many.*
(10:45)

Theme: The Suffering Servant
Date written: A.D. 60
Author: John Mark
Setting: Rome

Mark (his Roman name) and John (his Jewish name) was not a personal observer or witness of the life of Jesus. But he is a close friend of the apostle Peter, who passed on the details of his time with Jesus to John Mark. Whereas Matthew wrote his Gospel to a Jewish audience, Mark seems to target Roman believers. As he writes, he uses Latin, the language of the Romans, for certain expressions. Mark carefully explains Jewish customs and presents Jesus as the Suffering Servant. He focuses more on Jesus' deeds than His teachings. He demonstrates the humanity of Christ and describes His human emotions, His limitations as a human, and ultimately His physical death.

The Skeleton

▸ **Chapters 1–7:23** *Jesus' Ministry in Galilee*

Mark begins with Jesus' ministry years. Instead of presenting a detailed time line, Mark touches on key events of the Lord's work. The major focal points in Mark's account are Jesus' miracles and the rejection He faces from His hometown as well as the Jewish religious leaders.

▸ **Chapters 7:24–10:52** *Jesus Expands His Ministry*

As Jesus visits regions outside of Israel, He continues to heal people, confirming His credentials as the Messiah promised by the Old Testament prophets. Jesus also predicts His death and warns about the cost of following Him. He then begins to work His way toward Jerusalem, where He will be crucified. Along the way, Jesus proclaims that He "did not come to be served, but to serve, and to give his life as a ransom for many" (10:45).

▸ **Chapters 11:1–16:20** *Jesus Arrives in Jerusalem*

The day after Jesus enters Jerusalem, He expresses anger at the money changers and sellers who have set up shop in the temple and overturns their tables. The Jewish religious leaders question Jesus' authority and challenge Him with difficult questions, all of which Jesus answers with great ease and wisdom. Jesus is then arrested, tried, and crucified...and early on the first day of the week, He rises, and appears first to Mary Magdalene, then to other followers.

Putting Meat on the Bones

Many have asked the question, "Why four Gospels? Couldn't the story of Jesus have been given in one book rather than four?" The apostle John goes the other way and ends his Gospel with the observation that if all that Jesus had done and said had been written down, "even the whole world would not have room for the books that would be written" (John 21:25). Each of the Gospel writers gives the story of Jesus from his viewpoint and for his particular intended audience. As a result, each Gospel contains distinctive material. Taken together, the four Gospels form a complete testimony about Jesus Christ.

Mark's view comes from his time with Peter, the disciple who becomes the chief spokesman for this new religious movement. In Mark, the Lord is presented as an active, compassionate, and obedient Servant who constantly ministers to the physical and spiritual needs of others. At the same time Mark clearly shows the power and authority of this unique Servant, showing Him as no less than the Son of God.

Fleshing It Out in Your Life

Following Jesus' example, you should strive to serve God and others. The religious leaders of Jesus' day wanted to be served and rule over others. Jesus taught the exact opposite attitude. Real greatness is shown by service and sacrifice. Ambition, love of power, and position should not be your desire. Instead, seek to be a lowly servant.

Do you try to rule over people rather than serve them? What can you do to be a stronger servant?

Jesus was human and faced human problems. Mark makes that very real. How does knowing this inspire you to live out your faith?

Jesus was very angry with the money changers at the temple. Look around at our culture...who is Jesus probably just as upset with today?

Life Lessons from Mark

- Opposition to your beliefs should not keep you from carrying on the work God has called you to do.
- Follow Christ's call and seek a life of self-denial and personal sacrifice.
- Jesus came to serve, and you should desire to follow His example.

Where to Find It

Peter's mother-in-law healed .... Mark 1:31
Jesus walks on water .... Mark 6:45-52
Jesus cleanses the temple .... Mark 11:15-19
Judas agrees to betray Jesus .... Mark 14:1-2,10-11

The 12 Disciples

Brothers Peter and Andrew—fishermen
Brothers James and John—fishermen
Philip—fisherman
Bartholomew—also known as Nathanael
Matthew, also known as Levi—a tax collector
Thomas—also known as the twin
James—the son of Alphaeus
Thaddaeus—also known as Judas, son of James
Simon the zealot—a fierce patriot of Judaism
Judas Iscariot—greedy betrayer of Jesus

Luke

The Son of Man came to seek
and to save what was lost.
(19:10)

Theme: The Perfect Man
Date written: A.D. 60–62
Author: Luke, the beloved physician
Where written: Rome

It is evident from the opening lines of Luke's Gospel that it is addressed to a man named Theophilus. Luke's purpose is to give a true historical account of the unique life of Jesus. Luke is a doctor and the only Gentile (non-Jew) author of the New Testament books. He is writing to strengthen the faith of Gentiles, especially Greek believers. He also desires to give unbelieving Greeks an opportunity to consider the claims that Jesus Christ is the Perfect Man—the Son of Man—who came in sacrificial service to seek and save sinful men.

The Skeleton

▸ **Chapters 1–4:13** *Jesus' Preparation for Ministry*

In the early chapters of Luke we see the lives of John the Baptist and Jesus come together. The two are cousins born months apart. God calls John to proclaim the coming of Jesus to save people from their sins. Luke also shares one very rare glimpse into Jesus' childhood years. In it Jesus' parents find Jesus, at age 12, teaching the Jewish religious leaders at the temple in Jerusalem, where God's people worshipped. At around age 30, Jesus is baptized by John the Baptist.

▸ **Chapters 4:14–9:50** *Jesus' Ministry and Miracles in Galilee*

Jesus begins His ministry in His hometown of Nazareth, which is in the region of Galilee. His two primary activities are teaching and healing. It is during this time that Jesus calls His 12 disciples and performs most of His miracles, including raising a widow's dead son, calming the winds and waves on the Sea of Galilee, and casting demons into a herd of swine.

▸ **Chapters 9:51–19:27** *Jesus' Teaching Ministry*

While Jesus continues to do miracles, Luke now presents a greater emphasis on Jesus' ministry of teaching His disciples. In this section, Jesus teaches through many parables, including the parables of the Good Samaritan and the lost sheep. Along the way He teaches many important lessons that are practical for everyday life—lessons about money, prayer, and faithfulness.

▸ **Chapters 19:28–23:56** *Jesus' Final Week*

Luke provides a survey of Jesus' "passion week"—the last week of His life before His death on the cross. His triumphal entry into Jerusalem, His teachings to the Passover crowds, and His last moments with His disciples are described. After the Last Supper, Jesus is arrested and given mock trials. Pilate, the Roman governor, attempts to release Jesus, but the crowds want Him crucified. Afterward, Jesus is buried.

▸ **Chapter 24** *Jesus' Final Act—Resurrection!*

Death does not bring an end to Jesus. There is one further act—resurrection! On Sunday morning, the third day after the crucifixion, visitors to the tomb find it empty and hear the message from two angels that He is risen. The Lord conquers the grave exactly as He promised, and appears on a number of occasions to His disciples before He returns to heaven and the Father.

Putting Meat on the Bones

Luke has a strong interest in people and how their lives connect with Jesus' ministry. This may have been because Luke was a doctor trained to care for the physical needs of people. Luke also gives special notice to women. He writes about Mary, Elizabeth, and Anna and their part in

Jesus' early life. Mary and Martha, two sisters from Bethany, give us a glimpse of home life in New Testament times. The story of Zacchaeus and his desire to see Jesus shows Jesus' concern for even a despised tax collector. Luke's Gospel shows the Christian message to be for everyone. He also describes Jesus, the Son of Man, as the compassionate Savior for all people.

Fleshing It Out in Your Life

Jesus' love and compassion should serve as a powerful example to you as you go about your daily life. For example, you need to be like the Good Samaritan that Jesus described in chapter 10, who stopped to help a person who was suffering. And in the same way that Jesus went out of His way to support Mary and Martha after the death of their brother, Lazarus, you too need to go out of your way to support friends and family in their hour of need. No, you are not Jesus. But when you perform acts of love and show compassion, you point others to the Spirit of Jesus, who lives in you.

People were attracted to Jesus' love and message. What attracts you to Jesus?

If you invited Jesus over to your house for a day, what would you plan? Eat? Talk about?

If you had come upon the empty tomb, what would you have done? What do you do now to share the good news?

Life Lessons from Luke

- Jesus shows compassion for the hurting and the lost, and so should you.
- Jesus speaks about the attitudes and actions that should characterize your daily life—forgiveness, faithfulness, thankfulness, and commitment.
- Jesus shows a deep interest in people and their needs. He is not interested in their status, their race, or their gender. You too should develop the same kind of interest in the needs of others, regardless of who or what they are.

Where to Find It

The angelic announcement of Jesus' birth to the shepherds . . . . . Luke 2:8-14
The baptism of Jesus . . . . . Luke 3:21-22
The temptation of Jesus . . . . . Luke 4:1-13
The feeding of 5000 with bread and fish . . . . . Luke 9:12-17
The parable of the good Samaritan . . . . . Luke 10:29-37
The parable of the lost sheep and coin . . . . . Luke 15:3-10
The parable of the prodigal son . . . . . Luke 15:11-32
The widow's mites . . . . . Luke 21:1-4
The three denials of Jesus by Peter . . . . . Luke 22:54-62

The Land of Israel in the Time of Christ

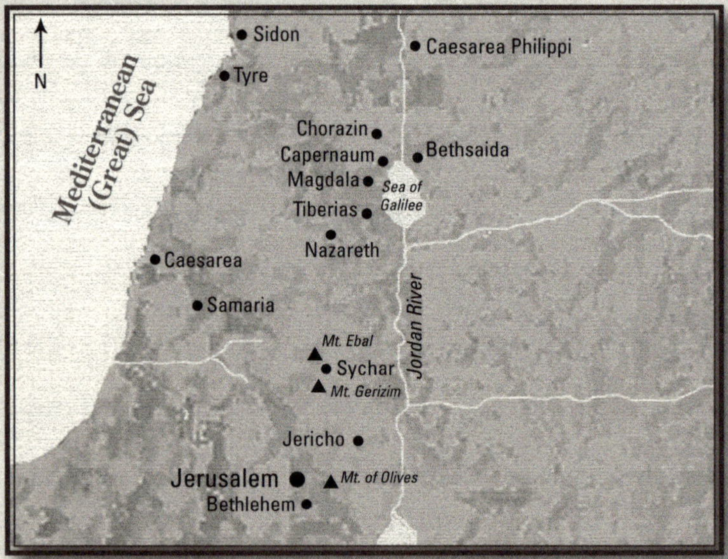

John

These are written that you may believe that
Jesus is the Christ, the Son of God,
and that by believing you may
have life in his name.
(20:31)

Theme: The Son of God
Date written: A.D. 80–90
Author: John, the disciple whom Jesus loved
Setting: Palestine

It has now been 50 years since Jesus' disciple, John, witnessed the earthly life of Christ. A lot has happened. The Christian faith has grown and spread throughout the Roman world. But with growth has come great suffering from the Roman government. All Christ's apostles have died or been killed except for John. Now an old man, John adds to what has already been written about Jesus in the first three Gospels. His record of Jesus presents the most powerful and direct case for the deity and humanity of the Son of God. Taken together with the Gospels by Matthew, Mark, and Luke, a reader will have a complete portrait of Jesus, the God-man. In Jesus, perfect humanity and deity are fused, making Him the only possible sacrifice for the sins of mankind.

The Skeleton

▸ **Chapter 1:1-14** *The Incarnation of the Word*

The introduction to John's Gospel reveals that Jesus Christ is the eternal God who became a man. He made Himself known to His creation and provides spiritual birth to those who receive Him.

▸ **Chapters 1:15–11** *The Public Ministry of Jesus*

Jesus performs miracles and talks with people such as Nicodemus, the woman at the well, and a sinful woman about the true worship of the true God.

▸ **Chapters 12–17** *The Ministry to Jesus' Disciples*

In the days before His death and resurrection, Jesus focuses on teaching His disciples about His divine purpose, the coming of the Holy Spirit, the importance of being united with Him, and how to live for Him in a hostile world. Jesus then prays for His followers—that they would see His glory, be protected from the world, and be set apart and unified so that they may be witnesses who attract others to belief in Him.

▸ **Chapters 17–21** *The Last Hours and Resurrection of Jesus*

Jesus is arrested, brought to trial, and crucified, all in fulfillment of Scripture. Then, three days later, He rises from the dead. As the Gospel closes, the risen Lord instructs Peter, who had earlier denied Him, to assume responsibility as a leader of Jesus' small band of believers and to feed His sheep, or His people.

Putting Meat on the Bones

John gives a clear statement of his purpose in writing: "These are written that you may believe that Jesus is the Christ, the Son of God, and that by believing you may have life in his name" (John 20:31). John, with all his heart, wants his readers to "believe" in Jesus as God and Savior. In fact, he uses the term "believe" about 100 times to get the message across. In Genesis, the Bible begins with man made in the image of God, while John begins with God made in the image of man, or as John describes it, "the Word became flesh" (1:14). Jesus is presented as "the Word," the visible form of the truth, the life, and the glory of the eternal God.

Later John shows the reason for Jesus' coming to earth in his statement, "God so loved the world that he gave his one and only Son, that whoever believes in him shall not perish but have eternal life" (John 3:16).

To further convince his readers of Jesus' true identity, John presents eight miracles—that is, "signs" or proofs. Only God could perform these miracles. And only the God-man could die as the perfect sacrifice in the place of sinners.

Fleshing It Out in Your Life

Only a fool would ignore road signs on a dangerous mountain road. Likewise, only a spiritual fool would ignore the signs of salvation. Look at the signs that tell you about Jesus Christ—signs that prove He is the Son of God. Do you yet believe? If so, you have life—everlasting life. Don't miss the signs God has placed before you. Pray for eyes that see!

Why is John 3:16 so powerful and so important?

How has God guided you in your faith?

If you are still watching for signs, revisit the Gospels and see how Jesus reveals who He is through the living Word.

Life Lessons from John

- Jesus is God in bodily form, and is the way, the truth, and the life.
- It is only by having a relationship with Jesus that you will experience God.
- You become a child of God by receiving Jesus.
- Jesus can forgive even your worst sins.
- Though you fail at times, Jesus extends His forgiveness to you and is willing to take you back.
- Forgiveness from God turns uselessness into usefulness.

Where to Find It

The Seven "I Ams" of Jesus

I am the bread of life . . . . John 6:35,48
I am the light of the world . . . . John 8:12; 9:5
I am the door . . . . John 10:7,9

I am the good shepherd . . . . John 10:11,14

I am the resurrection and the life . . . . .John 11:25

I am the way, the truth, and the life . . . . .John 14:6

I am the true vine . . . . John 15:1,5

The Eight Signs of Jesus' Divine Nature

1. Turning water to wine . . . . John 2:1-11
2. Healing the nobleman's son . . . . John 4:46-54
3. Healing the cripple at Bethesda . . . . John 5:1-9
4. Feeding 5000 with five loaves and two fish . . . . John 6:1-14
5. Walking on water . . . . John 6:15-21
6. Restoring sight to a blind man . . . . John 9:1-41
7. Raising Lazarus from the dead . . . . John 11:1-44
8. Giving the disciples a large catch of fish . . . . John 21:1-14

Acts

You will receive power when the Holy Spirit comes on you; and you will be my witnesses in Jerusalem, and in all Judea and Samaria, and to the ends of the earth.
(1:8)

Theme: The spread of the gospel
Date written: A.D. 60–62
Author: Luke, a Greek physician
Setting: Jerusalem to Rome

Jesus said in Matthew's Gospel that He would build His church, and the gates of hell would not stand against it. Acts is Luke's account of the growth of the early church. As a follow-up to what he wrote about the life of Jesus in the Gospel of Luke, Luke continues the history of what happens after Jesus returned to heaven. He once again addresses his writing to a Greek named Theophilus.

In Acts, the church starts with just 120 people in the upper room, where Jesus had the Last Supper with the disciples. But with the coming of the promised Holy Spirit, these few become empowered and boldly witness to others of the life-changing message of Jesus' resurrection. In spite of severe opposition and persecution, the fearless church experiences explosive growth. Acts 1:8 provides an outline for following Luke's 30-year record of the growth of the church, which begins in Jerusalem and ultimately extends to the world.

The Skeleton

▸ **Chapters 1–7** *The Witness in Jerusalem*

The good news of Jesus' resurrection is to be given first to the Jews. After the Holy Spirit comes upon the followers in the upper room, Peter preaches a powerful sermon and 3000 people respond. Later, after a dramatic healing of a man lame from birth, Peter delivers a second sermon, and thousands more come to believe in Jesus. The religious leaders become threatened by these amazing events. They even have Stephen—a powerful preacher of the truth—killed as an example to other Christians, hoping to stop this new religious movement centered on Christ.

▸ **Chapters 8–12** *The Witness in Samaria*

Stephen's death and the further persecution of Christians did diffuse some of the explosive growth in Jerusalem. But with the scattering of the church, the message about Christ spreads to Samaria, a neighboring region. Peter and John, two of Jesus' disciples, come to the region and confirm that God is at work here. Exercising their authority as apostles of Christ, they impart the Holy Spirit to these new believers.

▸ **Chapters 13–20** *The Witness to the Ends of the Earth*

Luke now switches his focus from Peter to a zealous Pharisee named Paul, who had earlier met the risen Lord Jesus and was converted while on his way to persecute Christians in Damascus. Paul's meeting with Jesus makes him an eyewitness of the resurrected Christ like the other apostles. Jesus calls Paul to take the message of His resurrection to the Gentiles. Paul and his team make three missionary journeys over a nine-year period to plant new churches and train up leaders.

▸ **Chapters 21–28** *The Witness Before Leaders*

Paul was told he was to be Jesus' "chosen instrument to carry my name before the Gentiles and their kings and before the people of Israel" (Acts 9:15). In these closing chapters, Paul speaks of Christ before the Jewish council known as the Sanhedrin. He next spends two years in Caesarea in jail, preaching the gospel to two Roman governors and a king. Finally he asks to defend himself before Caesar in Rome. Acts ends with Paul's journey to Rome, where he witnesses about Jesus while he awaits his trial before Caesar, the ruler of the Roman Empire.

Putting Meat on the Bones

Acts is the historical link between the Gospels and the letters of instruction (the *epistles*) that make up the remainder of the New Testament. Acts is the history of the church and its energizing force, the Holy Spirit. Acts could be viewed as "the Acts of the Holy Spirit" working in and through the apostles. Luke is not a detached bystander reporting historical facts, but one who is personally involved in the spread of the gospel. Yet he never names himself in his writings. Only occasionally as he writes does Luke include himself in the action with the pronoun *we*.

Fleshing It Out in Your Life

Do you consider yourself part of the "we" when it comes to sharing the gospel? Are you part of the action, or are you a bystander? You have been given the same call and the same power given to Luke and the early disciples. Don't stand on the sidelines watching others share their faith in the risen Christ. Step out in the power of the Spirit and share what you have seen and heard. Then step back and watch God's Spirit work through your testimony.

What does the Holy Spirit empower the apostles to do? Keep in mind that these apostles were ordinary people, like us, who were willing to follow God's extraordinary call.

What can you do with the power of the Spirit that you could not do before you gave your life to Christ?

How can you be a missionary, like Paul, without going to another country, state, or town?

Life Lessons from Acts

- Jesus has called you to be His witness.
- The Holy Spirit empowers you to carry out that witness.
- All ministries are important in the church.
- You are to faithfully witness of the resurrection and leave the results to God.

- As you witness, you will usually receive one of two responses to the gospel—acceptance or rejection!

Where to Find It

Peter's first sermon .... Acts 2:14-39
Peter's second sermon .... Acts 3:11-26
The deception by Ananias and Sapphira .... Acts 5:1-11
The first deacons chosen .... Acts 6:1-7
Paul's conversion .... Acts 9:1-18
The conversion of the Gentiles .... Acts 10:1-47
Paul stoned and left for dead .... Acts 14:19-20
The Council at Jerusalem .... Acts 15:1-41
Paul's journey to Rome .... Acts 27–28:16

Paul's Three Missionary Journeys

The Three Journeys	*Duration*	*Area of Focus*
Acts 13:2–14:28	one year	Cyprus, Galatia
Acts 15:36–18:22	two years	Corinth
Acts 18:23–21:16	four years	Ephesus

The Doctrinal Books

With the end of Acts and the historical books of the New Testament, the Bible moves to 22 letters (called *epistles*). They are letters of doctrine—teaching and instruction in Christian truth and practice.

The first nine epistles (Romans through 2 Thessalonians) are penned by the same human author, the apostle Paul. These letters contain many of the doctrines or essentials of the Christian faith. They are all addressed to Christian assemblies, or churches.

The next four epistles (1 Timothy through Philemon) are also written by Paul, but are addressed to individuals. Their contents center on personal relationships.

The final nine letters of the New Testament (Hebrews through Revelation) are addressed to groups scattered throughout the world. Their messages address the issues of persecution, false teachers, the superiority of Christ, and His soon return. Even though the book of Revelation focuses largely on God's prophetic plan for the future, it is also a letter of Jesus Christ. It was transmitted through the apostle John and affirms Christ's authority and His concern for the church. Revelation closes with a wonderful glimpse of the church's future home in heaven.

Romans

In the gospel a righteousness from God is revealed, a righteousness that is by faith from first to last, just as it is written: "The righteous will live by faith."
(1:17)

Theme: The righteousness of God
Date written: A.D. 56–57
Author: Paul
Setting: Corinth

Toward the close of his third missionary journey, Paul writes this letter to the church in Rome from the Greek city of Corinth. He has come from Ephesus, a city in what is now modern Turkey, where he spent three years planting and strengthening a church. As he prepares to travel to Jerusalem with an offering for the poor believers there, he stops long enough to write a letter to a church he has never visited. He writes to introduce himself to the church at Rome so the people can pray for him, encourage him, and help him with his future plans to minister in Spain. But being the teacher he is, Paul can't help but teach his new friends about the righteousness that comes from God—the great truths of the gospel of grace.

The Skeleton

▸ **Chapters 1–3:20** *The Problem of Righteousness*

Every person in the world is guilty of sin, which separates them from God and condemns all to eternity apart from Him. Even those who are morally good are, at heart, sinners, for "there is no one righteous…no one who seeks God" (Romans 3:10-11). Therefore, all deserve judgment and punishment.

▸ **Chapters 3:21–5:21** *The Provision of Righteousness*

God provides the solution to man's problem of sin and judgment by sending Jesus Christ to earth to take the judgment sinners deserve. Jesus, who is perfectly righteous and has no sin, became sin on the cross. He took man's sin and punishment upon Himself. This frees those who trust in Him of their sin and makes them righteous before God.

▸ **Chapters 6–8** *The Power in Righteousness*

Christians—those who believe in Christ as Savior—are declared righteous and possess new life. However, there is still the daily struggle with the sin that resides in the flesh. With the Holy Spirit's help, believers have the power to make right choices and refrain from sin. Also, there is no eternal blame, and nothing that can separate God's children from God's love.

▸ **Chapters 9–11** *The Promise of Righteousness*

Even though the people of Israel rejected the Lord Jesus Christ, God's promise to one day redeem and restore Israel still stands. God is not finished with Israel; there is coming a time when Israel's blindness will end, the people will be delivered, and they too will receive the righteousness of God.

▸ **Chapters 12–16** *The Pattern of Righteousness*

Christians have been declared righteous by God. They possess new life through the indwelling of the Holy Spirit. This inner transformation results in an outer transformation. What is true inside a person's heart will show up in a person's life. Some of the signs of a new or transformed life are yielding to God, submitting to government authority, loving one's neighbor, following Christ's example, bearing others' burdens, and serving in the church.

Putting Meat on the Bones

Paul had often wanted to visit the church in Rome but had been delayed. He had planted many other churches and raised up many new leaders for those churches, and now it is time for him to move on. He wants to preach in a new area, Spain, and the church at Rome is on the way to Spain. Paul feels a common bond with the believers in Rome. He longs to see them face to face and pass on to them what he has learned about God's salvation through Jesus Christ. Like an experienced trial lawyer, Paul presents the facts of the gospel and declares that all are lost without God's help. Paul explains that God gave help by sending His Son, the Lord Jesus Christ, to be the Savior of all who believe. The letter to the Romans is the most forceful, logical, and concise treatment on salvation ever penned. The book of Romans has influenced the history of Christianity more than any other epistle.

Fleshing It Out in Your Life

All men and women are sinners, and that includes you and me. Sin separates every person from God. But God has graciously extended an offer of salvation to all who place their faith and trust in Christ. Have you accepted God's offer of salvation? If you have, then you possess the righteousness of God in Christ. God now expects you to live a righteous life that honors Him.

With help from Romans, create a short explanation of salvation that you could use to share with a friend.

How can you put "love your neighbor" (see Romans 12:10-13) into action?

This week, commit to praying for a couple of people. Develop this great habit of lifting up others to God in prayer.

In what ways does your outer life reflect an inner transformation of righteousness?

Life Lessons from Romans

- Everything you receive as a Christian—your salvation, your spiritual growth, and someday your glorification—is a work of God's grace.
- Inward change will produce outward fruit. Whatever is true about your heart will show up in your actions.

- The righteousness of God is a gift that can be received only by faith, not earned by your works.
- Faithfulness in the little things will prepare you for greater tasks from God.

Where to Find It

All are without excuse and are accountable to God Romans 1:18-23
All have sinned . . . . Romans 3:23
Those justified by faith have peace with God . . . . Romans 5:1
The wages of sin is death . . . . Romans: 6:23
There is no condemnation to those in Christ . . . . Romans 8:1
The Holy Spirit prays for believers . . . . Romans 8:26
God has a plan for Israel . . . . Romans 9–11
Present yourself to God as a living sacrifice . . . . Romans 12:1
All are to submit to governing authorities . . . . Romans 13:1-7

The Holy Spirit

His Personhood

- The use of "He" and "Him" (John 14:17)
- His intellect (1 Corinthians 2:11)
- His will (1 Corinthians 12:11)
- His emotions (Ephesians 4:30)
- His fire quenched (1 Thessalonians 5:19)

His Ministry

- His caring for believers (John 14:16,26)
- His convicting of sin (John 16:8-11)
- His guiding (John 16:13)
- His glorifying Christ (John 16:14)
- His choosing (Acts 13:2)
- His directing (Acts 16:6-7)
- His interceding (Romans 8:26-27)
- His sealing of believers (Ephesians 4:30)

When Paul wanted the letter to the Romans delivered to the church at Rome, who do you think he chose to carry this important document? Which one of the leaders should be responsible? How many men should go—two, four, or more? You might be surprised to learn that the task was given to a woman named Phoebe. She is asked by Paul to carry this greatest of all documents hundreds of miles to Rome. What are her qualifications? Only that she is a servant of the church and a faithful helper of many, including Paul.

1 Corinthians

Whether you eat or drink
or whatever you do,
do it all for the glory of God.
(10:31)

Theme: Christian conduct
Date written: A.D. 55
Author: Paul
Setting: Ephesus

While the apostle Paul is teaching in Ephesus (a city in what is now modern Turkey) visitors arrive from the church at Corinth, which Paul had begun in Greece some three years before. One group of visitors reports disturbing news of division, immorality, and lawsuits within the body of believers. Another group has difficult questions concerning marriage and divorce, eating food offered to idols, public worship, and the resurrection of the body. Therefore Paul writes this first of two letters to believers in Corinth to firmly address their terrible or bad conduct and answer their questions.

The Skeleton

▸ **Chapters 1–2** *The Need for True Unity*

Paul is concerned about the divisions and hostility within the Corinthian church. He reminds the people that the message of the cross, empowered by the Holy Spirit, is the basis for true unity.

▸ **Chapter 3** *The Nature of True Spirituality*

Paul points out that as spiritual people, we should not live in a worldly manner. God wants all Christians to remember to whom they belong. That should affect the way they live their lives, for all believers will be judged for their works and rewarded for their service.

▸ **Chapters 4–11** *The Problems in the Church*

Because many of the believers in the church at Corinth are not living truly spiritual lives, the church has many problems. Paul warns the people not to become devoted to any individual leader (including himself). He condemns them for not dealing with sexual immorality, for suing each other, for neglecting God's teachings on marriage, and for taking the Lord's Supper too lightly.

▸ **Chapters 12–16** *The Resources for Problems*

Then Paul presents teachings intended to help this church get back on track. First, he reminds the people that they are all members of the body of Christ. As such, they all have a variety of gifts to offer each other. These gifts should be used with love as their prime motivation. Next, Paul emphasizes the importance of Christ's resurrection. When Christ rose from the dead He defeated death and made possible their salvation. It is the power by which they can live the Christian life.

Putting Meat on the Bones

Paul's letter to the Corinthians is filled with many exhortations for the Corinthian believers to act like Christians. Their most serious problem is worldliness. They are unwilling to let go of the culture around them. They are not separating themselves from their former evil ways. Their old beliefs were affecting their present behavior.

The corrupt Corinthian culture of Paul's day is much like our culture today. Sadly, the people in many of today's churches display the same spiritual immaturity Paul saw in the Corinthian believers.

Fleshing It Out in Your Life

What's the answer? It's the same for us today as then. Just as Paul attempts to correct the Corinthians through teaching, you and I need to correct our behavior with an accurate understanding of God's Word. Whether you realize it or not, your behavior is influenced by the world you live in, which is filled with wrong kinds of thinking. And wrong living is directly related to wrong thinking. With God's help, bring your behavior back in line with God's standards by reading, studying, and obeying God's Word.

How is your life becoming too worldly? How do you want to make it more godly?

What do you think Paul's message to today's churches and believers would be?

Write a short letter in response to Paul. Let him know what you are doing and hope to do to follow his wisdom.

Life Lessons from 1 Corinthians

- God has given you unique "spiritual gifts" to use for the support and growth of the body of Christ.
- Exercising a spiritual gift without showing true love is meaningless.
- God takes sexual sin very seriously.
- The Lord's Supper is important and should not be taken lightly.
- Christian leaders should be treated with respect and honor.
- Christians should not sue each other.

Where to Find It

Discipline for sinning Christians .... 1 Corinthians 5:9-13
Lawsuits in the church.................... 1 Corinthians 6:1-7
Sex in marriage.......................... 1 Corinthians 7:3-5
Divorce.................................1 Corinthians 7:10-16
Marriage and singleness .... 1 Corinthians 7:25-40
The Lord's Supper ....1 Corinthians 11:17-34
Instruction on spiritual gifts .... 1 Corinthians 12:4-31

What Is Love?

1 Corinthians 13:4-8

Love is patient.
Love is kind.
Love does not envy.
Love does not boast.
Love is not proud.
Love does not behave rudely.
Love is not self-seeking.
Love is not easily angered.
Love doesn't keep a record of wrongs.
Love doesn't delight in evil.
Love does not rejoice in iniquity.
Love rejoices in the truth.
Love bears all things.
Love believes all things.
Love hopes all things.
Love perseveres in all things.
Love never fails.

2 Corinthians

We do not preach ourselves, but Jesus Christ as Lord, and ourselves as your servants for Jesus' sake.
(4:5)

Theme: Paul's defense of his apostleship
Date: A.D. 56
Author: Paul
Setting: Philippi (on the way to Corinth)

After writing 1 Corinthians, Paul plans to stay at Ephesus a little while longer before going on to Corinth. His stay, however, is cut short by a riot of the tradesmen over the effect Christianity is having on the sale of idols. Paul sends his young disciples, Titus and Timothy, ahead to find out what effect his first letter is having on the Corinthian believers. As Paul travels toward Corinth, Titus finds him and reports that the Corinthians have repented of their resistance against Paul and his teaching. With great joy, but also with concerns about some new issues and attitudes, Paul writes this second letter.

The Skeleton

▸ Chapters 1–2 *The Personal Testimony of Paul*

Paul's follow-up letter to the Corinthians is a defense of his life and ministry, which some had called into question. He gives thanks to God for bringing him through tough times and giving him great joy. He also reflects on the amazing opportunity Christians have to be Christ's representatives to the world.

▸ **Chapters 3–7** *The Nature of Christian Ministry*

Paul begins defending his ministry, pointing to his many converts as proof and evidence of God's call on his life. Paul encourages believers that, although they will suffer for the cause of the gospel, they can be fearless in the face of death because it is not the end. He shares that true ministry is motivated by Christ's love, is blameless in its actions, and is pure in its lifestyle.

▸ **Chapters 8–13** *The Glory of Christian Ministry*

After hearing from his disciple Titus that the Corinthians had turned from their negative attitude, Paul now launches into the longest discussion in the New Testament of the principles and practice of giving money to support church ministries. Paul also uses his God-given authority, knowledge, sufferings, visions, and miracles as additional proof of his authority, urging the rebellious minority in Corinth to repent so he will not have to be stern with them when he arrives in person.

Putting Meat on the Bones

Titus is overjoyed to inform Paul of the repentance of the Corinthian church. But he also tells Paul that false teachers have arrived from the church at Jerusalem. These teachers openly reject the position of Paul as an apostle and start preaching false doctrine. Paul acts quickly and sends a second letter to the Corinthians. In it he warns the church against false teaching and defends himself as a true apostle. This letter contains more of Paul's personal history than any of his other letters. It is filled with details about Paul's sufferings and sorrows. He even discusses his "thorn in the flesh" (12:7-10), explaining how God used this trial to keep him humble and teach him God's sufficiency. Through all his suffering, Paul praises God's faithfulness to provide comfort to him so that Paul could now comfort others.

Fleshing It Out in Your Life

As you seek to live for Christ, you too will probably be bad-mouthed, misunderstood, undermined, and falsely accused. When that happens, do as Paul did. Look to Christ. Recall who you are in Him. Recall what

God has done in and through you. Rather than dread the trials that are coming your way, take courage in the fact that God is faithful. His strength is sufficient for any trial you are facing or will face in the future. He is the "God of all comfort" (2 Corinthians 1:3), and He promises to comfort you in all your distresses. But comfort from God is not an end in itself. God comforts you so you can then turn around and comfort others.

What trial in your life do you want to give over to God's strength?

Do you worry about the future a lot? Write out a prayer to God asking Him to take control of your future.

How can you show comfort to others? When has someone comforted you?

Life Lessons from 2 Corinthians

- God has established ministry leaders to shepherd His flock, or His people. These leaders are to be blameless, pure, and dedicated to service, and such leaders are deserving of your honor and respect.
- No Christian—including you—is immune from suffering. In many instances, God's workers suffer more than non-Christians.
- Trials are used by God to teach you humility and dependence on His grace rather than your own strength.
- You should give financially to God's work—sacrificially, with great joy, and with a sense of responsibility.

Where to Find It

God's comfort . . . . 2 Corinthians 1:3-7
Christian giving . . . . 2 Corinthians 8–9
Spiritual warfare . . . . 2 Corinthians 10:3-6
Paul's vision of heaven . . . . 2 Corinthians 12:1-6
Paul's thorn in the flesh . . . . 2 Corinthians 12:7-10

Key Content in...

First Corinthians: Practical help for Christians	*Second Corinthians:* Personal life of Paul
Addresses unbecoming conduct	Shares his heart and love
Answers questions on issues	Answers those accusing him
Advises against worldliness	Warns about false teachers
Adds information on the Last Supper	Supplies reasons for giving
Assures concerning the resurrection	Gives personal experience on suffering

Making the journeys that Paul made was not a matter of booking online and hitting the road. He faced many struggles and risks. He was shipwrecked three times during his travels! Read 2 Corinthians 11:25-27 to discover more about the many dangers he faced.

Galatians

Stand firm, then, and do not let yourselves be burdened again by a yoke of slavery.
(5:1)

Theme: Freedom in Christ
Date written: A.D. 49
Author: Paul
Setting: Antioch

Having just returned from Jerusalem to his home church in Antioch, Paul is shocked by some distressing news. He hears that many of the Galatians who had come to belief in Christ during his first missionary journey have bought into the false teaching that Gentile believers must submit to all the Jewish law before they can become Christians. Paul immediately writes this letter to defend justification by faith alone. He also warns the churches of the dreadful results of failing to believe the pure gospel of Christ alone for salvation.

The Skeleton

▸ **Chapters 1–2** *Concern for the Pure Gospel*

Paul begins by warning the people in the churches in southern Galatia (the cities of Antioch, Iconium, Lystra, and Derbe—Acts 13:14–14:23). He cautions them about those who are not teaching a gospel of faith in Christ alone. These teachers are adding the works of religious activity to the gospel, saying these good "works" are necessary for a person to please God. But this is legalism, which seeks to gain God's approval through one's actions. Christ, Paul explains, has already done everything for us that is necessary for our salvation.

▸ **Chapters 3–4** *Defense of the Pure Gospel*

Paul points to Abraham, the great Old Testament leader, and says, "Abraham was not saved by observing religious requirements, but by his belief in God." Because of Abraham's belief, God credited Abraham with righteousness. Paul explains that obeying the law cannot save anyone. In fact, it only condemns people of their sinfulness. Christians are made right with God not through the law, but because of God's grace.

▸ **Chapters 5–6** *Freedom in the Pure Gospel*

Paul instructs the Galatian Christians that they are to enjoy their freedom in Christ. They are not to try to earn God's favor through religious works or good deeds. True goodness does not come from self-effort, but from submitting to the Holy Spirit so He can create the fruit of righteousness. When it comes to successful Christian living, no one can brag about their own deeds, but only in the cross of Christ. Christ made it all possible.

Putting Meat on the Bones

Galatians is about justification by faith—being declared holy before God. Paul writes about this to his friends and divides his argument into three sections with three purposes: 1) He defends his authority as an apostle, which affirms his gospel message; 2) he uses God's Old Testament to teach the principles of justification by faith alone; and 3) he shows that freedom from the law does not mean lawlessness, but instead means that, by God's grace, believers are free to obey, love, and serve God.

Fleshing It Out in Your Life

If you are a Christian, you are no longer under the rules and judgments of the law. Christ has set you free from religious works. There is nothing so thrilling as knowing that your past is forgiven and you are free to live a holy life by the power of the Holy Spirit. However, with freedom comes responsibility. You are responsible to serve your Savior and do His will. You are not free to disobey Christ. Therefore, use your freedom to love and to serve, not to do wrong.

In your own words, describe the difference between being justified by the law and being justified by faith alone.

Freedom is a great word! And an even greater gift. What do you do with this gift of faith?

How would you explain God's grace to someone who doesn't know Christ?

Life Lessons from Galatians

- The gifts of salvation and God's love are given to you by God's grace.
- There is nothing you can do to gain favor with God.
- You cannot produce good works on your own, but only with the help of the Holy Spirit.
- When you yield yourself to God, He produces the fruit of the Spirit in your life.
- Christ alone makes possible everything you are as a Christian.

Where to Find It

Paul's three years in Damascus . . . . Galatians 1:17-18
Paul's visit with the Jerusalem Council . . . . Galatians 2:1-10
Paul's confrontation of Peter . . . . Galatians 2:11-21
"I have been crucified with Christ" . . . . Galatians 2:20
The purpose of the law . . . . Galatians 3:19-25
"You are all one in Christ Jesus" . . . . Galatians 3:28
The command to walk by the Spirit . . . . Galatians 5:16-18
The fruit of the Spirit . . . . Galatians 5:22-23
The principle of sowing and reaping . . . . Galatians 6:7

The Works of the Flesh

Galatians 5:19-21

Adultery	Fornication
Uncleanness	Lewdness
Idolatry	Sorcery
Hatred	Contentions
Jealousies	Outbursts of wrath
Selfish ambitions	Dissensions
Heresies	Envy
Murders	Drunkenness
Rivalries	And the like

The Fruit of the Spirit

Galatians 5:22-23

Love	Joy
Peace	Longsuffering
Kindness	Goodness
Faithfulness	Gentleness
Self-control	

Ephesians

Praise be to the God and Father of our Lord Jesus Christ, who has blessed us in the heavenly realms with every spiritual blessing in Christ.
(1:3)

Theme: Blessings in Christ
Date written: A.D. 60–62
Author: Paul
Setting: A Roman prison

One of the most important early churches was the church in Ephesus. Paul founded the church and spent three years teaching its members. Now, some five or six years later, Paul is a prisoner in Rome, awaiting a trial before Caesar. While he waits, Paul writes this letter. Unlike some of his other letters, this one is not about problems in the church. Instead, Ephesians is a letter of encouragement. In it Paul describes the nature of the church, which is not an *organization* but a living *organism,* the body of Christ. He then challenges his readers to act like the living body of Christ on earth.

The Skeleton

▸ Chapters 1–3 *The Powerful Blessings in Christ*

Paul opens his epistle with an awesome list of the spiritual blessings that have been given to every believer. Believers in Christ are chosen by God, redeemed by Christ, and given a heavenly inheritance through Christ. They have been adopted, redeemed, and given grace and citizenship. Through the power of the Holy Spirit they can experience the fullness of life in Christ. Each believer is a part of Christ's body, the church. God is building His people into a temple for Him to live in. Paul prays that his readers would understand their powerful blessings in Christ.

▸ **Chapters 4:1–5:20** *The Power to Live*

Paul now changes from emphasizing *doctrine* (or teaching) to focusing on *duty* and how it is to be performed. Paul explains that through the power of the Holy Spirit, believers are to put off the old self and live by the new self. This worthy walk leads to a holy lifestyle as Christians imitate God. This is what the Spirit-filled life is all about.

▸ **Chapters 5:21–6:9** *The Power to Love and Work*

In the same way that Christ loved His church, husbands are to love their wives, and wives are to willingly follow the godly leadership of their husbands. Life in Christ also means children are to obey their parents and parents are to lead their children with love. Finally, slaves (or, in today's society, workers) are to obey their employers, doing their work as if they were working for Christ. Paul challenges masters or bosses to lead properly, knowing that their ultimate master is Jesus Christ.

▸ **Chapter 6:10-24** *The Power for the Battle*

As believers walk with Christ, they will have problems with the enemy of their souls—the devil. However, they have weapons that God has provided for use against the devil's temptations and attacks. These weapons are spiritual ones, not physical. They are faith, prayer, and the Word of God. With these spiritual weapons, Christians can fight life's battles and gain the victory!

Putting Meat on the Bones

Paul writes this epistle to the Ephesian church to make the members more aware of their spiritual resources. First, he describes where these resources come from—their relationship with Christ and their position in Him. Paul then encourages his readers to draw upon those resources so they can live their Christian lives in victory. Put another way, the first half of the epistle describes a believer's *wealth* in Christ, and the last half challenges a believer's *walk* in Christ.

Fleshing It Out in Your Life

Everyone who has trusted in Christ possesses an endless supply of *spiritual blessings.* Unfortunately, most believers act as though they are *spiritual beggars* and live in defeat. Why is this so? Many are unaware of all the resources that are theirs in Christ, and fail to count on them. Do you understand what your resources are in Christ? If not, Ephesians will help you find out. If you know what your resources are, then "live a life worthy of the calling you have received" (Ephesians 4:1).

Describe your old self and your new self in the form of a commercial before and after testimony. Don't forget to list the benefits of the new self.

What does obeying your parents look like (Ephesians 6:1)? How do or don't you fulfill this command?

What are some of your spiritual blessings? Do you live a life that reflects your access to such powerful resources?

Life Lessons from Ephesians

- ▶ Remember that it is only in Christ that you can grow and mature spiritually.
- ▶ God has given you the tools you need to fight against the enemy.
- ▶ You must use God's resources to obtain spiritual victory.
- ▶ All your work is to be done as to the Lord.
- ▶ God gives instructions for success in your family life.

Where to Find It

Grieving the Spirit . . . . Ephesians 4:30
Redeeming the time. . . . . Ephesians 5:15-16
Roles and responsibilities in marriage . . . . .Ephesians 5:22-33
Roles of children and parents . . . . Ephesians 6:1-4
Roles of bosses and workers. . . . . .Ephesians 6:5-9
Spiritual armor of the believer . . . . Ephesians 6:10-17

The Armor of God

Ephesians 6:14-17

The waistband of truth
The breastplate of righteousness
The shoes of the gospel of peace
The shield of faith
The helmet of salvation
The sword of the Spirit, the Word of God

Shofar, So Good

The Jews are credited with creating many musical instruments. Here are some of the instruments mentioned in the Bible.

Shofar—This horn was made of a horn, of course. A ram's horn was steamed long enough for it to become pliable. Then the wide end was bent upward to create a trumpet shape. The shofar creates a very mournful sound.

Reed pipe—This little instrument was also used to express sorrow or mourning. Its wailing music would be played during times of death or sadness.

Harps, lutes, and lyres—A celebration wouldn't be complete without the sound of a stringed instrument. The harps of Bible times were smaller, more portable versions of the harps we see today. The lutes and lyres were also festive-sounding instruments. The lyre was typically played with a pick, whereas the lute was played by plucking with the fingers.

Tambourines—Where there was dancing, there was probably a tambourine. At parties, weddings, and feasts, tambourines would be played and women often danced and sang along.

Philippians

Rejoice in the Lord always.
I will say it again: Rejoice!
(4:4)

Theme: The joy-filled life
Date written: A.D. 62
Author: Paul
Setting: Prison

It has now been four or five years since Paul made his last visit to Philippi, where he began a church during one of his missionary journeys. The Philippian church had always given money to help meet Paul's needs, and this was no exception. Having heard that Paul was in prison, they send another contribution, and along with it, a man named Epaphroditus. This man was to minister personally to Paul's needs. Unfortunately, Epaphroditus becomes ill and almost dies. Paul, who realizes his own death could be close, writes this letter to thank the Philippians for their gift. Concerned for Epaphroditus and afraid that the Philippians might be worried about him, Paul decides to send Epaphroditus home along with this letter. In the letter Paul describes his circumstance in prison, encourages the believers in Philippi toward greater unity, and warns them against false teachers.

The Skeleton

▸ **Chapter 1** *Paul's Difficult Circumstances*

Even though Paul is in chains, he is not discouraged because, as he says, his circumstance has "served to advance the gospel" (Philippians

1:12). Paul is confident that Christ will be glorified even if he dies for his faith in Christ, and affirms that good can come from suffering for Christ's sake.

▸ **Chapter 2:1-18** *Paul's Loving Encouragement*

Paul begins the teaching portion of Philippians by encouraging believers to live in unity with one another. The key to unity is to be like-minded and serve others. Christians are to follow in the steps of Christ, who is the greatest example of humility—He was willing to die on the cross for our benefit.

▸ **Chapter 2:19-30** *Paul's Faithful Friends*

Next Paul expresses his appreciation for Timothy, who has proven his character and served alongside Paul with diligence. Paul hopes to send Timothy to the Philippians soon. But Paul does not forget to praise Epaphroditus, who ministered to Paul to the point of exhaustion and became sick. These two friends, Timothy and Epaphroditus, are examples of the self-sacrifice that ought to mark the lives of all Christians.

▸ **Chapters 3:1–4:1** *Paul's Firm Warnings*

The Christian journey is not an easy one. The Philippians can expect enemies and problems, and they will need to hang in there and press toward the goal of spiritual growth and maturity. When life becomes discouraging here on earth, they need to remember that they are citizens of heaven, which is their real home.

▸ **Chapter 4:2-23** *Paul's Final Exhortations*

Though life is difficult, Paul says believers in Christ should not be anxious or allow negative thoughts to pull them down. Rather, they are encouraged to rejoice in the Lord and give everything to Him in prayer. When they do, the peace of God will guard their hearts.

Putting Meat on the Bones

The key word in this letter is "joy." In one form or another, it is used 19 times. When Paul wrote, "Rejoice in the Lord always" (4:4), he was not sitting in comfort or in pleasant surroundings. Instead, he was a captive in a Roman prison. Yet Paul could rejoice even while in prison because of his passion for knowing Jesus Christ more and more. This is the secret of a joyful Christian life. Joy is not based on circumstances, but in the confidence that comes from a relationship with Jesus Christ.

Fleshing It Out in Your Life

Everyone wants to be happy. Therefore many people make happiness a lifelong search by spending money, traveling to new places, and experiencing new and exciting activities. But this kind of happiness depends on positive circumstances. What happens when your circumstances are not so positive or joyous? Often your happiness disappears and despair sets in. But joy is different. You have joy because you know that God is at work in your life in spite of your circumstances. True joy comes from knowing Christ personally and depending on His strength rather than your own. Do you know true joy and contentment? Do you know Christ personally, and are you depending on His strength rather than your own?

Is joy a part of your life? As a Christian, your joy should be evident. How can you celebrate your faith and be joyful?

Paul was in prison and still he expressed devotion to God. What do you feel "imprisoned" by in your life right now? Pressure at school? Home? Temptations? Tiredness? Sadness? A friend's betrayal? Find a way to express your devotion to God in spite of your circumstances. Your situation might look a lot different after doing this.

How can you recognize a false teacher? What should you do if you hear false teachings?

Life Lessons from Philippians

- Difficult circumstances should not prevent you from sharing the gospel.
- Christ humbly sacrificed Himself for the good of others, and you are called to follow His example.
- Unity comes when you put others ahead of yourself and care for their needs.

- You are commanded not to worry, but rather to give all your concerns to God and allow Him to take care of them.
- Even your most difficult circumstances can have positive benefits and be a cause for rejoicing.

Where to Find It

God will finish what He begins in you . . . . Philippians 1:6
To live is Christ, and to die is gain . . . . Philippians 1:21
Christ is your example of humility . . . . Philippians 2:5-11
Everyone will confess Jesus as Lord . . . . Philippians 2:10-11
You may know Christ and His power . . . . Philippians 3:10
Your citizenship is in heaven . . . . Philippians 3:20
You are to rejoice always . . . . Philippians 4:4
You can do all things through Christ . . . . Philippians 4:13
God will supply all your needs . . . . Philippians 4:19

Christ in Philippians

Christ is our life (1:21)
Christ is our model of humility (2:5)
Christ is our hope (3:21)
Christ is our strength (4:13)

Colossians

In Christ all the fullness of the Deity lives in bodily form, and you have been given fullness in Christ, who is the head over every power and authority.
(2:9-10)

Theme: The importance of Christ
Date written: A.D. 60–61
Author: Paul
Setting: Prison

Colosse was a small city about 100 miles east of Ephesus. The founding pastor of the church in Colosse was a man named Epaphras, who had been converted by Paul while on a visit to Ephesus. Paul had ministered in Ephesus for three years. Paul had never visited the church in Colosse, but Epaphras has now come to Rome to visit Paul and report his concerns about a false philosophy that is being taught in Colosse. Paul immediately pens this letter to warn the Colossians against this teaching that is lessening the value of Christ. He writes to give them a proper understanding of Christ's attributes and accomplishments.

The Skeleton

▸ **Chapter 1:1-14** *The Heart of Paul*

Paul greets the Christians in Colosse and thanks God for the spiritual fruit seen in their lives. He prays that they would be filled with the knowledge of God's will for their lives. When believers know and understand God's desires for them, they are able to be spiritually productive.

▸ **Chapters 1:15–2:7** *The Truth About Christ*

Apparently some false teachers in Colosse were saying there was more to the Christian life than Christ. They taught that it was necessary to also gain some kind of "deeper knowledge" and observe special religious traditions. Paul warns of these serious errors and says that Christ is all one needs. Christ alone is the head of the church, the hope of future glory, and the source of true wisdom and knowledge.

▸ **Chapter 2:8-23** *The Believer's Sufficiency in Christ*

The false teachers in Colosse are encouraging the Christians to seek some kind of higher knowledge and observe certain rules. Paul argues that believers are already complete in Christ in every way, including their salvation. There is no need for them to bind themselves to rules and regulations.

▸ **Chapters 3–4** *The Believer's Character in Christ*

Rather than follow man-made rules, Paul instructs that Christians are called to put aside their old ways (anger, bad language, lying, and so on) and put on the character of the new man—mercy, kindness, humility, meekness, longsuffering, patience, and forgiveness. In their lives, their homes, their work, their schoolwork, and their friendships, believers are to live as God-pleasers, not men-pleasers.

Putting Meat on the Bones

Paul wants the Colossians to understand the supremacy of Christ. First, he explains that a proper view of Christ is the cure for false teaching. Christ is sufficient. Nothing else needs to be added if one has Christ as Savior. Second, since Christ is supreme, the believers in Colosse are to live in obedience to Christ both in behavior and attitude. They are to be merciful, kind, humble, meek, patient, forgiving, and loving.

Fleshing It Out in Your Life

Because Christ is supreme, submission is not optional. As you are obedient to His commands, He provides the power for the transformation of every area of your life, including your home life and your time at school. Is Christ supreme in your life? Read the short epistle of Colossians and gain a better understanding of the sufficiency of your Savior for your every area of need.

Christ is all you need. Knowing this, are there things in your life that you give too much importance or value?

In Christ you are complete. In what ways does the world try to tell you that you are lacking and not good enough?

What fruit does your life display as a result of your faith and obedience?

Life Lessons from Colossians

- When it comes to salvation and living the Christian life, the Lord Jesus Christ has done it all for you.
- You are totally sufficient in Christ and have no need of special or unique knowledge, experiences, or religious rules.
- Christ is supreme, and your commitment to Him should be total.
- Living the Christian life means you put off the qualities of the world and put on the character of Christ.

Where to Find It

Do not lie to one another .... Colossians 3:9
Bear with one another........................ Colossians 3:13
Forgive one another .... Colossians 3:13
Admonish one another .... Colossians 3:16

Christ in Colossians

Christ is our redemption (1:14)
Christ is the embodiment of deity (1:15)
Christ is the Creator and Sustainer of all things (1:16-17)
Christ is head of the church (1:18)
Christ is the author of reconciliation (1:20)
Christ is the basis of our hope (1:27)
Christ is the source of power for living (1:29)

1 Thessalonians

We believe that Jesus died and rose again
and so we believe that God will bring with Jesus
those who have fallen asleep in him.
(4:14)

Theme: Concern for the church
Date written: A.D. 51
Author: Paul
Setting: Corinth

It is not clear exactly how long Paul was in Thessalonica, a city in northern Greece. It could have been as little as three weeks. But because of the response Paul's message of salvation in Christ received from many Gentiles, jealous Jews turned the townspeople against Paul. To avoid the mob, Paul had to flee under the cover of darkness. Still concerned for these new believers, Paul sends his companion Timothy to see how they are doing while he travels on to Athens and Corinth. Timothy meets Paul in Corinth, and the book of 1 Thessalonians is the result of Timothy's good report from this new church.

The Skeleton

▸ Chapter 1 *Paul's Evaluation of the Church*

The witness of the church in Thessalonica had quickly spread throughout the entire region—so much so that as Paul traveled along, he had no need to say anything about the church. Paul takes great pride in the spiritual health of the people in this new church. Their missionary zeal, their dedication to the truth, their conduct in the face of persecution, their unselfish love, and their devotion to ministry are clearly seen by all.

▸ **Chapters 2–3** *Paul's Conduct and Concern*

Paul reviews how he and his companions, Silas and Timothy, brought the gospel to those in Thessalonica, how they accepted the message, and how he now longs to be with them. Because of his concern, he sends Timothy back to encourage them in their Christian faith. Paul then ends with a prayer for even greater growth in Christ among the Thessalonians.

▸ **Chapter 4:1–12** *Paul's Exhortation*

This chapter begins the central thrust of Paul's message. Paul reminds the Thessalonians to continue to please God in their daily lives by avoiding sexual sin, loving each other, and living for Christ in a non-Christian world.

▸ **Chapters 4:13–5:28** *Paul's Reminder of the Believer's Hope*

Even though Paul's ministry in Thessalonica was brief, the new church had already come to hope for their Savior's return. Paul reminds them of the blessed hope that Jesus is coming again. Therefore, "the day of the Lord" can be a day of rejoicing rather than a day of judgment. Paul closes with an exhortation for the people to honor their church leaders, and for wisdom about how to treat each other. Paul ends with a blessing that God would keep them holy until Christ's return.

Putting Meat on the Bones

The Thessalonian Christians are living in hope of the soon return of Christ. Paul has taught them that Christ's second coming is the conclusion of salvation history. For that reason, the Thessalonians did not want to miss it! Timothy brings news to Paul that they are concerned because some of the Christians among them have already died. They wonder, *Will these departed souls miss Christ's return?* In this first letter, Paul informs them that the deceased believers haven't missed out on Jesus' return. He assures them that even their dead will have a part in Christ's return.

Fleshing It Out in Your Life

No one knows the time of Christ's return. However, one day all believers, both alive and dead, will be united with Christ. Looking forward to His return on a daily basis should comfort you as you deal with your everyday difficulties. Knowing that Christ will return should motivate you to live a holy and productive life. So live in expectation of Christ's return at any moment. Don't be caught unprepared.

How do your peers persecute or make life difficult for believers?

What is a good and godly response to give those who persecute you?

How can you prepare for Christ's return? Why is this important to think about?

Life Lessons from 1 Thessalonians

- You are to honor your church leaders.
- Your testimony is a powerful witnessing tool.
- Godly living may cause persecution.
- The promised return of Christ should motivate you toward holy living.

Where to Find It

A picture of a model church .... 1 Thessalonians 1:8-10
A picture of Paul's ministry .... 1 Thessalonians 2:1-12
Timothy's report on the church .... 1 Thessalonians 3:6-10
The second coming of Christ .... 1 Thessalonians 4:13-18
The day of the Lord .... 1 Thessalonians 5:1-4
The frequency of prayer .... 1 Thessalonians 5:17
The quenching of the Spirit .... 1 Thessalonians 5:19

The Details of Christ's Second Coming

Christ is preparing a place in heaven (John 14:1-3)

Christ's coming will be rapid (1 Corinthians 15:51-52)

Christ will descend from heaven...(1 Thessalonians 4:16)
...with a shout
...with the voice of an archangel
...with the sounding of the trumpet of God

Christ's coming will cause...(1 Thessalonians 4:16-18)
...the dead in Christ to be raised first
...those believers who are alive to be "caught up"
...both those dead and alive to meet the Lord in the air
...all to be with the Lord forever

2 Thessalonians

The Lord is faithful, and he will strengthen and protect you from the evil one.
(3:3)

Theme: Living in hope
Date written: A.D. 52
Author: Paul
Setting: Corinth

This is the second letter Paul sends to the Thessalonian believers. It is written just a few months after 1 Thessalonians, while Paul is in Corinth. Word came to Paul from Thessalonica that some people misunderstood his teaching about the second coming of Christ. His statements that Christ could come at any moment had caused some to stop working at their jobs and to begin sitting around waiting for Christ's return. Others are viewing their continuing persecution as signs that this must be "the day of the Lord," or the last days. Responding quickly, Paul sends this second letter to the young church.

The Skeleton

▸ **Chapter 1** *Paul Comforts the Discouraged*

As he did in the first letter, Paul commends the Thessalonians for their faith in Christ. Then he consoles the victims of suffering and persecution with the knowledge that when Christ returns, He will reward the faithful and punish the wicked. He also prays that God will be glorified through their faithful service.

▸ **Chapter 2** *Paul Corrects a Misunderstanding*

Paul tells those who believed that "the day of the Lord" had already come that they are wrong. He warns that mass unbelief and rebellion will occur before that day. That day, Paul writes, will be pictured by the rise of "the man of lawlessness" and others who practice evil and reject the truth. Paul then prays that the Thessalonian believers will stand firm in their faith.

▸ **Chapter 3** *Paul Condemns Idleness*

Paul begins this last section of his letter with a request for prayer that the gospel would spread swiftly and that God, who is faithful, will continue to guard them from the evil one.

Paul then finishes with a word of warning for those believers who have stopped working and have built their life around waiting for the Lord's second coming. Paul is very clear that looking forward to Jesus' return should not keep believers from taking care of the basic responsibilities of life, including work. He uses himself as an example of one who worked for his food while he was with the Thessalonians instead of relying on others to meet his daily needs.

Putting Meat on the Bones

Even when people try their best to be clear in their speaking and writing, misunderstandings can occur. That's what happened with Paul's first letter to the Thessalonians. Some people had become discouraged because they thought their present persecution meant they had missed the Lord's return. They thought they were actually in "the day of the Lord" and experiencing the awful tribulation to come in that day. They did not understand that persecution is always to be expected by those who live their faith in the Lord. And for others, the hope of the soon return of Christ had given them an excuse for laziness.

Fleshing It Out in Your Life

Paul's letter should keep you from becoming discouraged or afraid when you are persecuted or see evil increasing. God is still in control, no matter how bad things look or become. He has a plan for your future, and this hope should give you strength to keep moving forward instead of stopping and doing nothing. Paul encourages you to stand firm, keep working, keep doing good, and keep waiting for Christ.

Is there an area of your life that feels out of control? Pray to God and give Him full control of this area.

How does your faith give you hope for the future?

What are some ways that you "stand firm" in your life?

Life Lessons from 2 Thessalonians

- Your expectation of Christ's return should not keep you from living life in a responsible manner.
- God is with you in your suffering and will use it to grow you and bring glory to Himself.
- Make sure you properly understand what Scripture says, for it will affect how you live.
- God expects you to do your part at home, at school, or at work if you have a job, and not expect others to make up for your lack of responsibility.

Where to Find It

Comfort in persecution . . . . 2 Thessalonians 1:5-12
Second coming of Christ . . . . 2 Thessalonians 2:1-12
Profile of a Christian . . . . 2 Thessalonians 2:13-17
Paul's request for prayer . . . . .2 Thessalonians 3:1
Warning against laziness . . . . 2 Thessalonians 3:6-15

Profile of "the Man of Lawlessness"

• Called "the man doomed to destruction"	2 Thessalonians 2:3
• Called the "little" horn	Daniel 7:8
• Called "the ruler who will come"	Daniel 9:26
• Called "the antichrist"	1 John 2:18
• Called "the beast"	Revelation 13:2-10

Details from 2 Thessalonians 2:3-12 About "the Man of Lawlessness"

- He comes with a great apostasy.
- He is held in check until "the one who now holds it back"—the Holy Spirit—is taken out of the way.
- He proclaims himself to be God.
- He sits in the temple of God.
- His coming is the work of Satan.
- His coming is with power, signs, lying wonders, and deception.
- He will be consumed by the breath of God.

1 Timothy

If I am delayed, you will know how people ought to conduct themselves in God's household, which is the church of the living God.
(3:15)

Theme: Instructions for a young disciple
Date written: A.D. 64
Author: Paul
Setting: Macedonia/Philippi

Timothy has been one of Paul's closest disciples since he was first recruited by Paul for service some 15 years earlier. Paul has just been released from his first imprisonment in Rome, and revisits several of the cities in which he had ministered, including Ephesus. When Paul leaves Ephesus, he asks Timothy to stay behind as his personal representative. Paul then goes on to Macedonia, while Timothy now finds himself serving as pastor of the church at Ephesus. Paul hopes to eventually return to Timothy, but in the meantime, he writes this letter to give Timothy practical advice for his ministry.

The Skeleton

▸ **Chapter 1** *Instruction About False Doctrine*

Paul immediately opens this letter with a warning about the growing problem of false teaching about the law of Moses. Paul writes that the law is good because it reflects God's holy and righteous standard. Its purpose is to show people their sin and their need for the saving gospel of Jesus Christ. At this point the aging apostle rehearses his dramatic conversion and his calling to the ministry. He also reminds Timothy of his own divine calling when he was probably a teen and charges Timothy to fulfill it without wavering in doctrine or conduct.

▸ **Chapters 2–3** *Instruction About the Church*

Having given Timothy his marching orders, Paul now addresses some issues about church worship. Public prayer should be a part of the worship service and the responsibility of the men in the church. The women, on the other hand, should focus on developing the inner quality of godliness. Next, Paul addresses the qualifications of two groups of leaders—bishops (or overseers) and deacons.

▸ **Chapter 4** *Instruction About False Teachers*

Having already warned about false teachers, Paul now tells how to recognize them, and how to respond to them. Paul also explains that God's teachers, by contrast, defend their people by proclaiming God's truth. Paul exhorts Timothy to do this as well.

▸ **Chapter 5** *Instruction About the Pastorate*

Next, Paul gives practical advice on caring for the young, the old, and the widows. He also addresses the honor due to church leaders and how to select them.

▸ **Chapter 6** *Instruction About Worldliness*

Paul concludes by describing the motives of false teachers. They are in ministry for personal profit and are greedy. By contrast, Timothy is told to guard his motives when it comes to money, to stand firm in his faith, to live in a godly manner so that no one could accuse him of any wrong, and to exhort the rich to share their wealth.

Putting Meat on the Bones

Bank tellers are taught to spot counterfeit bills by becoming very familiar with the real thing. This same technique applies to detecting false teachers and their wrong teachings. We must know the truth in order to spot error. Timothy knew the truth, for he had heard Paul preach and teach it for 15 years. Therefore it was only natural for Paul to give

Timothy the responsibility of defending the faith by teaching the truth. Armed with sound teaching, the Ephesians could defend themselves against false teachers and their teachings.

Fleshing It Out in Your Life

Do you know the truths in God's Word well enough to spot a false teacher or teaching? Are you prepared to defend the Christian faith with your current level of biblical knowledge? If so, follow Paul's example and find younger-in-the-faith Christians and begin mentoring them. If you are not as mature as you would like to be, follow the example of Timothy and gain wisdom by learning from a more mature Christian.

So much is at stake! False teaching is much more harmful than a fake dollar bill. A false dollar only affects you physically. But false teaching affects the soul. Paul calls false doctrine the "doctrines of demons" (1 Timothy 4:1 NKJV). Get to know your Bible both on your own and with the help of a mentor so you can defend your faith and protect others from the worst of all errors—spiritual error.

Paul was a great mentor and teacher for Timothy. What advice from Paul is also helpful for your faith growth?

What have you learned from studying the Bible that will help you recognize false teachings?

Paul spends time talking about roles within the church. Are you investing yourself in the growth and ministry of your church? Yes, you are young…but you are an important part of your church family.

Life Lessons from 1 Timothy

- As a young person, use the spiritual qualifications of leaders as a guide for your own growth to maturity.
- As a young person, take note of the relationship Paul had with his young disciple. Find someone like Paul, who can give you guidance and counsel not for just a few weeks or months, but for years if needed.
- As a young person, follow the example of Timothy and imitate the lives of more mature believers.

- As a young person, be reminded of the profound effect you can have on your brothers and sisters and those at school.

Where to Find It

The roles of men and women in public worship... 1 Timothy 2:8-15
The qualifications for a bishop/elder .... 1 Timothy 3:1-7
The qualifications for a deacon............... 1 Timothy 3:8-13
The profile of an apostate...................... 1 Timothy 4:1-3
The financial support of widows .... 1 Timothy 5:9-16
The financial support of elders.............. 1 Timothy 5:17-21
The sinful love of money...................... 1 Timothy 6:6-10

The Titles and Qualifications of Leaders in the New Testament

Bishop or overseer .... 1 Timothy 3:1-7
Elder .... Titus 1:5-9
Pastor .... 1 Peter 5:2

(Note: The above terms for leaders are used for those in the church who feed, lead, watch over, and warn God's people—see Acts 20:28-32. These terms are also used interchangeably in the New Testament.)

Deacon or server ....Acts 6:1-6; 1 Timothy 3:8-13

Timothy started studying the Scriptures when he was a young boy. He grew in knowledge as he grew in life. He eventually became a pastor in Ephesus.

2 Timothy

Do your best to present yourself to God as one approved, a workman who does not need to be ashamed and who correctly handles the word of truth.
(2:15)

Theme: A charge to faithful ministry
Date written: A.D. 67
Author: Paul
Setting: Rome

Paul is in prison and alone except for the presence of Luke, who has been his faithful friend and doctor for many years. Paul is also aware that the end is near. But before he dies, Paul wants to pass on the baton of his ministry to Timothy, his trusted assistant. Concerned that Timothy may be in danger of spiritual burnout, Paul writes to encourage him to continue being faithful to his duties. Timothy is to hold on to sound doctrine, to avoid error, to expect persecution for preaching the gospel, and above all, to put his confidence in the Word of God as he preaches it.

The Skeleton

▸ **Chapter 1** *The Prerequisites for Faithful Ministry*

Paul opens his letter to his "dear son" (1:2) with tenderness and love. He reminds Timothy of his resources for the ministry—a genuine faith that had been modeled for him by his mother and grandmother, his calling and giftedness, a desire to hold tightly to the truth of God's Word, and a loyalty that will last even under the most difficult of times.

▸ **Chapter 2** *The Pattern for Faithful Ministers*

Paul now challenges Timothy to prepare others to follow him in the ministry. Timothy is to discipline himself like a soldier, an athlete, and a farmer, and to follow Paul's example of endurance. In his dealings with others, Timothy must not get caught up in useless discussions. In his dealings with himself, he must flee youthful desires and keep his life pure.

▸ **Chapter 3** *The Perils of Faithful Ministry*

Paul, the ever-watchful leader, foresees difficult times of growing unbelief and wickedness, during which men and women will be more open to false teaching. Paul exhorts Timothy to never waver in his use of the Scriptures to combat this growing problem. In fact, it was these same Scriptures that God had used during Timothy's childhood to make Timothy "wise for salvation" (2 Timothy 3:15). These Scriptures are "God-breathed" (God-inspired) and will now equip Timothy to combat false teaching and heresy.

▸ **Chapter 4** *The Proclamation of Faithful Ministers*

Paul's final advice to Timothy is that a man of God must be ready to preach the Word of God at any time and at any place in all the ways necessary to reach people with the truth. Paul closes this very personal letter with an update on his situation in Rome. He states his longing to see Timothy before the end, and asks him to come to Rome and bring certain articles, particularly what he calls "the parchments" (1 Timothy 4:13), probably portions of the Old Testament.

Putting Meat on the Bones

If you knew you were going to die in the near future, what information would you want to pass on, and who would you want to pass it on to? That was Paul's situation. He was on "death row," waiting his execution for preaching the gospel of Christ. The letter of 2 Timothy is his last will and testament. Of all the people Paul has known over the years, he chooses to write one last letter to his spiritual son in the faith, Timothy. Instead of trying to drum up sympathy for himself or stir up action against an unjust, godless government, Paul writes to comfort, encourage, and motivate Timothy.

Paul's message to Timothy has also come to the rescue of other distressed Christian workers down through the centuries. He reminds all Christian workers of what is truly important and what will ultimately provide strength and power—the Word of God. To the very end, Paul is thinking of the personal and spiritual needs of others more than he is thinking of himself.

Fleshing It Out in Your Life

How does Paul's utter disregard for himself strike you? Are you so busy focusing on yourself and your perceived needs that you are failing to notice the truly needy people around you? Look outside yourself. You are sure to find plenty of unhappy people who could use a helping hand or a word of encouragement, especially a message from God's Word delivered to them...by you!

If Paul had been writing to you, what resources or assets of faith would he have identified in your life?

Do you ever experience burnout? What encouragement can you draw from this letter?

Paul chose to encourage people even as he faced death. What tough thing are you experiencing? How can you still reach out to others during this difficult time?

Life Lessons from 2 Timothy

- Your Christian life is to be a disciplined life.
- Your sincere faith can have a positive effect on your family and others.
- By contrast, phony faith can have a negative effect.
- Scripture, empowered by God's Spirit, is the instrument that brings people to salvation.
- Scripture is essential for encouraging a life of godliness.
- Mentoring, as modeled by Paul, is a long-term commitment.

Where to Find It

"God did not give us a spirit of timidity" . . . . .2 Timothy 1:7
"I know whom I have believed" . . . . .2 Timothy 1:12
The mandate for discipleship .2 Timothy 2:2
A diligent workman for God is not ashamed . . . . .2 Timothy 2:15
The inspiration of Scripture. . . . . 2 Timothy 3:16-17
"I have fought the good fight" . . . . 2 Timothy 4:6-8

The Word of God Is Important

2 Timothy 3:16-17

Because It Is...

- Inspired by God—it is God-breathed
- Profitable for doctrine—it instructs in divine truth
- Essential for reproof—it rebukes wrong behavior
- Necessary for correction—it points the way back to godly living
- Helpful for instruction in righteousness—it trains in right behavior
- Able to make you complete—it is capable of making you proficient in all you do
- Always there to equip you—it prepares you for the demands of righteous living

Titus

You must teach what is
in accord with sound doctrine.
(2:1)

Theme: A manual of conduct
Date written: A.D. 62–64
Author: Paul
Setting: Macedonia

While on his way to Rome for his first imprisonment, Paul had briefly visited Crete, an island in the Mediterranean Sea. After his release, Paul returns to Crete for ministry and leaves Titus there. Titus is to continue the work Paul started while Paul goes on to Macedonia. Titus is a trusted and longtime disciple of Paul's who served with Paul on his second and third missionary journeys. Paul now writes to Titus in response to a letter from Titus or a report that comes to him from Crete. Paul gives personal encouragement and counsel to a young pastor who is being opposed by ungodly men within the new churches. He gives instruction on how those young-in-the-faith believers are to conduct themselves before a pagan society that is eager to speak out against this new religion and its people.

The Skeleton

▸ **Chapter 1** *The Conduct of Church Leaders*

Paul opens with a brief greeting. He then gives the first of three statements: God purposed to save and grow His chosen ones by His Word and bring them to eternal glory (Titus 1:1-4).

Paul goes on to inform Titus of one of his major duties—that of appointing qualified leaders in the churches on Crete. These leaders are to refute false teachers and encourage the people in the church to live godly lives in front of their sinful neighbors.

▸ **Chapter 2** *The Conduct of Church Members*

Paul instructs Titus to speak solid words of truth to men and women, different age groups, and slaves so that they show a pattern of good works and gain a good reputation before the unbelieving world. Then Paul gives his second statement touching on the basis for godly living: Jesus Christ, through whom we receive God's gracious gift of salvation, redeems us so that we may be His special people—a people who are zealous to do good works (Titus 2:11-14). Paul then urges Titus to teach these truths boldly.

▸ **Chapter 3** *The Conduct of Believers in General*

Titus is to remind the church members of their responsibilities in society—they are to be subject to rulers, obey God, and be ready for every good work. They are to speak no evil, and be peaceable, gentle, and humble toward all people. Paul then gives his third statement: He reminds his readers that they were all once foolish and disobedient, yet God brought salvation to them not on the basis of their works but His mercy. They are heirs of eternal life, having been made righteous by His grace (Titus 3:4-7).

Paul next exhorts Titus to deal firmly with complainers who cause division and strife. He closes his letter by asking Titus to come to him. Paul then gives a final challenge to the people to continue to be involved in good works and not be unfruitful.

Putting Meat on the Bones

The book of Titus is important because it stresses the need for right living among Christians as a testimony to the godless world around them. The problem of sexual sin among the Cretans was not much different than that found in other cities where Christianity was taking root. Paul writes Titus about preparing the people in the churches to live as positive witnesses for Jesus Christ.

Fleshing It Out in Your Life

Whether it's A.D. 62 or today, the total witness of all church members must have the same message. There cannot be arguing and strife. And there must be godly behavior outside the church as you come in contact with unbelievers. Have you thought about your conduct both inside and outside the church? Ask God to give you insight into your behavior at church, and in public. May your godly behavior help promote unity within your youth group, and may your good works outside the church be a bright light leading others to the Savior.

How are you a witness to others at school, home, and even at church?

Do you ever catch yourself acting differently at church than you do while at school? Which behaviors do you need to work on so that you are consistently faithful to God's teachings?

Think of a time when you showed authentic faith to others. How did it feel? How did others respond?

Life Lessons from Titus

- Spiritual leadership starts with what you are before it moves to what you are to do.
- Your conduct exposes your true spiritual condition.
- Your conduct is essential in your witness.
- Each age group and gender in the church has specific roles and responsibilities that, when fulfilled, reflect positively on God and His Word.

Where to Find It

God's selection of believers . . . . Titus 1:1-2
Christ's deity . . . . Titus 2:13
Christ's death for sinners . . . . Titus 2:14
A Christian's duty to obey the government . . . . Titus 3:1
The Holy Spirit's ministry . . . . Titus 3:5

The Ministry of Good Works

Christians are to be an example of good works	Titus 2:7
Christians are to be excited about doing good works	Titus 2:14
Christians are to be ready for every good work	Titus 3:1
Christians are to be careful to continue doing good works	Titus 3:8

Philemon

Perhaps the reason he [Onesimus] was separated from you for a little while was that you might have him back for good—no longer as a slave, but better than a slave, as a dear brother.
(Verses 15-16)

Theme: Forgiveness
Date written: A.D. 60–62
Author: Paul
Setting: Prison

A runaway slave from Colosse by the name of Onesimus makes his way to Rome and, in God's grand design, becomes a Christian under Paul's ministry. Amazingly his master and owner, Philemon, had also been saved under Paul's ministry several years earlier. Now Paul, a prisoner, wants to do the right thing and send Onesimus, his new friend and fellow believer, back to his master, Philemon. Paul writes this letter asking his "dear friend and fellow worker" (verse 1) Philemon to forgive his runaway slave and receive him back as a new brother in Christ.

The Skeleton

▸ Verses 1–3 *A Greeting from a Good Friend*

Paul usually dictated his letters, but because this letter was so different, he decides to write it personally. He addresses it to Philemon, a Christian leader in Colosse, but also names Philemon's wife, Apphia, and their son, Archippus, in the letter. He even addresses the entire church that meets in their home. They are all his beloved friends.

▸ **Verses 4-7** *The Character of One Who Forgives*

Paul thanks God for Philemon's love and faithfulness toward Jesus Christ and all the believers in Colosse, who have been refreshed by Philemon's ministry. Paul's praise of Philemon is honest and heartfelt.

▸ **Verses 8-18** *The Actions of One Who Forgives*

Paul bases the request he is about to make on Philemon's character, rather than ordering Philemon to pardon and receive Onesimus. Paul doesn't use Onesimus' name until after he describes the dramatic change that has occurred in Onesimus' life. He tells Philemon that once Onesimus was of some use to Philemon. But now he is useful in his service to Paul, and he can also be useful in a similar way to Philemon. Paul pleads with Philemon to receive Onesimus back like he would receive Paul himself. Evidently Onesimus had stolen from his master, so Paul says Philemon is to put Onesimus' debt on his (Paul's) account.

▸ **Verses 19-25** *The Motive of One Who Forgives*

After Paul asks that Onesimus' debt be put on his account, Paul reminds Philemon of his greater spiritual debt as one of Paul's converts. Paul explains that this opportunity is a real test of Philemon's ability to forgive. Paul expresses confidence in the outcome—that Onesimus may be freed from slavery or given permission to engage in ministry—or both! Paul is hoping to be released from prison before long and asks that a room be prepared for his arrival.

Putting Meat on the Bones

The book of Philemon, along with the books of Ephesians, Philippians, and Colossians, are referred to as "prison epistles" because they were written while Paul was in prison for several years in Rome. In this shortest of the four prison epistles Paul tactfully appeals to his friend not to punish his runaway slave, Onesimus, but to forgive and restore him as a new Christian brother. This request would probably have been impossible to fulfill under normal circumstances. Slaves had a tough life, and those who had run away or stolen from their master—or, like Onesimus, done both—would be in serious trouble. Philemon had every right under Roman law to punish or even kill Onesimus. But Christ's death makes forgiveness possible. In Christ, Philemon and anyone who names the name of Jesus can have the forgiveness of sins. Forgiveness is a very foundational aspect of Christianity.

Fleshing It Out in Your Life

Because of your forgiveness in Christ, you can and should be willing to forgive others. Your ability to forgive others is proof of the forgiveness you have received from God. Is there someone who has wronged you and, until now, you have been unwilling to forgive? Examine your heart. A forgiven Christian is a forgiving Christian.

When is the last time you were forgiven by someone?

When is the last time you forgave someone?

When you pray, do you ask God for forgiveness? Make it a priority to bring your sins to God in prayer.

Life Lessons from Philemon

- Coming to Christ does not relieve you of your past sinful actions.
- You must obey the law even though you might not agree with it.
- Forgiveness is most Christlike when it is given to the undeserving.
- Being a go-between on behalf of others is an important part of your Christian life.

Where to Find It

Paul's praise of Philemon . . . . Philemon 4-7
Paul's appeal to Philemon . . . . Philemon 8-14
Paul's vision for Onesimus . . . . Philemon 15-17
Paul's confidence in Philemon . . . . Philemon 18-21

~ Bible Bio Profile ~
The Apostle Paul

- He met the risen Lord Jesus Christ.
- He was a pioneer missionary and church planter.
- He was a discipler of men.
- He worked as a tentmaker to support his ministry.
- He began his formal ministry after the age of 40.
- He made his first missionary trip after the age of 45.
- He wrote his first epistle at the age of 49.
- He preached the gospel until he was put to death at about age 65.
- He wrote 13 God-inspired books of the New Testament.
- He was the most influential man in the New Testament other than Jesus Christ.

Hebrews

Therefore, since we have a great high priest who has gone through the heavens, Jesus the Son of God, let us hold firmly to the faith we profess.
(4:14)

Theme: The superiority of Christ
Date written: A.D. 67–69
Author: Unknown
Setting: A community of Jewish Christians

Persecution is a real threat to the Jewish Christians in the new churches of the first century. Many find themselves persecuted as they try to live out their faith in Christ while living in Jewish communities where the Old Testament is the focus of religion. The unknown writer of the book of Hebrews believes that many Jewish Christians are in danger of slipping back into Judaism (the practice of the Old Testament law) because of growing opposition. They need to grow and become stable in their faith. By showing the superiority of Christ over all the Old Testament laws and sacrifices, this author exhorts these early believers to stay true to the gospel of Jesus Christ.

The Skeleton

▸ Chapters 1–4:13 *Christ, a Superior Person*

Hebrews opens with the author showing that Christ is superior to the prophets. The writer explains that even though angels are special beings, Christ is superior to the angels because He is God's Son. Christ is also superior to Moses, the great lawgiver, who was merely God's servant, because Christ is God's Son. Unlike Moses, Christ can lead His people into a peaceful place to live. Even though Joshua led the Israelites into their inheritance, there is a better home for God's people in the future. Christ, from His superior position, will provide that final and perfect home.

▸ **Chapters 4:14–10:18** *Christ's Superior Priesthood*

Throughout this section, the author uses a priest named Melchizedek (who lived before the Jewish priesthood was set up) as an illustration of the priesthood of Christ. The Old Testament priesthood was very important to the Jews. But Christ's priesthood is superior to the Old Testament priesthood. The writer says the priesthood of Christ was far better, superior, the best—perfect! Over and over the author makes it clear Christ is the only priest who was permanent and sinless, therefore the perfect priest—our Great High Priest. In other words, with Jesus as High Priest, the Old Testament priesthood became out-of-date. Christ offered Himself as a sinless and voluntary sacrifice once and for all, which means His work on the cross makes it possible for our sins to be removed from us—forever! By contrast, the old priesthood had to offer animal sacrifices continually, and these sacrifices could never bring about the forgiveness and removal of people's sins.

▸ **Chapters 10:19–12:29** *Christ's Superior Faith*

The author sums up all he has been saying about Christ by warning his readers of the danger of throwing away their superior faith, which is based on a superior Savior. Trust in God is defined and illustrated with the lives of many Old Testament believers such as Abraham, Sarah, David, Samuel, and others. The readers need to fix their eyes on Jesus, the author and perfecter of genuine faith, who endured great hostility and suffering on the cross. Those who believe in Him will sometimes have to endure difficulty from the world and expect God's discipline if it's needed for developing personal holiness.

▸ **Chapter 13** *Superior Christian Behavior*

This last chapter focuses on some of the basic behaviors of Christian living. These behaviors are the result of the readers' dedication to Christ. This superior behavior will be seen in loving relationships, a lack of wanting other people's things, and contentment and obedience. This kind of Christlike behavior helps portray the true gospel to the world, encouraging others to believe in Christ, which brings glory to God.

Putting Meat on the Bones

The Jewish religion was divinely designed and expressed true worship and devotion to God. The commandments, rituals, and the prophets described God's promises of the Messiah and revealed the way to forgiveness and salvation. But then Jesus Christ, the Messiah, came and fulfilled the law and the prophets. He eliminated the need for sacrifices, conquered sin, and provided eternal life through His death on the cross.

The message of Jesus was hard for the Jews to accept. Many were violently opposed to the gospel of Christ. Those who did accept Jesus as the Messiah often found themselves drifting back into their old religious ways, especially as persecution increased. Hebrews was written to these people with the key message that Christianity is superior to the Jewish religion and every other religion because Christ is superior and He alone is completely sufficient for salvation.

Fleshing It Out in Your Life

Faith is confident trust in God and the salvation He provides in His Son, Jesus. Jesus is the only one who can save you from sin. If you trust in Jesus Christ for your complete salvation, He will change you completely. That change and your growth will enable you to face trials, stay true to God when you are suffering, and build your character. Don't allow persecution, temptation, or other religious systems to cause you to hesitate in your commitment to Jesus. Your Savior is superior. Your faith placed in your Savior is superior. And your final victory through your Savior is assured.

How have you experienced transformation?

What are you facing right now that is building your character? How is genuine faith helping?

Write a letter encouraging other teens to stay true to God. In the letter, use what you've learned in Hebrews.

Life Lessons from Hebrews

- ▶ The superiority of Christianity is based on the superiority of Christ.
- ▶ Salvation in Christ and freedom from sin are gifts from God, but you are given the responsibility to grow and strengthen your faith and trust in God.
- ▶ The process of growing your faith in God takes time.
- ▶ Maturity keeps you from being easily swayed in your beliefs.
- ▶ You can have victory in your trials when you keep your eyes focused on Christ.

Where to Find It

The ministry of God's Word .... Hebrews 4:12-13
The king of Salem, Melchizedek .... Hebrews 7:1-22
God's definition of faith .... Hebrews 11:1
God's "hall of faith" .... Hebrews 11
The race of faith .... Hebrews 12:1
God's discipline of His children .... Hebrew 12:3-11

A Comparison of the Two Sacrifices

The sacrifices under the law were:	The sacrifice of Christ was:
A reminder of sin	The removal of sin
Offered continually	Offered once
The blood of animals	The blood of Christ
A covering for sin	The cleansing of sin
Involuntary	Voluntary

Is that a cricket in your teeth?

Common foods eaten during Bible times include barley, almonds, cucumbers, figs, bread, beans, fish, deer meat, chicken, grapes, olive oil, nuts, apples, cheese, eggs, and honey.

Oh, and how about a little wild goat or a few crickets for an after-school snack?

Forget your table manners? No problem. People in Bible times frequently ate food served on animal skins while seated on the ground or while reclining on couches (John 12:2). And bread was often used as the utensil so they didn't have to worry about which fork was for the salad. People would dip their bread into the beans or soup or whatever was being served in the main pot.

James

Faith by itself, if it is not accompanied by action, is dead.
(2:17)

Theme: Genuine faith
Date written: A.D. 44–49
Author: James
Setting: Jerusalem

The book of James is the earliest New Testament epistle or letter. It was written by James, a leader of the church in Jerusalem. The people in the Jerusalem church—the first church—had been scattered to a number of Roman provinces because of persecution. James wants to instruct and encourage them in their struggles. James explains genuine faith will produce real changes in a person's conduct and character. He presents a series of tests by which a person's faith in Christ can be measured. If real change is absent, then readers should examine themselves to make sure they are not showing signs of dead faith—which is really no faith!

The Skeleton

▸ Chapters 1–2 *Actions of Faith*

James, the half-brother of Jesus, opens with a one-verse greeting to the Jewish Christians scattered everywhere. Then he immediately begins sharing how genuine faith is proved and strengthened by the outward test of trials. James explains that trials are designed to produce growth, staying power, and trust in God as believers turn to Him for wisdom and help. Regarding temptation, James explains:

- Temptations are inward tests of faith.
- Temptations do not come from God.
- Temptations are handled by responding to God's Word, by doing and not merely hearing God's Word.

James goes on to examine Christian faith by explaining that true faith does not favor the rich over the poor. True faith will "love your neighbor as yourself" (2:8). James then points to Abraham and Rahab from the Old Testament as good examples of those whose faith was shown by their actions.

▸ **Chapter 3** *Evaluation of Faith*

James refers to the tongue as another test of how true faith acts—faith tames the tongue, or the mouth. He then says wisdom is a further evidence of faith. Just as you can identify a tree by its fruit, you can know the kind of wisdom a person possesses by his or her actions. James also shows the difference between ***human*** wisdom, which leads to confusion and chaos, and *God's* wisdom, which leads to peace and goodness.

▸ **Chapters 4:1–5:6** *Conflicts of Faith*

Worldliness is putting physical pleasures and things before God. It is harmful to faith, and it produces greed, envy, fighting, and pride. The only thing that overcomes worldliness is submitting to God with a humble heart. A for-real Christian will not complain or take God for granted. Instead, he or she will place their life and plans into His hands. This will keep a believer from spending too much time trying to get rich...which leads right back to pride and selfishness.

▸ **Chapter 5:7-20** *Forbearance of Faith*

James ends by asking his readers to be patient as they endure suffering. They can take comfort in knowing that someday the Lord will return. They are to follow the examples of the prophets and men like Job, who suffered with patience. In all such cases, the Lord was merciful. Therefore, James's readers are to pray in the midst of their suffering and sickness. They could be confident that prayer makes a difference. James closes by urging his readers to reach out to those who stray from the truth and stop living God's way. He states that their souls are in danger of eternal separation from God.

Putting Meat on the Bones

Christians often hurt their witness to others by their actions. They say they trust God and are His people, yet they continue to live in a worldly way. Claiming to have true faith and giving all the right answers while still pursuing worldly goals can have a bad effect on how unbelievers view the gospel.

Fleshing It Out in Your Life

James reminds you that genuine faith changes lives. You must put your faith in Christ into action. It's easy to say you have faith, but true faith produces loving actions toward others. Your faith must not be head knowledge only, but it must be lived out by heart actions. The proof that your faith is genuine is a changed life shown by practical Christian living. James 1:19 says believers are to be "quick to listen, slow to speak, and slow to become angry." You can't get much more practical than that!

When has your tongue gotten you in trouble? How can you use your words for righteous purposes?

If someone who just met you were to spend a couple hours with you, would he or she know you are a Christian? Why or why not?

What is your biggest temptation to be worldly? How can you counter that temptation with God's wisdom?

Life Lessons from James

- Genuine faith will produce real changes in your life.
- Temptation is not sin, but if it's not dealt with, it can lead to sin.
- Being wealthy is not a sin, but selfishness is. God gives you money to help meet the needs of others.
- Prayer plays a key role in the ministry of the local church.
- God does not favor some people more than others, and you shouldn't either.

Where to Find It

The benefits of trials .... James 1:2-4
The solution to a lack of wisdom .... James 1:5-8
The nature of temptation .... James 1:12-15
The fact that faith without works is dead .... James 2:17
The untamable tongue .... James 3:1-12
The patience of Job .... James 5:11

The Divine Nature of God: God Is...

The giver of wisdom (1:5)
Not tempted by evil (1:13)
The giver of every good gift (1:17)
Unchanging (1:17)
The Father of lights—the Creator (1:17-18)
The Righteous One (1:20)
Our Father (3:9)
The giver of grace to the humble (4:6)
The lawgiver (4:12)
The sovereign Lord (4:15)

1 Peter

To this you were called, because Christ suffered for you, leaving you an example, that you should follow in his steps.
(2:21)

Theme: Responding to suffering
Date written: A.D. 64–65
Author: Peter
Setting: Rome

First Peter was written around the time Rome was burned by the emperor, Nero. The persecution of Christians had been increasing, and its strength will only get worse as Nero spreads the false rumor that the fires were started by Christians! Peter writes this letter to Christians throughout the Roman Empire to show them how to have victory in the midst of the hostility without losing hope. They should not become resentful, but trust the Lord and look for His return. Peter believes that if his readers will live obediently in the midst of a hostile society, they can be good witnesses for God.

The Skeleton

▸ **Chapters 1:1–2:10** *Remembering God's Great Salvation*

Addressing believers in several Roman provinces, Peter begins by thanking God for the gift of salvation. Then Peter explains that trials will refine their faith. In spite of their difficulties, they should believe in God's plan of salvation, just as many in the past did. Even the prophets of old who wrote about it believed it, even though they did not understand it.

But now salvation has been shown in Christ. In response to such a great salvation, Peter tells his readers to live holy lives, to respect and trust God, and to be honest and loving in their relationships with others. They are to become like living building stones with Christ, who is the "chosen and precious cornerstone" upon which the church is to be built (2:6).

▸ **Chapters 2:11–4:6** *Recalling Christ's Example*

Peter next explains how believers should live in the world during difficult times. They should be godly, live like Christ in all their social roles, whether as employers or workers, husbands or wives, younger or older, church members or neighbors. Peter desires that any suffering that comes should not be for doing the wrong things, but for doing godly things! He points his readers to Jesus Christ as their example for obedience to God in the midst of great suffering.

▸ **Chapter 4:7-19** *Rejoicing in the Lord's Return*

Peter warns that the end of the world is at hand and the Lord's return is near. Therefore, Christians need to be serious and watchful in their prayers, and to love one another. They are to be hospitable, use their spiritual gifts to serve each other, and rejoice in their suffering—all of which brings glory to God.

▸ **Chapter 5** *Revealing Some Special Instructions*

Peter gives these final words of instruction: Leaders are to watch over their people; younger people are to obey their leaders; and all are to humbly submit to each other. In humility, believers are to put their troubles into God's hands because He cares for them. Believers are also to resist the devil, who walks about like a roaring lion. Peter then concludes with a great statement of hope: God is working through all that is going on in the lives of his readers—even their struggles—to produce strength of character, which will bring glory to God.

Putting Meat on the Bones

Peter wrote this letter to Christians who were going through persecution because of their faith in Christ. He wrote to comfort them and remind them of their salvation and hope of eternal life. He urged them to live holy lives and to realize that those who suffer for their faith become partners with Christ in His suffering.

Fleshing It Out in Your Life

Today, many Christians around the world are suffering for what they believe. You may or may not be in that situation. But all Christians should expect persecution, for Jesus said, "In this world you will have trouble" (John 16:33). When your faith is seen by others, you can expect some people to make fun of you and not want to be your friend. But Peter says you don't have to be afraid of such treatment. Though you live in this world with those who pick on you, you are also a citizen of heaven and will live in eternity with Christ. This should give you strength and hope to stand firm when your faith in Christ is tested. You need to see each test of your faith as an opportunity to have your faith made stronger. As you face suffering for Jesus, remember Peter's words: "To this you were called, because Christ suffered for you, leaving you an example, that you should follow in his steps" (1 Peter 2:21).

Why do you think following and obeying others is so hard? Who or what do you need to submit to that you have been avoiding?

What have been your biggest tests of faith so far? What helped you through them?

Imagine that you are encouraging others to become citizens of heaven. How would you promote it?

Life Lessons from 1 Peter

- You are expected to submit to your teachers and others in charge.
- Your conduct should point unbelievers to Christ, especially those in your family.
- You should not be surprised when people make fun of your faith.
- You can face persecution victoriously as Christ did if you rely on Christ for strength.

Where to Find It

Desire for the pure milk of God's Word	1 Peter 2:1-2
Submission to governments	1 Peter 2:13-17
Submission of wives	1 Peter 3:1-6
Responsibility of husbands	1 Peter 3:7
Teaching about spiritual gifts	1 Peter 4:10-11
Responsibility of spiritual leaders	1 Peter 5:1-4
Devil pictured as a roaring lion	1 Peter 5:8

~ Bible Bio Profile ~
The Man Called Peter

- Was a fisherman
- Was one of the first to be called to serve with Jesus
- Was one of the 12 disciples
- Was one of the inner group of three disciples, along with James and John
- Was hotheaded in speech and actions
- Denied Christ three times
- Was restored by Christ to "feed" His sheep—His people
- Preached the first sermon after the founding of the church
- Had difficulty with receiving Gentiles into the church
- Supplied John Mark with eyewitness accounts of the life of Jesus
- Wrote 1 and 2 Peter
- Was, according to historical rumor, crucified upside down in Rome

2 Peter

We have the word of the prophets made more certain, and you will do well to pay attention to it, as to a light shining in a dark place, until the day dawns and the morning star rises in your hearts.
(1:19)

Theme: Warning against false teachers
Date written: A.D. 67–68
Author: Peter
Setting: A Roman prison

About three years after Peter wrote his first letter, he writes a second one. In it he expresses alarm about the false teachers who have invaded the churches in the region of Asia Minor (modern-day Turkey). These evil people have already caused many problems, and Peter knows that their false teachings and sinful lifestyles will continue to have a bad effect on the churches they have become part of. Therefore, Peter writes this letter from his prison cell to warn believers about the dangers of false teachers. To be prepared for what's coming, his readers need to know a few things...

The Skeleton

▸ **Chapter 1** *Know the Bible*

After a brief opening, Peter says that the cure for a lack of growth in the Christian life is the knowledge of truth. His readers must continue to develop their Christian character, which will give them assurance of their salvation. He explains that his days are numbered and they need to heed his warning and listen to his message and the words of the Bible.

▸ **Chapter 2** *Know the Enemy*

Peter next gives a very clear picture of the false teachers, who are becoming widespread in these last days. They will do or say anything for money. They laugh at the things of God. They do what they feel like doing. They are proud and boastful. Their crafty words are capable of misleading Christians. But God will deliver His people and punish those who seek to destroy their faith.

▸ **Chapter 3** *Know the Future*

Peter again tells his readers what they can expect from false teachers. They scoff at the idea of Christ's second coming, and they claim that God does not involve Himself in world affairs. But Peter points out three times when God did or will intervene: creation, the flood, and the coming destruction of the heavens and the earth. He explains that what seems like an unfulfilled promise on God's part is due to His patience in waiting for more people to come to salvation through Christ. So the day of the Lord *will* come, and God *will* establish a new heaven and earth. In light of this coming day of the Lord, Peter exhorts his readers to pay attention to holiness, steadfastness, and growth.

Putting Meat on the Bones

In his first letter Peter wrote to comfort and encourage believers in the midst of persecution, suffering external attacks by the enemy of their souls. Now three years later he is writing to warn the churches of inside attacks through lack of growth and false teaching. In Peter's mind, the cure for these two problems is growth in the grace and knowledge of Christ. The best cure for error is a growing understanding of the truth. This growth comes from the Word of God, which contains everything a believer needs for "life and godliness" (1:3).

Fleshing It Out in Your Life

Warnings come in many forms—lights, signs, sounds, smells, and the written word. No one who values their life would fail to respond to one or all of these forms of warning. Are you reading God's warnings of spiritual danger as found in the Bible? And are you responding to them? Don't turn your back on God's warnings. Do what 2 Peter 3:18 says and grow in the grace and knowledge of Jesus. Spiritual growth will keep you faithful and give you the wisdom to defend against the ways of Satan and his false teachers.

Have you taken self-defense classes? Second Peter offers spiritual defense lessons. Which lessons will you use first?

There are Christians in other parts of the world who are persecuted for their faith. Do research on these areas, and commit to praying for these brothers and sisters in Christ.

What three areas of spiritual growth do you need to work on the most? How will you go about gaining godly wisdom?

Life Lessons from 2 Peter

- You are commanded to grow in your knowledge of God.
- Your growth combats spiritual laziness and deception by the enemy.
- Do not fail to heed the warnings of Scripture.
- Each day that the Lord delays His return is to be a day devoted to holy living and faithful service.

Where to Find It

Our sufficiency in Christ . . . . 2 Peter 1:2-3
The origin of Scripture . . . . 2 Peter 1:20-21
A brief history of God's judgment . . . . 2 Peter 2:4-11
God's view of time . . . . .2 Peter 3:8

The Day of the Lord

2 Peter 3:10-13

It will be a day of punishment for ungodly men.
It will come like a thief in the night.
The heavens will be dissolved.
The earth will be burned up with fire.
A new heaven and a new earth will be created.

1 John

We proclaim to you what we have seen and heard, so that you also may have fellowship with us. And our fellowship is with the Father and with his Son, Jesus Christ.
(1:3)

Theme: Fellowship with God
Date written: A.D. 90
Author: John
Setting: Ephesus

John is now advanced in age and probably the only apostle and original disciple of Christ still alive. But John continues to be active in ministry. As the last remaining apostle, his words are well respected in the churches of Asia Minor. In this letter (as well as in 2 and 3 John) he writes to these churches with a pastor's heart.

It has been about 50 years since Jesus physically walked the earth. Most of the eyewitnesses of Christ's ministry had died by now, but John was still alive to talk about Jesus. He had walked and talked with Jesus. He had seen Him heal the sick and raise the dead. He had watched Him die and witnessed His resurrection and return to heaven. John *knew* God—he had fellowship with Him and watched Him teach, serve, and minister to others. Now, out of concern for a new group of believers, John wants his readers to know what it means to have fellowship with God. At the same time, he warns that false teachers have entered the churches, denying that Jesus had actually come in the flesh. They openly reject the physical birth of Christ, and John writes from personal experience to correct this error.

The Skeleton

▸ Chapters 1:1–2:2 *The Basis of Fellowship*

John opens his letter by giving his credentials as an eyewitness to the person of Christ. Jesus was not merely a spirit, but one who could be physically touched. John's purpose is to pass on his personal knowledge of Christ's life and ministry to his readers so they may share in the same sweet fellowship John enjoyed with Jesus. This fellowship is made possible by the blood of Jesus, which cleanses believers and satisfies the Father's righteous demands against sin. As a result, believers will walk in this light of God's fellowship and willingly confess sin, knowing that they have a spokesman with the Father, Jesus Christ.

▸ Chapter 2:3-27 *The Companions of Fellowship*

Fellowship with God has actions that are connected with it. These actions are the constant companion of a believer. One who stays with God will live in obedience and walk in Christlikeness. He or she will love fellow believers, separate from the world, confess Jesus as the Son of God, and have the anointing of the Holy Spirit.

▸ Chapters 2:28–3:23 *The Mark of Fellowship*

The basic theme of 1 John is summarized in this way: Fellowship with Christ comes through a close relationship with Him. This happens when a person is regenerated, or born again. The person in fellowship with Christ practices holy living and looks forward to His appearing. He or she has a dislike for sin, and loves the family of God (unlike Cain, who murdered his brother Abel). A believer's love is seen in self-sacrifice, which gives one assurance of being a child of God.

▸ Chapters 3:24–4:21 *The Proof of Fellowship*

John now introduces the important idea of the indwelling of believers by God, the Holy Spirit. When the Spirit of God lives in a person, the Spirit causes certain beliefs and behaviors: 1) the belief that Jesus actually had a physical birth, was God in human flesh, and there will one day be eternal life and fellowship with Jesus; and 2) the behavior of Christlike love for others.

▸ **Chapter 5** *The Assurance of Fellowship*

John finishes by listing a number of ways believers can be sure of their fellowship with God. They will 1) believe in Jesus Christ; 2) have love for both the Father and the Son; 3) keep God's commandments; 4) experience victory over the world; 5) experience the witness of the Holy Spirit; 6) possess eternal life; and 7) be assured of answered prayer.

Putting Meat on the Bones

Many wonder about the true identity of Jesus. Was He just a good man—maybe one of the best who ever lived? Was He a man with illusions of grandeur—a man with a Messiah complex? Was He really the God-man, 100 percent God and 100 percent man? Hearing such speculations about Jesus could cause a person to wonder or even doubt. John rushes to give his readers a set of essentials of the Christian faith. Basic to the Christian faith is that Jesus alone is qualified to offer up the perfect sacrifice for our sins—His body. He and He alone is capable of satisfying God the Father's requirement for the payment of the debt of sin.

Fleshing It Out in Your Life

John is writing this letter to take away any doubts believers might have and to give assurance that, if you believe in the Son of God, you have eternal life. John does this by painting a clear picture of Jesus, the Christ, the Son of God, God in a body. Do you yet believe in the Son of God? If you do, John says, "This is the testimony: God has given us eternal life, and this life is in his Son" (1 John 5:11-12). Armed with this testimony of your fellowship with God, you are to live in holiness, love your fellow believers, and long for His return.

Are you in fellowship with other believers? How do you encourage fellowship in your life?

What would you say to someone who expressed doubt that Jesus was God?

John was an eyewitness to Jesus' life. You are an eyewitness to how Jesus works in your life. Write a paragraph describing the power of this experience. Only you can express your testimony in words!

Life Lessons from 1 John

- Love is a mark of your fellowship with God.
- You are commanded to love others as Jesus did.
- You must resist sin, and when you do sin, you must confess your wrong to God.
- Fellowship with God is a promise, but it is also a duty for how you are to live your life.

Where to Find It

The spirit of Antichrist (a false Jesus) . . . . 1 John 4:1-3
"Perfect love drives out fear" . . . . 1 John 4:18
The essentials for eternal life . . . . 1 John 5:12

~ Bible Bio Profile ~
Facts About John, the Disciple Whom Jesus Loved

John 21:20

- Job: fisherman
- One of John the Baptist's followers before following Jesus
- One of the three disciples closest to Jesus, along with his brother, James, and Peter (Matthew 17:1; 26:37)
- Nicknamed by Jesus, along with his brother, James, as the "Sons of Thunder" (Mark 3:17)
- Asked for a special position in Jesus' kingdom
- Leaned on Jesus' breast during the Last Supper
- Ministered with Peter (Acts 3:1; 4:13; 8:14)
- Became a "pillar" in the Jerusalem church (Galatians 2:9)
- Exiled to the island of Patmos (Revelation 1:9)
- Longest-living disciple
- Wrote five New Testament books (the Gospel of John; 1, 2, 3 John; Revelation)

2 John

If anyone comes to you and does not bring this teaching [of Christ], do not take him into your house or welcome him. Anyone who welcomes him shares in his wicked work.
(Verses 10-11)

Theme: Christian wisdom
Date written: A.D. 90–95
Author: John
Setting: Ephesus

The apostle John is still dealing with the same problem he addressed in his first epistle—that of false teachers. In this second letter John is concerned with false teachers who are roving around and seeking to win people over to their teachings in the churches that are under John's care. John is writing to a woman who may have given help to these false teachers. John fears they may be taking advantage of her kindness, and warns her not to become friends with any who do not tell the truth.

The Skeleton

▸ **Verses 1-3** *The Greeting*

John calls himself "the elder" as he sends greetings to an unknown "chosen lady" and her children. He describes a Christian's relationship with God as living in truth and love.

▸ **Verses 4-6** *The Commendation*

The apostle praises his readers for their walk in obedience to God.

He reminds them that this commandment to be friends involves loving one another.

▸ **Verses 7-11** *The Warning*

John now urges his readers to watch out for deceivers who deny that Jesus Christ was actually born as a man. They are "antichrists," he explains, so do not in any way show friendship to them. Do not even give them a greeting. To do this is seen as sharing in their evil deeds.

▸ **Verses 12-13** *The Blessing*

John closes this brief letter saying he has more to say but will wait until he comes.

Putting Meat on the Bones

John has seen truth and love firsthand—he has been with Jesus! He is so affected with these ideals that all his writings—the Gospel of John, 1 John, and now 2 John—are filled with them. Truth and love are vital to the Christian and part of a Christian's life. In this short letter to a friend, John advises her to follow the truth, love God, and invite into her home only those who follow the basic teachings of the faith. At the same time, she is to avoid those who are trying to destroy these basic beliefs.

Fleshing It Out in Your Life

John's concern applies to today as well. Your service to Christians is to be done in wisdom. You are not called to blindly accept anyone who claims to be a believer. Make sure they are not false teachers. How are you to determine truth from error? First, read and study God's Word. Next, compare what others are teaching with what the Bible says. And then avoid those who don't follow the teachings of Christ.

How can you counter false teachings?

Loving one another sounds good, but it can be hard to put into practice. How can you show love to someone who is difficult to like?

You may be young, but the wisdom of God is on your side. Write down a few questions you have about faith, God, or Jesus. Now dig into the Bible to find the answers. Ask a trusted leader or teacher to help you.

Life Lessons from 2 John

- Walking in obedience to the truth should be an ongoing habit in your life.
- Be careful! False teachers are clever. Look at their lives and their message to see if they match with Scripture.
- It is right to avoid those who would destroy the truth of Christ.
- Disagreeing over minor issues is not a reason for avoiding Christian friendships.

Where to Find It

Greetings to "the chosen lady" . . . . Verse 1
Walking in the truth . . . . Verse 4
Walking in God's commandments . . . . Verse 6
Definition of a deceiver and an antichrist . . . . Verse 7
Admonition not to receive into your home those who deny Christ. . . . . Verse 10

Some Who Showed Kindness in the Bible

Abraham to three angelic beings	Genesis 18:1-8
Lot to two angels	Genesis 19:1-11
Laban to Abraham's servant	Genesis 24:11-61
The Shunammite woman to Elijah	2 Kings 4:8-10
Mary and Martha to Jesus and His disciples	Luke 10:38-42
Priscilla and Aquila to Paul	Acts 18:2
The New Testament widows	1 Timothy 5:9-10

3 John

Dear friend, you are faithful in what you are doing for the brothers, even though they are strangers to you.
(Verse 5)

Theme: Christian hospitality
Date written: A.D. 90–95
Author: John
Setting: Ephesus

This is John's third letter written to those under his care and leadership. This letter deals with Christian hospitality and friendships. In John's day, church leaders traveled from town to town helping to establish new churches and strengthen existing ones. These church workers depended on fellow believers for a place to stay. This letter includes three different messages about three men: John commends Gaius for his ministry of hospitality; he condemns the self-serving ministry of Diotrephes; and he congratulates Demetrius for his good testimony.

The Skeleton

▸ Verses 1-8 *Gaius's Hospitality*

John again calls himself "the elder" as he responds with joy to a report that his "dear friend Gaius" is walking in the truth. John acknowledges Gaius's actions toward traveling teachers and missionaries. These travelers take no money from unbelievers and depend entirely upon the hospitality and goodness of faithful Christians like Gaius. John encourages Gaius to continue to provide help to their ministries.

▸ **Verses 9-10** *Diotrephes's Lack of Hospitality*

John now shifts to a negative example—a man named Diotrephes. His pride would not allow him to help these traveling teachers sent out by the apostle. If anyone in the local church tries to help one of these teachers, Diotrephes has that person removed from the church. John believes he must exercise his authority and plans to confront Diotrephes for his un-Christianlike conduct.

▸ **Verses 11-13** *Demetrius's Good Testimony*

John cautions his readers not to pattern their lives after what is evil, such as the conduct of Diotrephes in verses 9-10. Diotrephes's evil actions go against the very thing John has preached passionately about in his first two letters—we are to love one another. On the other hand, Demetrius's life is a testimony of what is good. He is highly spoken of by all, including John himself, and his very life is a living example of the truth.

Putting Meat on the Bones

Love, humility, and a knowledge of the truth are key to Christian hospitality and friendships. Gaius showed perfect hospitality and welcomed those who believed and taught the truth. Diotrephes's pride would not allow him to show hospitality to those who needed and deserved it. Demetrius was another who did what was right in the area of "stranger love"—showing hospitality to believers in need.

Fleshing It Out in Your Life

Third John is a great reminder of the positive role of helping others in or outside the church...and the negative power of pride in a church leader. When your parents invite a missionary to stay in your home and you are asked to give up your room, follow the Bible's advice and "offer hospitality to one another without grumbling" (1 Peter 4:9). Be faithful to extend hospitality when you can. Don't let pride keep you from obeying God's command to receive and care for others. Be sure to show love to one another.

Why is humility in action such a contrast to today's culture?

Have you ever been shown great hospitality? How did it make you feel?

Think of ways you can reach out this week to others. Now go do those things!

Life Lessons from 3 John

- Try to walk in the truth. It will give you a spirit of loving hospitality.
- Realize Christian teachers, leaders, and missionaries need your help.
- Support and help your youth workers in their ministries to your group.
- Encourage your youth workers so they don't get discouraged.
- If you are a leader in your youth group, be like Gaius and Demetrius.

Where to Find It

Blessings of health and prosperity of soul . . . . Verse 2
Joy due to the truth in others . . . . Verse 3
Joy in knowing your "children" walk in truth . . . . Verse 4
Reasons for helping Christian workers . . . . Verses 5-8
Warning against desiring preeminence . . . . Verse 9
Command to imitate what is good, and not what is evil . . . Verse 11

Sibling Spotlight: The Apostles James and John

- James and John were brothers.
- James was the older brother.
- James and John were fishermen from Galilee.
- James and John were the sons of Zebedee.

- Jesus called them "Sons of Thunder" (Mark 3:17).
- John was one of the three most intimate associates of Jesus.
- John identified himself as "the disciple whom Jesus loved" (John 21:20).
- John is sometimes referred to as "the apostle of love."
- John was exiled late in life to the island of Patmos, where he wrote the book of Revelation.
- James was the first apostle to be martyred.
- John's manner of death is unknown.

Jude

Dear friends, although I was very eager to write to you about the salvation we share, I felt I had to write and urge you to contend for the faith...
(Verse 3)

Theme: Battling for the faith
Date written: A.D. 68–69
Author: Jude
Setting: Jerusalem

Although Jude had earlier rejected Jesus as the Messiah, he and his three half-brothers of Jesus believed in Jesus after His resurrection. Because of his family relationship with Jesus and because he had seen Jesus' life, ministry, and resurrection, Jude has a burning passion to let others know about the salvation that comes in Christ. But as he writes, he switches his topic to a matter that is on his heart at this time. Jude is concerned about the threat of false teachers in the church. He wants all to know the response Christians should have concerning this threat. Therefore, Jude urges his readers to be alert and take action against false teachers.

The Skeleton

▸ Verses 1-4 *The Reason for Writing*

Jude begins by referring to himself as "a servant" of Jesus and as the brother of James, who was the leader of the Jerusalem church, the author of the book of James, and the half-brother of Jesus. Jude is about to write a letter on salvation when grim news forces him to put aside this topic. In light of those who are denying Christ and using the grace of God to justify sinful behavior, Jude writes this timely word of rebuke and warning.

▸ **Verses 5-16** *The Danger of False Teachers*

Jude begins this section by reminding his readers that false teachers will meet their doom just as three other groups in the Old Testament met theirs: 1) quarrelsome unbelievers who died in the wilderness; 2) fallen angels who sinned greatly before the flood and who are in chains until judgment; and 3) men who exhibited wrong sexual behavior and were destroyed in the destruction of Sodom and Gomorrah. False teachers are described by Jude as being ruled by their bodies, rejecting authority, and scorning the angels. Jude compares false teachers to three spiritually rebellious men in the Bible—Cain (from Genesis), and Korah and Balaam (from Numbers). Jude says their evil is like hidden reefs, airy clouds, uprooted trees, wild waves, and wandering stars, and that they deserve to be judged by God.

▸ **Verses 17-25** *The Duty to Fight for God's Truth*

After exposing the behavior of false teachers, Jude reminds his readers that others have warned about these men. He urges them to protect themselves against this fierce attack of unbelief. They must build themselves up in the Bible, pray in the Spirit for God's will, and look for Christ's second coming. While fighting for God's truth, they are to be kind to those who deserve it and, if necessary, to carefully pull others out of the fires of unbelief so they themselves do not become spiritually dirty. Jude then returns to the theme of salvation. He closes with one of the most familiar praises in the Bible (verses 24-25), emphasizing the power of Christ to keep His followers from being overpowered by the enemy.

Putting Meat on the Bones

It is human to fight for survival and defend what is most important—home, family, and freedom. God's truths in the Bible are of great value and are under attack. Through the centuries many have opposed both God's people and His truth. These enemies of God twist the truth to deceive and destroy the unsuspecting. But God's truths still stand and are being proclaimed by those who have committed their lives to Jesus

Christ. It is an important responsibility and a privilege to be a part of those who share and defend God's Word.

Fleshing It Out in Your Life

What value do you place on God's Word? His church? His people? Today, as in years gone by, false teachers have invaded our churches, Bible colleges, and Christian institutions. What price are you willing to pay to defend God's truth? Are you ready to stand with Jude and "contend for the faith that was once for all entrusted to the saints" (verse 3)? If so, then you stand with Jude and many others who fight the good fight of faith as they engage the forces of evil for the souls of men.

Do you sit on the sidelines or do you jump in and defend the faith?

God's Word does not let you down even when you are unsure about life. Write down a few truths from the Bible that will help you stand strong this week.

How can you help your friends grow in their faith?

Life Lessons from Jude

- As long as Satan is alive and well, false teachers will threaten the church with error. Do what you must to know the truth.
- Mark it well: One of the revealing features of a false teacher is his fearless, ungodly behavior.
- False teachers act as if God will not punish their godless behavior.
- Genuine servants of God will faithfully point to Christ with their words and their conduct.
- Sitting on the sidelines is not an option for Christians. You are to earnestly battle for the faith.

Where to Find It

Warning from Jude of the fact of apostasy .... Verse 4
Description of Michael, the archangel .... Verse 9

Warnings from the apostles of the fact of apostasy . . . Verse 18
Blessings of knowing and following God . . . . Verse 24
Blessing of the all-wise God, our Savior . . . . Verse 25

Jude's Description of an Apostate (one who has left his faith)

Godless (verse 4)
Immoral (verse 4)
Denies Christ (verse 4)
Rebels against authority (verse 8)
A grumbler (verse 16)
A faultfinder (verse 16)
Mocks the truth (verse 18)
Divisive (verse 19)
Worldly (verse 19)
Lacks the Holy Spirit (verse 19)

Revelation

The revelation of Jesus Christ, which God gave him to show his servants what must soon take place. He made it known by sending his angel to his servant John. . .
(1:1)

Theme: The unveiling of Jesus Christ
Date written: A.D. 94–96
Author: John
Setting: Isle of Patmos

By this time, John is the only survivor of the original 12 disciples. He is old and has been sent to Patmos, a small island in the Aegean Sea off the coast of Ephesus, for his faithful preaching of the gospel. While on Patmos, John receives a series of visions that describe the future history of the world. The visions reveal Jesus Christ as the divine Shepherd who is concerned about the condition of the church, as the righteous Judge who will punish the wicked, and the victorious King who will establish His kingdom forever.

The Skeleton

▸ Chapter 1 *The Vision of the Glorified Christ*

The apostle John is told to write about "what you have seen, what is now and what will take place later" (verse 19). John sees the exalted Christ and describes Him in a way similar to the visions of God in the Old Testament (see Daniel and Ezekiel). Jesus is seen moving among His churches with a desire that His people be pure and free of sin.

Seeing the awesome glory of the Lord, John falls at Jesus' feet in fear and dread.

▸ **Chapters 2–3** *The Letters to the Seven Churches*

In John's vision, Jesus speaks to seven different churches about their spiritual health. Most of the churches receive both praise for their good deeds and rebuke for the problems in their midst. Christ commends those who take a stand for truth and are willing to suffer for Him, and condemns those who have lost their love for Him, tolerated sin, or become too much in love with worldly riches.

▸ **Chapters 4–5** *The Scene in Heaven*

Chapter 4 opens with a scene in heaven—John sees God upon His throne surrounded by many who worship Him day and night. One of the songs of worship declares, "You are worthy, our Lord and God, to receive glory and honor and power, for you created all things, and by your will they were created" (4:11). Chapter 5 continues the worship of the Holy Lamb of God by angels, elders, and living creatures. In addition, Christ, the only One worthy, opens seven seals that signify God's unfolding punishments and judgments upon the earth.

▸ **Chapters 6–20** *The Pouring Out of Judgment*

John reveals what will take place during the last days, or the seven-year Tribulation. Jesus opens the first of the seven seals on a scroll, thus beginning the destruction. Then come the seven trumpet judgments followed by the seven bowl judgments. These describe the series of judgments in which God pours out His wrath upon the earth. Yet even in this time of judgment, God's mercy shines as brightly as ever as He continues to reach out to the lost with the message of salvation through Jesus Christ. During this time the Antichrist—the adversary of Christ—will gain worldwide power and unleash terrible persecution against Christians. In the end, Christ will return to earth, destroy the Antichrist, and set up His kingdom forever.

▸ **Chapters 21–22** *The Coming of Eternity*

A new heaven and earth will descend from heaven because the present earth has been destroyed. Within this new heaven and earth resides the new Jerusalem, where there will be no more sin, no more death, and no more suffering. God then brings in an eternal kingdom marked by holiness, peace, and love. All Christians look forward to this future kingdom with great hope.

Putting Meat on the Bones

The word "revelation" (1:1) means "to uncover or to reveal." God has been revealing Himself to mankind from the very first verse of the Bible in Genesis. Beginning with His first act of creation, God has been unfolding His eternal plan for man. Throughout history He has been guiding the human race toward His ultimate purpose of redeeming His lost creation. Along the way and throughout time, man has resisted God. Man has rebelled and suffered the consequences. But there has always been a small group of people who have desired to know and follow God. Their path of godly living has not been easy. They have been persecuted and killed for their love of God. But now the book of Revelation shows that the end is coming. God's promise of the coming King is about to happen. Jesus, the Suffering Servant, the ultimate revelation of God, is returning in all His glory and power. He will conquer all who have and would defy Him and rescue His chosen people. History will be complete. Time will cease, and all creation will again be dissolved into eternity.

Fleshing It Out in Your Life

This book is truly "the revelation of Jesus Christ" (1:1). From the beginning to the end of this glorious book Christ's glory, wisdom, and power are described. The future events described within this book are more relevant today than at any other time in history. As you watch the daily news, you see the mysteries of this book being revealed through modern political and economic policies and military interventions. The signs are there that the King is coming in judgment. For any believer who is compromising with the world, this book is a call to refocus on Jesus and His will. For any who has lost his or her excitement for the Lord's return, this book should stir them up to a higher level of commitment while watching and waiting for the Lord. Do you believe in His return? And are you prepared for it?

A lot of Christians think that Revelation is hard to understand. But if you spend some time studying it, you'll discover that it is full of assurances. Write down some of these assurances and discuss them with your church group or a friend.

Compromise, or giving in to the world, will lead to destruction, but knowledge of God leads to life. What knowledge have you gathered along this study journey?

Your life is one of God's creations. As carefully as He planned the unfolding of the world, He planned the unfolding of your own future. Yield yourself to God's control of your future by first giving Him control of today.

Life Lessons from Revelation

- God controls all people and events—what He says will happen in the future *will* happen! This should give you confidence for the future.
- In the end, justice and holiness will prevail. Sin will not continue forever. This should give you strength for each and every day of your life.
- Christians will one day become free from this sin-filled world and know perfection and glory in heaven. This should give you hope for eternity.
- God is worthy of worship at all times. This should give you reason to praise Him…now!

Where to Find It

The seven seal judgments 5:1–8:1
The seven trumpet judgments .8:2–11:19
The seven bowl judgments 15:1–16:21
The battle of Armageddon 19:17-19
The casting of Satan into the lake of fire 20:10

Jesus' Comments to the Seven Churches

(2–3)

Church #1: The loveless church—Ephesus
"You have forsaken your first love" (see 2:4)

Church #2: The persecuted church—Smyrna
"I know your afflictions and your poverty" (2:9)

Church #3: The lax church—Pergamos
"You tolerate sin" (see 2:14-15)

Church #4: The compromising church—Thyatira
"You permit the teaching of immoral practices" (see 2:20)

Church #5: The lifeless church—Sardis
"You are dead" (3:1)

Church #6: The obedient church—Philadelphia
"You have kept my word and have not denied my name" (3:8)

Church #7: The lukewarm church—Laodicea
"You are neither cold nor hot" (3:15)

The Seven Churches in Revelation 2–3

A Final Word

As you finish this book and your journey down the hallways of time, you should have a better understanding of God's work in history. Hopefully you have also made many applications of God's truth and developed a greater appreciation for the relationship He extends to you through His Son, Jesus Christ. Faithful obedience to God's Word is life-changing and results in a closer walk with God.

Before you close the covers of this book, purpose to act on these final steps:

- Purpose to open your heart to the Person of Jesus Christ and the salvation and forgiveness of sin which God extends to you through Him, if you have not already done so. "For there is no other name under heaven given to men by which we must be saved" (Acts 4:12).
- Purpose to continue to "grow in the grace and knowledge of our Lord and Savior Jesus Christ" (2 Peter 3:18).
- Purpose to share God's message of love and redemption with others—the truth that "God so loved the world that he gave his one and only Son, that whoever believes in him shall not perish but have eternal life" (John 3:16).

Bare Essentials for Using Your Bible

Themes of All the Books of the Bible

The Old Testament

Genesis	Beginnings
Exodus	Deliverance
Leviticus	Instruction
Numbers	Journeys
Deuteronomy	Obedience
Joshua	Conquest
Judges	Deterioration and deliverance
Ruth	Redemption
1 Samuel	Transition
2 Samuel	Unification
1 Kings	Disruption
2 Kings	Dispersion
1 Chronicles	Israel's spiritual history
2 Chronicles	Israel's spiritual heritage
Ezra	Restoration
Nehemiah	Reconstruction
Esther	Preservation
Job	Blessings through suffering
Psalms	Praise
Proverbs	Practical wisdom
Ecclesiastes	All is vanity apart from God
Song of Songs	Love and marriage
Isaiah	Salvation
Jeremiah	Judgment
Lamentations	Lament
Ezekiel	The glory of the Lord
Daniel	The sovereignty of God
Hosea	Unfaithfulness

Joel	The day of the Lord
Amos	Judgment
Obadiah	Righteous judgment
Jonah	God's grace to all people
Micah	Divine judgment
Nahum	Consolation
Habakkuk	Trusting a sovereign God
Zephaniah	The "great day of the LORD"
Haggai	Rebuilding the temple
Zechariah	God's deliverance
Malachi	Disobedience rebuked

The New Testament

Matthew	The kingdom of God
Mark	The Suffering Servant
Luke	The Perfect Man
John	The Son of God
Acts	The spread of the gospel
Romans	The righteousness of God
1 Corinthians	Christian conduct
2 Corinthians	Paul's defense of his apostleship
Galatians	Freedom in Christ
Ephesians	Blessings in Christ
Philippians	The joy-filled life
Colossians	The supremacy of Christ
1 Thessalonians	Concern for the church
2 Thessalonians	Living in hope
1 Timothy	Instructions for a young disciple
2 Timothy	A charge to faithful ministry
Titus	A manual of conduct
Philemon	Forgiveness
Hebrews	The superiority of Christ
James	Genuine faith
1 Peter	Responding to suffering
2 Peter	Warning against false teachers
1 John	Fellowship with God
2 John	Christian discernment
3 John	Christian hospitality
Jude	Contending for the faith
Revelation	The unveiling of Jesus Christ

How to Study the Bible —Some Practical Tips

One of the noblest pursuits a child of God can embark upon is to get to know and understand God better. The best way we can accomplish this is to look carefully at the book God has written, the Bible, which communicates who He is and His plan for mankind. There are a number of ways we can study the Bible, but one of the most effective and simple approaches to reading and understanding God's Word involves three simple steps:

Step 1: Observation—*What does the passage say?*
Step 2: Interpretation—*What does the passage mean?*
Step 3: Application—*What am I going to do about what the passage says and means?*

Observation

Observation is the first and most important step in the process. As you read the Bible text, you need to look carefully at what is said, and how it is said. Look for:

- *Terms, not words.* Words can have many meanings, but terms are words used in a specific way in a specific context. (For instance, the word *trunk* could apply to a tree, a car, or a storage box. However, when you read, "That tree has a very large trunk," you know exactly what the word means, which makes it a term.)
- *Structure.* If you look at your Bible, you will see that the text has units called *paragraphs* (indented or marked ¶). A paragraph is a

complete unit of thought. You can discover the content of the author's message by noting and understanding each paragraph unit.

- *Emphasis.* The amount of space or the number of chapters or verses devoted to a specific topic will reveal the importance of that topic. (For example, note the emphasis of Romans 9–11 and Psalm 119.)
- *Repetition.* This is another way an author shows that something is important. One reading of 1 Corinthians 13, where the author uses the word "love" nine times in only 13 verses, communicates to us that love is the focal point of these 13 verses.
- *Relationships between ideas.* Pay close attention, for example, to certain relationships that appear in the text:

  —Cause-and-effect: "Well done, good and faithful servant! You have been faithful with a few things; I will put you in charge of many things" (Matthew 25:21).

  —Ifs and thens: "If my people, who are called by my name, will humble themselves and pray and seek my face and turn from their wicked ways, then will I hear from heaven and will forgive their sin and will heal their land" (2 Chronicles 7:14).

  —Questions and answers: "Who is he, this King of glory? The LORD Almighty—he is the King of glory" (Psalm 24:8).
- *Comparisons and contrasts.* For example, "You have heard that it was said...But I tell you..." (Matthew 5:21-22).
- *Literary form.* The Bible is literature, and the three main types of literature in the Bible are discourse (the epistles), prose (Old Testament history), and poetry (the Psalms). Considering the type of literature makes a great deal of difference when you read and understand the Scriptures.
- *Atmosphere.* The author had a particular reason or burden for writing each passage, chapter, and book. Be sure you notice the mood or tone or urgency of the writing.

After you have considered these things, you then are ready to ask the "Wh" questions:

Who?	Who are the people in this passage?
What?	What is happening in this passage?
Where?	Where is this story taking place?

When? What time (of day, of the year, in history) is it?

Asking these four "Wh" questions can help you notice terms and identify atmosphere. The answers will also enable you to use your imagination to re-create the scene you're reading about.

As you answer the "Wh" questions and imagine the event, you'll probably come up with some questions of your own. Asking those additional questions for understanding will help to build a bridge between observation (the first step) and interpretation (the second step) of the Bible study process.

Interpretation

Interpretation is discovering the meaning of a passage, the author's main thought or big idea. Answering the questions that arise during observation will help you in the process of interpretation. Five clues (called "the five C's") can help you determine the author's main point(s):

- *Context.* You can answer 75 percent of your questions about a passage when you read the text. Reading the text involves looking at the near context (the verse immediately before and after) as well as the far context (the paragraph or the chapter that precedes and/or follows the passage you are studying).
- *Cross-references.* Let scripture interpret scripture. That is, let other passages in the Bible shed light on the passage you are looking at. At the same time, be careful not to assume that the same word or phrase in two different passages means the same thing.
- *Culture.* The Bible was written long ago, so when we interpret it, we need to understand it from the writers' cultural context.
- *Conclusion.* Having answered your questions for understanding by means of context, cross-reference, and culture, you can make a preliminary statement of the passage's meaning. Remember that if your passage consists of more than one paragraph, the author may be presenting more than one thought or idea.
- *Consultation.* Reading books known as commentaries, which are written by Bible scholars, can help you interpret Scripture.

Application

Application is why we study the Bible. We want our lives to change. We want to be obedient to God and to grow more like Jesus Christ. After we have observed a passage and interpreted or understood it to the best of our ability, we must then apply its truth to our own life.

You'll want to ask the following questions of every passage of Scripture you study:

- How does the truth revealed here affect my relationship with God?
- How does this truth affect my relationship with others?
- How does this truth affect me?
- How does this truth affect my response to the enemy Satan?

The application step is not completed by simply answering these questions. The key is *putting into practice* what God has taught you in your study. Although at any given moment you cannot be consciously applying *every*thing you're learning in Bible study, you can be consciously applying *some*thing. And when you work on applying a truth to your life, God will bless your efforts by, as noted earlier, conforming you to the image of Jesus Christ.

Helpful Bible Study Resources

Concordance—Young's or Strong's
Bible dictionary—Unger's or Holman's
Webster's dictionary
The Zondervan Pictorial Encyclopedia of the Bible
Manners and Customs of the Bible, James M. Freeman

A One-Year Daily Bible Reading Plan

January

	Genesis
❑ 1	1–3
❑ 2	4–7
❑ 3	8–11
❑ 4	12–15
❑ 5	16–18
❑ 6	19–22
❑ 7	23–27
❑ 8	28–30
❑ 9	31–34
❑ 10	35–38
❑ 11	39–41
❑ 12	42–44
❑ 13	45–47
❑ 14	48–50
	Exodus
❑ 15	1–4
❑ 16	5–7
❑ 17	8–11
❑ 18	12–14
❑ 19	15–18
❑ 20	19–21
❑ 21	22–24
❑ 22	25–28
❑ 23	29–31
❑ 24	32–34
❑ 25	35–37
❑ 26	38–40

	Leviticus
❑ 27	1–3
❑ 28	4–6
❑ 29	7–9
❑ 30	10–13
❑ 31	14–16

February

❑ 1	17–20
❑ 2	21–23
❑ 3	24–27
	Numbers
❑ 4	1–2
❑ 5	3–4
❑ 6	5–6
❑ 7	7–8
❑ 8	9–10
❑ 9	11–13
❑ 10	14–15
❑ 11	16–17
❑ 12	18–19
❑ 13	20–21
❑ 14	22–23
❑ 15	24–26
❑ 16	27–29
❑ 17	30–32
❑ 18	33–36
	Deuteronomy
❑ 19	1–2
❑ 20	3–4
❑ 21	5–7
❑ 22	8–10
❑ 23	11–13
❑ 24	14–16
❑ 25	17–20
❑ 26	21–23
❑ 27	24–26
❑ 28	27–28

March

❑ 1	29–30
❑ 2	31–32
❑ 3	33–34
	Joshua
❑ 4	1–4
❑ 5	5–7
❑ 6	8–10
❑ 7	11–14
❑ 8	15–17
❑ 9	18–21
❑ 10	22–24
	Judges
❑ 11	1–3
❑ 12	4–6
❑ 13	7–9
❑ 14	10–12
❑ 15	13–15
❑ 16	16–18
❑ 17	19–21
	Ruth
❑ 18	1–4
	1 Samuel
❑ 19	1–3
❑ 20	4–6
❑ 21	7–9
❑ 22	10–12
❑ 23	13–14
❑ 24	15–16
❑ 25	17–18
❑ 26	19–20
❑ 27	21–23
❑ 28	24–26
❑ 29	27–29
❑ 30	30–31

	2 Samuel
❑ 31	1–3

April

❑ 1	4–6
❑ 2	7–10
❑ 3	11–13
❑ 4	14–15
❑ 5	16–17
❑ 6	18–20
❑ 7	21–22
❑ 8	23–24
	1 Kings
❑ 9	1–2
❑ 10	3–5
❑ 11	6–7
❑ 12	8–9
❑ 13	10–12
❑ 14	13–15
❑ 15	16–18
❑ 16	19–20
❑ 17	21–22
	2 Kings
❑ 18	1–3
❑ 19	4–6
❑ 20	7–8
❑ 21	9–11
❑ 22	12–14
❑ 23	15–17
❑ 24	18–19
❑ 25	20–22
❑ 26	23–25

	1 Chronicles
❑ 27	1–2
❑ 28	3–5
❑ 29	6–7
❑ 30	8–10

May

❑ 1	11–13
❑ 2	14–16
❑ 3	17–19
❑ 4	20–22
❑ 5	23–25
❑ 6	26–27
❑ 7	28–29
	2 Chronicles
❑ 8	1–4
❑ 9	5–7
❑ 10	8–10
❑ 11	11–14
❑ 12	15–18
❑ 13	19–21
❑ 14	22–25
❑ 15	26–28
❑ 16	29–31
❑ 17	32–33
❑ 18	34–36
	Ezra
❑ 19	1–4
❑ 20	5–7
❑ 21	8–10
	Nehemiah
❑ 22	1–3
❑ 23	4–7
❑ 24	8–10
❑ 25	11–13

Esther

❑ 26	1–3
❑ 27	4–7
❑ 28	8–10

Job

❑ 29	1–4
❑ 30	5–8
❑ 31	9–12

June

❑ 1	13–16
❑ 2	17–20
❑ 3	21–24
❑ 4	25–30
❑ 5	31–34
❑ 6	35–38
❑ 7	39–42

Psalms

❑ 8	1–8
❑ 9	9–17
❑ 10	18–21
❑ 11	22–28
❑ 12	29–34
❑ 13	35–39
❑ 14	40–44
❑ 15	45–50
❑ 16	51–56
❑ 17	57–63
❑ 18	64–69
❑ 19	70–74
❑ 20	75–78
❑ 21	79–85
❑ 22	86–90
❑ 23	91–98
❑ 24	99–104
❑ 25	105–107
❑ 26	108–113
❑ 27	114–118

❑ 28	119
❑ 29	120–134
❑ 30	135–142

July

❑ 1	143–150
	Proverbs
❑ 2	1–3
❑ 3	4–7
❑ 4	8–11
❑ 5	12–15
❑ 6	16–18
❑ 7	19–21
❑ 8	22–24
❑ 9	25–28
❑ 10	29–31
	Ecclesiastes
❑ 11	1–4
❑ 12	5–8
❑ 13	9–12
	Song of Songs
❑ 14	1–4
❑ 15	5–8
	Isaiah
❑ 16	1–4
❑ 17	5–8
❑ 18	9–12
❑ 19	13–15
❑ 20	16–20
❑ 21	21–24
❑ 22	25–28
❑ 23	29–32
❑ 24	33–36
❑ 25	37–40
❑ 26	41–43

❑ 27	44–46
❑ 28	47–49
❑ 29	50–52
❑ 30	53–56
❑ 31	57–60

August

❑ 1	61–63
❑ 2	64–66
	Jeremiah
❑ 3	1–3
❑ 4	4–6
❑ 5	7–9
❑ 6	10–12
❑ 7	13–15
❑ 8	16–19
❑ 9	20–22
❑ 10	23–25
❑ 11	26–29
❑ 12	30–31
❑ 13	32–34
❑ 14	35–37
❑ 15	38–40
❑ 16	41–44
❑ 17	45–48
❑ 18	49–50
❑ 19	51–52
	Lamentations
❑ 20	1–2
❑ 21	3–5
	Ezekiel
❑ 22	1–4
❑ 23	5–8
❑ 24	9–12
❑ 25	13–15
❑ 26	16–17

❑ 27 18–20
❑ 28 21–23
❑ 29 24–26
❑ 30 27–29
❑ 31 30–31

September

❑ 1 32–33
❑ 2 34–36
❑ 3 37–39
❑ 4 40–42
❑ 5 43–45
❑ 6 46–48

Daniel
❑ 7 1–2
❑ 8 3–4
❑ 9 5–6
❑ 10 7–9
❑ 11 10–12

Hosea
❑ 12 1–4
❑ 13 5–9
❑ 14 10–14

❑ 15 **Joel**

Amos
❑ 16 1–4
❑ 17 5–9

❑ 18 **Obadiah** and **Jonah**

Micah
❑ 19 1–4
❑ 20 5–7

❑ 21 **Nahum**

❑ 22	**Habakkuk**
❑ 23	**Zephaniah**
❑ 24	**Haggai**
	Zechariah
❑ 25	1–4
❑ 26	5–9
❑ 27	10–14
❑ 28	**Malachi**
	Matthew
❑ 29	1–4
❑ 30	5–7

October

❑ 1	8–9
❑ 2	10–11
❑ 3	12–13
❑ 4	14–16
❑ 5	17–18
❑ 6	19–20
❑ 7	21–22
❑ 8	23–24
❑ 9	25–26
❑ 10	27–28
	Mark
❑ 11	1–3
❑ 12	4–5
❑ 13	6–7
❑ 14	8–9
❑ 15	10–11
❑ 16	12–13
❑ 17	14
❑ 18	15–16

	Luke
❑ 19	1–2
❑ 20	3–4
❑ 21	5–6
❑ 22	7–8
❑ 23	9–10
❑ 24	11–12
❑ 25	13–14
❑ 26	15–16
❑ 27	17–18
❑ 28	19–20
❑ 29	21–22
❑ 30	23–24

	John
❑ 31	1–3

November

❑ 1	4–5
❑ 2	6–7
❑ 3	8–9
❑ 4	10–11
❑ 5	12–13
❑ 6	14–16
❑ 7	17–19
❑ 8	20–21

	Acts
❑ 9	1–3
❑ 10	4–5
❑ 11	6–7
❑ 12	8–9
❑ 13	10–11
❑ 14	12–13
❑ 15	14–15
❑ 16	16–17
❑ 17	18–19
❑ 18	20–21
❑ 19	22–23
❑ 20	24–26

❑ 21	27–28
	Romans
❑ 22	1–3
❑ 23	4–6
❑ 24	7–9
❑ 25	10–12
❑ 26	13–14
❑ 27	15–16
	1 Corinthians
❑ 28	1–4
❑ 29	5–7
❑ 30	8–10

December

❑ 1	11–13
❑ 2	14–16
	2 Corinthians
❑ 3	1–4
❑ 4	5–9
❑ 5	10–13
	Galatians
❑ 6	1–3
❑ 7	4–6
	Ephesians
❑ 8	1–3
❑ 9	4–6
❑ 10	**Philippians**
❑ 11	**Colossians**
❑ 12	**1 Thessalonians**
❑ 13	**2 Thessalonians**

❑ 14 **1 Timothy**

❑ 15 **2 Timothy**

❑ 16 **Titus** and **Philemon**

Hebrews

❑ 17 1–4
❑ 18 5–8
❑ 19 9–10
❑ 20 11–13

❑ 21 **James**

❑ 22 **1 Peter**

❑ 23 **2 Peter**

❑ 24 **1 John**

❑ 25 **2, 3 John, Jude**

Revelation

❑ 26 1–3
❑ 27 4–8
❑ 28 9–12
❑ 29 13–16
❑ 30 17–19
❑ 31 20–22